COLLATERAL
CARNAGE

Chris Saper

Author photograph by Bill Dooling Photography, AZ
Editing by Lourdes Venard of Comma Sense and Kate Schomaker, Reedsy
Video production by Shelley Stark Kingrey and Chris Smith, BigIsland Productions
Formatting by Polgarus Studio
Photography Cover from **Shutterstock.com**

Subjects include: conspiracy, corruption, drug profits, lobbying, greed, Congress, veterans, PTSD, stock manipulation, murder.

GET MY AWARD-WINNING "SHORT-SHORT",
A GLIMPSE INTO A FUTURE DYSTOPIA
"Skybox"

For every writer, it's important to develop relationships with readers, but it's especially so for debut writers like me. Nothing is more important to an author than being able to communicate with readers who enjoy and, I hope, will recommend a fun read to others.

Here's what I promise:

I will never share or sell your information.

You will never get inundated by too many emails (well, at least not from me)– I'll only send them to you with periodic news, information about new releases or to let you know about special offers that might run from time to time.

Just for signing up for my mailing list, I'll email you a Free copy of my award-winning story, "Skybox". You'll find the sign-up link at the back of this book, right after the last page.

There's more than one road to hell. And you can forget about good intentions. I should know. I'm a PTSD therapist.
— Claire Wilheit, MSW, December 2024

PROLOGUE

Paul Sweeney, Sgt, US Army

Paul Sweeney slumped back into his couch and thumbed through his high school yearbook for the thousandth time. *Good luck in the future, Paul! Have a great summer!* The usual drivel written by casual acquaintances who thought they knew him but would barely recognize him now. The ready, quirky smile and contagious laugh for which he was known had vanished after his return from the Middle East. The TV droned on in a feeble attempt to put him to sleep.

While his physical injuries had healed completely, Paul's experiences left him with severe posttraumatic stress disorder, which in turn opened the door to years of self-medication in desperate attempts to escape his memories and the depression that attended them. He'd spent the past six months repeatedly trying to get help from the VA. Paul popped open another beer and swallowed his antidepressant.

"Breaking News!" A red banner appeared below the reporter who was talking on screen. "Police have cordoned off the grisly scene behind me, here at the downtown VA center. It appears that another veteran has taken his own life in the parking lot of the medical center. Stay tuned for more news on this developing story."

Paul hurled the nearly full can of beer against the wall. He put his head in his hands. The bubbly contents were still forming a puddle on the floor when he stood and picked up his phone to call his doctor at the VA.

1

"It's Paul Sweeney…yes, I've thought about it and would like to start your new medication program…this afternoon?…yes, I'll be there. I'll leave right now."

Plucking his keys from the kitchen table, Paul headed out to his car. He had just enough time to make his appointment.

Paul traveled with a gun under the front seat, never sure if each day might be the last day he could bear. But today wouldn't be that day. From everything he'd been told, the experimental drug developed by researchers at the Phoenix VA would be a life saver.

CHAPTER 1

Friday, January 5

Owen Block was an asshole.

Just thinking about him threatened to put Claire Wilheit in a foul mood. She'd deliberated long and hard before calling in sick this morning. It wasn't that Claire disliked the clinical work; she thought that she was helping her patients, at least a little. It was the Lucident workplace she hated. Really, she just needed to get off her ass and find another job. But if she was going to go, she'd rather it be on her terms.

Claire jabbed the paintbrush into the last of the small splintered divots on the screen door, hoping the thick fluid would just fill them up. It didn't. They just sucked the paint from the bristles, drinking in latex and begging for more.

She'd spent most of the day in her small backyard, finally putting paid to the screen door task. Three months ago, she'd removed the damaged door from its jamb and set it against the side of her garage, where she saw it so often it just became part of the landscape, as so many long-ignored things tend to do. Claire felt bad for calling in sick —she knew the other PTSD therapists would have to pick up her patient load. She hoped the day off would steel her against the disagreeable task awaiting her.

She pulled long strips of blue painter's tape from the edges of the screen door jamb, looping and crumpling them in her left hand as she went. Claire surveyed her work with satisfaction, pleased by the crisp, straight painted edges along the wood at the top of the screen. But as she pulled off the last strip of tape, a half inch of fresh paint came with it. *Shit*, she thought. Claire chucked her ruined paintbrush onto the spattered drop cloth. *Now I've got to repaint that section.* Despite her best efforts to rescue what otherwise might be a perfect Phoenix winter day, she was failing miserably. As she tossed the crumpled tape into the trash bag, she caught her reflection in the kitchen window, noting that her face no longer looked so skeletal. She absently rubbed at the tiny, faded scars on her left wrist, narrow white lines that ached in the cold weather and too often brought up painful memories.

Unwelcomed as they were, Claire's thoughts returned to her boss at Lucident. How this supposedly cutting-edge company had hired Owen Block to manage the outpatient clinic was beyond comprehension. During their twice-weekly meetings he had never once stood up to greet her when she entered his office. She wasn't sure whether that was because she was a woman or because she had a good four inches on him. Probably both. But it didn't matter because she couldn't do anything about it. Where would she file a complaint anyway? Lucident's parent company AllMed, was a giant corporation, and held one of the biggest government contracts ever awarded. It was widely viewed as a prototype for the final dismantling and privatization of the Department of Veteran's Affairs—not just in providing direct patient care but for its apparent revolutionary research into new drug therapies. Nothing would move this behemoth off its course, and she knew well that consequences of even the smallest disruption in big bureaucracies always landed on the little guy. Which, in this case, would be Claire.

She sighed and bundled up the trash. The paintbrush was in such bad shape she threw it away too.

Claire glanced at her watch. At least her timing was good. The last rays of afternoon warmed her face, inviting her to put thoughts of work and bad painting projects aside. Just enough time for a quick jog before tackling the last and most distasteful task on her plate: reviewing her deposition. It wasn't due until Monday morning, so she still had plenty of time to work on it.

Claire locked her back door and left the back yard through the gate to the alley. She began her run.

Therapist Robert Kingston looked across the desk at his boss, a small man who'd scratched his way up into lower-level middle management, most likely reaching his level of incompetency long before assuming his role at Lucident.

"I have told you repeatedly that I want reports every Wednesday and every Friday between 11:30 and noon. Not one minute earlier, not one minute later." Owen Block's voice rose, indignation coloring his neck and jowls. "No later than noon. It's almost 4:50 on Friday afternoon." He tapped his watch to make the point.

Just enter the damn report and let me out of here. Robert felt his own flush rise as he ignored the berating words. He focused on the single small window gracing Block's compact office, slowing his breathing before speaking. He didn't bother justifying why he was late, having to cover the extra patient appointments that always resulted when someone called in sick. Block was already well aware of that fact.

"Mr. Block, why don't I just create the summary on the proper form and file it for you?"

"Why don't you just sit here and wait for me to finish. You know, just in case I might have a question."

Robert took the hard plastic seat to the left of Block's desk and watched in silence as his boss started to insert the report into the corporate form. No sooner had Block begun to type, his phone buzzed. Block glanced at the incoming message.

"Wait here. I'm going to the men's room. Don't leave."

Fifteen minutes passed, then twenty. Robert's annoyance edged into concern. *Where the hell is Block,* thought Robert. *The restrooms were only down the hall.* Ten more minutes. Fidgeting, he bumped the table. The computer screen sprang back to life, and with it the summary form Block had been inputting. Robert glanced over, then did a double take.

That's not my report. Robert took a quick look around to see if Block was coming back. The office suite was silent. He grabbed his cell phone and took a photo of the open screen. He sat back down, heart racing. Now, at 5:18, the winter sun was setting, dimming Block's already dingy office. Robert wanted to get home. It had already been a long week but disobeying a direct order from his boss would no doubt result in a written warning.

Robert walked through the office cubicle farm, a now empty maze of desks, some cluttered, others evidently occupied during the day by employees scoring high on the OCD scale. He headed toward the men's room. It was situated right next to the elevator banks, across from the women's room. The interior lights of the building were set to dim at exactly 5:15 every day, and they were dim now. Without any visible exterior windows, the hallways took on a slightly sinister air. His footsteps echoed in the cavernous hallway, underscoring its emptiness.

He tried to open the men's room door. Locked. Cracking open the door to the women's room, just enough to be heard, Robert called out, "Hello? Anyone here?"

No answer, no sound at all, just the slightest echo of his words bouncing off the hard surfaces of the small, utilitarian restroom. He knocked on the men's room door. "Mr. Block?"

No answer.

Robert stepped up to the elevator and pushed the call button. Nothing.

"Are you kidding me?" he muttered aloud. His first thought was that Lucident was too cheap to leave the elevators on overnight, but on second thought, that was probably against some kind of safety code. *More likely, the janitorial crew was working its way down to the fourth floor and just had the elevators stopped at each floor as they cleaned the upper offices and restrooms.*

Maybe Block's in the lobby. Robert took the main staircase four flights down. No Block. It was now nearly dark outside, the auto security grates shut, sealed for the night. While security grates had been commonplace in commercial buildings for years, the newer grates in buildings like the ones that housed the Lucident offices were made with an alloy designed to thwart cell tower or satellite transmissions. Robert tried the front door. Locked. *Shit.* He couldn't even call outside the building for help.

He walked back up the stairs. Unless he could find Block, his only chance of getting out of here tonight was to be sure he didn't miss the janitors as they worked their way down the floors. *Do they start at the top? How many floors in this building? Eight?* He had no idea how long it took to clean each floor, but unless he could catch the janitors, he'd be stranded overnight.

The hallways and floors echoed. Robert couldn't remember ever seeing any other building occupants—other than the bean-counters working in the cubicles outside Block's office—in the three years he'd been making his visits to corporate. The notion that he might be alone in the building was starting to set off faint warning bells. He wasn't even sure that janitors were on duty.

Robert returned to Block's office and propped open the office suite doors, so he could hear the bell when, and if, the elevator got to his floor.

Robert pushed aside the nameplate that read "Owen Block—Managing Director" and took Block's seat. He touched the mouse, and the screen flashed to life again, displaying the full report Block had been working on.

Patient name: Alex Stanton
Date/time of service: 01.05.2024 3:00pm
ID number: LA1A-418
Intake diagnosis: Transitional posttraumatic stress disorder—TPTSD
Intake treatment plan: Admit to inpatient psych; continue A1A protocol, outpatient treatment TBD.
Revised diagnosis: Malignant PTSD

That's definitely not my report. Alex was just fine when he left my office at 3:20 today. Alex was hospitalized? Had some kind of crisis happened? Or had Block just made a mistake?

Bumping the mouse was one thing. Deliberately snooping beyond the open screen was quite another. But they were his damn patients, so the hell with it. Robert opened the next patient file. Another patient, this one deceased. *No. That's not right either.* Robert looked at the dates and then scrolled back. He continued scrolling through the last dozen patient reports he'd delivered to Block. Two more patients admitted to inpatient psych service. One more dead: Paul Sweeney. *Paul?* Paul had made more progress in his therapy than any of Robert's other patients. In fact, Robert thought of him as a true success story. Sure, Paul had missed his last two appointments, but that wasn't all so unusual. *What the hell?*

The reports of each of the five patients had been altered only slightly in its content, but the discharge diagnoses now all read "malignant PTSD," which reflected none of his current or even recent patient load. All his outpatients carried the less serious "transitional PTSD" diagnosis, meaning they had definite issues but were likely to respond well to therapeutic and pharmaceutical intervention.

Robert read on, scrolling to the next group of summaries, patients of a therapist named Claire Wilheit. Three of the last nine of her reports also showed deceased patients, all carrying the same label: malignant PTSD. The last entry in the file notes that Ms. Wilheit left the firm without notice, employment terminated as of 5:00 p.m. Signed, Owen Everett Block. On January 5th. Today. The closing note mentioned that Lucident's human resources department would arrange for her final paycheck to be deposited.

Robert clicked on the link next to Wilheit's termination note and found himself on the first page of her personnel file. He looked at the photo ID precisely inserted into its little two-inch-by-three-inch picture box on the form. He remembered seeing her several times over the past year or so, usually passing her on the elevator as he reported to Owen Block's office like clockwork on Wednesdays and Fridays, no earlier than 11:30 and no later than noon. According to Wilheit's file, her reports were required to be delivered between 11:00 and 11:30 promptly every Wednesday and every Friday. Of course, he didn't see her today because he was late getting to Block's office. He summoned a vague picture of Claire Wilheit: tall and lanky, with dark-framed glasses and short, wavy brown hair that always looked like she forgot to brush it.

Robert opened the section of her personnel file titled "Supervisor notes." Block's entry read:

"Second warning not to attempt to access inpatient files. Employment to be terminated. Signed, Owen Everett Block." It was dated the last day of December.

He returned to Claire's patient log. It was the same as his, except that her patients were scheduled at exactly ten minutes after the hour, not on the half hour. Probably to ensure patient confidentiality. *Given the company's obsession with privacy*, thought Robert, *nothing should be a surprise.*

Was she fired? His first impression had been that she must have been either incompetent or oblivious, although the written warning in Wilheit's personnel file made him wonder. Nonetheless, Wilheit's caseload looked dismally served: almost a third of her patients were deceased. Yet after reviewing his own caseload along with the fabricated reports on Block's computer, it was obvious that his own performance, according to the official patient outcomes, was far worse. What failed to register was the fact that although Claire's official termination by Owen Block occurred at 5:00 p.m. today, Robert had been in Block's office since 4:40, and there was no one in the office who could have effected the termination.

Robert checked the clock: almost 8:00 p.m. He'd completely lost all track of time reviewing files. *What was taking the janitors so long?* There had been no elevator bell, absolutely no sound coming from anywhere on the floor. The complete silence was one that could only accompany isolation. He was alone. The warning bells that had once been faint now began to clang.

CHAPTER 2

It was a beautiful night. The scent of dead, yet still fragrant sagebrush perfumed the evening and cleared Claire's mind. She turned the corner toward her house and slowed to a walk to cool down after her run. Her thoughts wandered and they summoned a long-ago memory, when she was about seven and her sister Stacy four years older.

"Claire, give me the leash."

"Just let me walk Cotton to the end of the block, please, Stacy…"

"No. I said give me the leash!"

Stacy wrenched the leash from Claire's left wrist, twisting and pulling harder than necessary.

"Owww! You're hurting me!"

Claire screamed in pain, holding her wrist to her chest. Leash trailing, Cotton took off running. Right into the path of a truck. The driver didn't stop.

Both girls screamed.

"Claire, look what you've done!"

"I didn't do any—"

"You killed my puppy. I hate you!"

Stacy turned and started running toward home, leaving a shocked and badly hurt younger sister to follow in her wake.

By the time Claire stepped onto the front porch, her mother was there with open arms to offer comfort. "You poor thing. Stacy told me what happened. Let me see your hand." One look and she said, "Let's put some ice on that. I'll call your dad to let him know we're going to the emergency room, and to, umm, get Cotton," eliciting an even louder wail from Claire. As the girls' mom put ice into a washcloth, she said, "I'm sorry you hurt your hand, honey, but you know not to let the leash go without handing it to someone. Stacy, you were very brave to try to save Cotton." Stacy's terrifying glare was fixed on Claire. Miserable, Claire knew she'd never be able to set the story right. This wasn't the first time this kind of thing had happened. Even though she was only seven, she knew the consequences of challenging her older sister. Worse, she knew it probably wouldn't be the last time, either. Claire and her mother headed to the nearby hospital, where they were told that several of the tiny bones in her wrist were broken and that there had been significant injury to the ligaments and soft tissue in her hand. Surgery would be required.

Claire pushed the unpleasant memory back into the past where it was supposed to stay.

Having spent most of the day on her painting project, Claire started the coffeemaker. She pushed a pile of books to one side of the dining room table to clear a workspace. This was her last chance to make any corrections in the document responding to Stacy's lawsuit. She still had two days to complete her review, but she didn't want to ruin the whole weekend. Better to just get it over with now.

Claire saw the lawsuit for what it was: another meritless conflict whose only function was to amuse her sister, whose married wealth bored her to tears. The suit alleged that Claire had taken possession of almost $900,000 in proceeds from her parents' life insurance policy without the equal property division required in the will. Claire, of course, never received any such monies and frankly had no reason to believe that a life insurance policy ever existed. Their parents' once comfortable estate had dwindled to less than $70,000 at their deaths, almost entirely due to Stacy's pushing them to invest in a "foolproof" real estate opportunity in a long-ago bankrupt company owned and operated by her husband.

After burial expenses and estate and income taxes, each sister reaped some $22,000 and change. Claire used her inheritance to make a down payment on her tiny, historic home, which once opened onto a lovely, small city park in which she could no longer walk, run, or read. All she could see from her yard was its block perimeter wall. She had no idea how her sister spent her $22K; Claire would have bet dollars to donuts it was on some self-indulgent luxury item, but honestly, she could give a shit. She just wanted to be done with the lawsuit and get Stacy out of her life for good.

Claire grabbed her tote.

"Goddammit!" The deposition wasn't in the tote, and neither was her personal laptop. *How the hell did I leave that stuff anywhere?* She closed her eyes briefly and thought she remembered putting it into her bag as she was leaving work yesterday afternoon just after five o'clock.

She'd gotten home just before six last night and put the bag in the hallway near the dining room, same as always, easy to grab the following morning on the way out the door again. Claire hadn't left the house all day. She could see herself in her office, putting on her fleece jacket and changing into her sneakers for the walk home, stuffing the work shoes into the top of the tote. *No,* she thought, *that wasn't right.* She'd decided against wearing the fleece jacket and now saw herself setting the laptop and paperwork on her desk to add the jacket to the tote. In her rush to leave the office and get the day's reports to the drop box outside Block's office, she'd left the sheaf of papers and small laptop on the desk in her own office. She could picture it perfectly now.

"Well, fuck me. Just fuck me!" she yelled at the bag, shoving the dining room chair hard against the table. All clinic buildings were closed over the weekends. To make the Monday deadline, she'd have to go back and get it before the skeleton evening shift of therapists left for the night at nine. Next week would be too late. Stacy's lawyers had threatened to force a summary judgment to demand payment of some $450K that Claire had never seen. She cursed herself for procrastinating. She'd waited until the last minute because, well, because the task was just so unpleasant.

It was just after eight at night. Claire's walk back to the treatment center would take only about fifteen minutes. The Phoenix streets tended to roll up fairly early, even on weekend nights. The "temporary" curfew established two years ago to try to curtail gang activity, but now continued with a life of its own. Most residents avoided going out at night anymore since the streets were sporadically patrolled by members of the Arizona Freedom Brigade. Formed several years ago, the Brigade was a functioning group of mostly heavily armed men, who had a reputation of being aggressive and ham-handed. Brigade members patrolled major intersections and surface streets to assure citizens that "law and order would continue to prevail" as long as the Brigade was there to protect them.

Hardly anyone bought into this charade, and most saw the Brigade for exactly what they represented: privatized vigilante law enforcement, enjoying a stamp of approval by the local powers that be, then ultimately legitimized on a federal level. There were fewer families in Arizona every year. Most people who had the means to leave migrated to the northern states in order to live in areas where their kids could get a decent public education, basic health care, and enjoy the waning amount of natural beauty that still remained somewhere between sea and shining sea. The threatening and sometimes physical harassment tactics foisted upon the citizens of the Great State of Arizona by Brigade members—who always claimed that they feared for their lives and that force was the only option left—were ubiquitous and rarely prosecuted.

The Brigade had secured a large ongoing federal operating grant, since Arizona's state budget, like those of other southwestern states, was completely overwhelmed with deportation costs. Congress had shifted the deportation responsibility to the states in attempts to balance the federal budget. But in terms of reducing overall costs, it was a ridiculously transparent failure. In Phoenix, as well as several other major urban areas, state and local officials found that privatizing police work was a simple way of managing the budget shortfalls. Not a good way, just an expedient one, held out triumphantly by elected officials who campaigned for reelection after reelection on the success of a "balanced budget." Budgets were restructured so the regular police force was on duty during the weekday shifts, and the Brigade took over patrol from 10:00 p.m. through 7:00 a.m., plus weekends. The police were happy. The politicians were happy. The citizens, not so much.

Claire had lived in Phoenix all her life, and her running schedule allowed her to investigate virtually every garbage collection alleyway and dead-end side street in the two square miles surrounding her neighborhood. Not that there were all that many alleys and shortcuts through vacant lots left, but enough that she could maneuver most of the route unnoticed by the Brigade, which mainly patrolled the larger intersections and more heavily trafficked routes along the north-south light rail line. She pulled on her navy-blue hooded sweatshirt, tucked her keys and phone into her pocket, and stepped out her back door and into the chilly desert evening.

Robert glanced back at the computer screen. At this point, even if Block returned tonight, Robert would just explain that he was trying to send an email to get someone to let him out of the building. More than plausible. *Screw it*, he thought and began to read.

The summary reports were filed in reverse chronological order, and there were a lot of them. The therapists' caseloads were brutal, with an expectation of seeing fourteen patients per day, five days per week. And that was on a regular day. When one of the therapists called in sick, as had happened today, the others were expected to step in to carry the day's caseload. So today he had seen sixteen patients, which was the whole reason he was late to Block's office to begin with. On the other hand, Lucident was a for-profit venture, and full schedules translated directly into higher revenue. *Well, no kidding*, Robert thought, *this country has been in continuous Middle Eastern ground wars since 2003, with no end in sight. So yeah, there's a damn conveyor belt of PTSD veterans out there.* To think that there was now an entire generation of US citizens who had never known anything *but* foreign wars saddened him beyond words.

Robert stepped to the small window in Block's office and regarded the quiet night, frustrated and confused. Eventually he let his gaze wander down to the clinic building he'd left what seemed like so many hours ago.

CHAPTER 3

Owen Block opened his eyes, vaguely disoriented. He felt like he'd had too much to drink over too many hours' time, kind of like a daytime hangover you might get if you started a Labor Day picnic with a Bloody Mary at brunch and stepped directly into a happy hour that lasted until midnight. He sat up, uncomfortable on the vinyl floor of what looked to be the men's room. Slowly his vision began to clear, along with his brain.

What the hell had happened? He recalled having to deal with Kingston—*I swear to Christ that guy is dust, I don't need assholes like that reporting to me*—and getting the text on his phone.

Hey babe! Can't wait to see you later at my place, can you run down to three and get my keys before the building closes down—you'll get to my place first— meet you in front of the elevator on three. I'll be home by eight. Best night ever! – O

For at least the thousandth time over the past few weeks, Owen simply could not believe that a woman like Olivia could ever possibly be interested in him. She was beautiful—only about an inch taller than him, big plus— lush, and if he were being honest with himself (not really a long suit with Owen), probably a lot smarter. But she loved having him be the boss, in a restaurant, in bed, and just the thought of seeing her to pick up her keys made him get hard enough to be a little uncomfortable in his Jockeys (he'd just bought all new underwear, low rise, nice colors a woman like Olivia might like, but not as comfortable as his old boxers, and yes, why do all the movie writers think that only women buy underwear when they take on a new lover?

Anyway, he didn't just get the briefs; he bought three pairs of pricey silk boxers, which he just knew she'd find irresistible). Shortly after meeting her, Owen joined a gym for the first time in his life.

With growing awareness, Block remembered that he had left Kingston in his office for the five minutes or so it would take to dash down to the third floor, grab the keys and possibly a quick feel, and get back to his report. *When was that? What time was it?* The restroom lights were dim, matching the little sliver of light snaking its way under the bathroom door from the hallway outside. Block scooted on his butt to the door and felt for the handle to ease his return to a standing position, only to find the door locked from the outside. He slumped back to a sitting position on the smooth vinyl surface. Wispy snatches of memory came and went—but when Block briefly surfaced through his mental haze, he pictured the last image he could recall. Olivia waiting at the elevator just outside the restrooms on three; she was stepping toward him with a big smile, keys in her outstretched hand. Then a stinging at the back of his neck, and then—well, nothing at all. He struggled to focus, fighting a dizziness that was worsening by the second, and realized he was losing the battle. He closed his eyes again.

CHAPTER 4

Claire loved the wintry desert nights. The climate shift over the past ten years had been gradual but steady. Phoenix had been in the worst drought on record for as long as she could remember, and its status had simply never changed. All the water-gulping trees and lawns were long gone. *God*, thought Claire, *I remember the lawns, as pretty as they were ridiculous in this environment, almost as absurd as the glut of eighteen-hole golf courses surrounding the valley.* Most of the flora in Phoenix had just withered up and collapsed where it once grew, tacky-looking at best. At worst, it was a constant fire hazard. All that really remained were the occasional palm and a few oleanders and Palo Verde trees, whose deep roots had spared them premature death. But at night, the open skies and dry air were liberating. So few people drove cars anymore that there was little street noise, and after curfew, the only sound was a background rustle created by slight breezes passing over dried-up plant life yet to be cleared by city workers.

Claire checked her watch. Just a little after eight. She picked up her pace as she navigated the alleys and stayed largely out of sight for the eighteen-block trip. While she didn't really anticipate any issue at the moment, a post-curfew stroll could definitely create problems she would prefer to avoid.

As she jogged, free-floating thoughts moved through her mind's eye.

Three months ago, she'd called it quits with the surgeon she'd been dating. When they'd met, Don's charm and energy swept her up in a romantic whirlwind. He told her that she was "the one" and sent flowers every week, taking her to upscale social events where he was usually one of the sponsors or keynote speakers. He showed up the week before every event with a new gown he'd picked out, so she'd be sure to have something "suitable" to wear. He'd asked her what she would like for her birthday, insisting that she just make a list of what she'd buy if she ever won the lottery. It was a fun exercise, and Claire's list was populated with items like a new mountain bike, a weekend ski trip, some artificial turf for her backyard (she'd never be able to justify the expense on her own), and scuba lessons. On her birthday, Don took her out to dinner and gave her an oversized envelope. "Happy Birthday, Claire!" Inside was a gift certificate to one of the pricey Scottsdale salons for a complete "make-over" including hair restyling, makeup lessons, and a $300 credit toward makeup products. He "suggested" that she would be more attractive as a blonde. So she went blonde.

He upped the pressure on her to move in with him and to get out of her little "starter home." Eventually the tarnish beneath the gold became too obvious to ignore, and one day, she packed up the few things he'd left at her house and set the box on the concrete stoop outside her back door for him to collect. When she got home from work, the box was gone and there was a tear in the screen and a splintered area along the bottom of the wood frame. She had removed the door from its hinges and set it along the side of the house, where it sat until she finally couldn't stand to look at it anymore and last week had finally picked up a gallon of paint to set things right. *God. I'm no better now at picking men than I was in high school. Maybe I should stick to the friends-with-benefits thing.* She was so sick of people who barged into her life to wrest from her what little manner of control she'd managed to put in place. At least she had returned her hair to its natural color. Not a big thing, but a start.

Claire's route took her to the patient entrance at the front of the therapy office building on Monterey. She took the walkway around the south side of the building, where the staff entrance was situated. A quick glance around told her she was alone. She touched her key fob to the door. Nothing happened. As she was about to try a second time to unlock the door, it pushed open toward her as two janitors rolled a trolley through the door. They nodded at Claire, and she said, "Good night." She slipped inside.

Inside the staff entrance, a small vestibule, about ten by twenty feet, acted as buffer space to the actual treatment rooms, but its primary function was to prevent costly air-conditioned air from rapidly dissipating in the staggeringly, unbelievably hot summer months now lasting from early March to late November. Now there were just three short months of winter, when the days were glorious and nights still chilly. The rest of the year, Phoenix was just a hellhole.

After stepping up to the entryway to her office, Claire swiped the electronic key fob to open her office door. Nothing. She tried again.

Now what! How could this day possibly get any worse? She slammed her fist against the door, and it banged open, obviously unlocked. Claire felt a little embarrassed, even though no one was around to witness her fit of frustration. The lights were on their after-hours "dim" setting, but the beam from her phone was enough to illuminate her room.

There was nothing on her desk, no deposition, no laptop, nothing. Generally speaking, therapists tend to avoid having any personal items in their work spaces. Claire's desk always had the requisite box of tissues, a fresh yellow legal pad (patients still felt better about watching their therapists taking actual handwritten notes than having to listen to them entering data on a keyboard), and a plain coffee cup holding a bunch of No. 2 yellow pencils and a couple of cheap generic ballpoint pens. Gone. Behind her chair, there was a small credenza that housed a printer and a secure two-drawer filing cabinet where she locked the Lucident clinic computer at the end of each day and where she also kept additional patient notes. The credenza had a cubby area that held extra legal pads and tissue boxes, a space where she could keep some water bottles and a few personal things—tampons, hairbrush, just basic stuff. She slid open the credenza doors.

The cubby was empty. And the file cabinet was gone.

She sat down at her desk, stunned. She was clueless about what had happened to her office. The deposition and her laptop were gone, along with everything else. Her office looked just as it did on her very first day at work, an odd-looking corporate skeleton, impassionate and sterile, awaiting its new occupant.

Confused, Claire left her office and exited the building. Her mind was racing. What happened to her office? And where was her stuff? Was there any way she could piece together the deposition via email? Her lawyer was okay. Well, "okay" would be pushing it. He was more like marginal, nearing retirement. No one would ever describe him as a go-getter, all of which probably explained a lot about why Claire could afford him. She'd tried a few times during the past month or so but never had any luck reaching him after hours; she had no expectation that he would be available to assist her over the weekend.

Claire leaned against the side of the clinic building. As she crouched down to adjust her shoelaces, she let her eyes wander as she planned her route home, looking up at the corporate offices, all dark except one small window on the fourth floor. She could see a figure silhouetted by the light of what looked like a TV—no, not flickering, maybe a computer screen. The figure was waving frantically, and it looked like it was waving right at her.

Robert hesitated less than a second before grabbing his backpack and Block's laptop, snapping the cord that tethered the laptop to the desk. Running out the door, through the hallway, and down the main stairwell, Robert hoped he could get to the lobby before the dark figure disappeared. Jacket flapping, he took the steps two and three at a time, nearly flying over each landing. He reached the lobby windows and could see the figure outside, still staring up at the small fourth floor window.

He banged on the lobby window and opened his phone, waving its lit-up screen wildly, trying to catch the shadowed figure's attention.

"Over here! Hey, over here!" Robert was yelling now, despite realizing no one would be able to hear him through the safety glass. The figure straightened and slowly turned toward him.

The figure, as it turned out, was a she. Claire crossed the parking lot and stepped up to the glass lobby windows, trying to see through the grate's opening to the man inside trying desperately to communicate with her. He opened his phone and typed: "Locked in, can you get help?" He held the phone right up to the glass.

Offering him a half smile, she typed back, and placed her own phone against the glass. "Why don't you just leave through the emergency exit?" His expression suddenly changed to one of complete puzzlement.

"What?" he typed.

"Go back toward the elevator and walk around it to your right—big sign that says *Exit*."

"But the alarm will go off!" he typed back.

Claire shrugged and lifted her hands slightly, palms up. She mouthed the words, "Up to you."

He looked at her and took off in the direction of the exit.

She rolled her eyes, marveling at how oblivious people could be. She had to acknowledge the irony—how oblivious does someone have to be to lose the very stuff she needed to set her life back on course? The man had looked at her and smiled back, a little crooked, and she realized she'd seen that smile before—he was one of the therapists! What the hell was this guy's name? She concentrated, trying to locate a memory that had never been formed. She walked around to the south side of the building to meet him at the emergency exit. *What on earth was he doing here at this time of night?*

Robert flew out of the emergency exit–only door, letting it slam shut behind him. He breathed deeply a few times to slow his heart rate. The night temperature delivered an unexpected chill, courtesy of his sweat-soaked shirt.

A woman's voice spoke, a touch of humor in the inflection. "Glad that worked out for you."

Robert turned and faced the woman he now recognized as Claire Wilheit, whose employee photo he'd seen just an hour or so ago.

"Claire?"

Puzzled that he knew her name, she couldn't recall when they had been introduced. "I'm sorry, I recognize your face but don't remember your name?"

"Robert, Robert Kingston, but that's probably because, well, we've never actually met. Listen, thanks for coming by, I might have been stuck in there overnight if you hadn't happened along when you did."

"You could always have used the emergency exit."

"But I was worried about the alarm…"

There were no alarm bells ringing. He felt more than a little foolish. He checked his watch: 8:56. *Wow, that was pretty close*, with 9:00 p.m. (okay, well, actually 9:05) being the last-man-out deadline for all of the clinic locations. A few minutes later and Claire would have been long gone. Still almost an hour until curfew. Robert began to relax a bit. His walk home would take only about fifteen minutes, and a brisk pace would help warm him up a little.

"Okay, well, nice to meet you, Robert Kingston," Claire said, holding out her hand. "I'll probably see you around next week." She turned toward the parking lot and began to walk west, toward the park and home.

Robert quickly stepped forward and gently touched her arm. "What do you mean, next week? I thought you left the company."

"What are you talking about? I was just coming back to my office to look for someth…what are you talking about?"

"Um, well, it's kind of a long story, and if you let me walk you home, I'll tell it to you. Anyway, it's on my way back home, so it's not a problem—plus, it's dark, and I might need rescuing again." Although rattled by the evening's events, Robert had the presence of mind to hope he came off as charming.

"How do you know where I live?" Claire's tone was somewhere between surprised and accusatory, dashing any hope that she had, in fact, been remotely charmed.

"Uh, well, that's part of the story."

Neither of them noticed the light that remained in the small window on the fourth floor, or the silhouetted figure that watched them leave.

CHAPTER 5

Claire and Robert walked briskly and spoke in low tones as Robert relayed the beginning of his day's tale, starting with his late arrival to Owen Block's office and the extended workday that seemed to have set everything into play. They crossed Central Avenue, hopping over the light rail track, and headed into the parking lot of the old abandoned shopping mall, once the pride of downtown Phoenix. There were a few monolithic office complexes that filled space formerly occupied by large retail department stores. The days of strolling through beautiful stores, decorated for every season, looking at the latest fashions, jewelry, you-name-it, had pretty much gone by the wayside, as online shopping offered convenience, better prices, and safety. Robert felt a bit sad about that, too.

"Oh, yeah, well, that was me who called in sick today. I swear to God, coming face-to-face with that narcissistic prick was just more than I could stand."

Robert gave her a half smile. "And is that your professional opinion, Ms. Wilheit?"

"Actually, the narcissistic prick part *is* my professional opinion, but the part about not being able to tolerate looking at him is just fact." She smiled back.

Robert continued. "When I saw you outside, I just grabbed Block's computer and ran for the lobby—"

"What?" She stopped right in the middle of the parking lot. "You *stole* Block's computer?"

"Well, I guess, kind of, but it's what I saw in my file, in yours…"

"You were in *my* file? What were you doing in *my* file?" Claire whirled to look directly at Robert. She was beginning to doubt her judgment in agreeing to let him walk her home.

"It's what was in *my* file," Robert said, "that made me look further—there's something really wrong going on here, and I, well, I just grabbed the whole thing. There's something wrong with your file, too, including the fact that your employment was terminated at five o'clock today. Please, just let me show you when we get a chance to look, but it's dark and late, and curfew's coming."

"What are you talking about? Terminated?" Claire was well beyond confused, but the spontaneity in Robert's blurted-out comments put her mind a bit more at ease. "Okay. Look. Let's pick up our pace, and you can show me what you're talking about once we get to my house. You don't want to be out after ten on your own way home." They hurried to the other side of the lot, facing Third Avenue, just about fifteen more blocks to Claire's place. Their pace didn't allow for much conversation. "Let's cut through here." Claire motioned to an alleyway on her right. "It's a shortcut that will drop us right at my backyard. It's only about a hundred yards up ahead on the left."

The alleyways in the older historic Phoenix neighborhoods hearkened back to the days when garbage pickup happened out of sight, before the city began supplying residents with big plastic trash bins, blue for recyclables and green for all the other stuff people throw away. It didn't stop the curbs from being eyesores on collection days, but at least there was some uniformity to the unsightly view. In any case, most of the old alleyways were too narrow to accommodate the garbage trucks of the twenty-first century, so they sat unused, except for occasional homeless people, druggies, teenagers getting themselves into trouble, and trash storage until the bins could be rolled out to the front curbs. Still, the alleys were, for people like Claire, great places to run or walk, away from front windows and nosy neighbors.

"Hey, it's me, Smith. I just got here." The lone figure in Block's office spoke quietly into the odd-looking phone. "No, I just watched the last two employees leave, so we're clear here until morning. But we've got a big problem, Noble. There's no laptop here.

"We're set for a 2:00 a.m. pickup, right outside the emergency exit, Noble. I'll only contact you if there is a problem. Until then, I'm going to look around some more. Maybe I'll be able to find the computer." He hung up before Noble could respond.

Smith, Lucident's security manager, walked through the cubicle maze and down to the fourth-floor men's room. He knocked three times, then three more.

"You can come out now. We'll just have a little time to kill until pickup." He heard the lock on the men's room door disengage, and two figures stepped out and stretched. The taller man said, "I'll just go down to three and make sure everything's as expected."

Smith returned to Block's office. Owen Block's office was simply not big enough to offer unnoticed hiding spots for the missing computer. Smith double- and triple-checked every little nook and cranny and, unsurprisingly, still came up empty. The snapped cord dangled next to the desk. Where was that damned thing?

He opened his own small tablet and typed in his access code. Within a couple of seconds, he was in the corporate systems' folders, searching for *Block, Owen*. Block's file opened, granting access to all the computer files that he'd modified during the past twenty-four hours. *Man*, Smith thought, *I love technology when it works.* He decided to begin his review at 4:00 p.m., trying to piece together Block's movements over the past several hours.

There was nothing in Block's input records until 4:50, when *Kingston, Robert* popped up as an entry. Smith's face took on an intense expression as he looked at the files' movements. He could see only one open file, for one of Kingston's patients, an Alex Stanton. He noted the discharge disposition notation, entered at 4:42, but then Block's entry stopped. The computer, however, hadn't been shut down. Interesting.

Smith exited the supervisor's files and moved into the campus building security files. He reviewed each of the outpatient therapists' computer activity and correlated them with their respective schedules. The last employee to leave the clinic building was a therapist named Claire Wilheit, who had attempted to access the outer clinic office at 8:28 and then her office a few seconds later. She had called in sick today and shouldn't have been in the clinic at all. He closed his eyes to think.

CHAPTER 6

Stacy Atkins sipped some vodka out of the crystal tumbler, looking at her husband as he gazed south over the Scottsdale skyline at night. "Only forty-eight hours until that coffin gets its last nail."

"Quit being so fucking dramatic." Curt Atkins was annoyed. "It won't really matter what she says in the deposition if we can't find the insurance policy."

"Well, Curt, I've ransacked all of my parents' stuff in storage, and it is nowhere in their files—not with their lawyer, not in the safe deposit box. It can't be anywhere else except in my sister's house."

"And I told *you* that I'd take care of it. I should be hearing from my guys any minute."

She was sick to death of his officious outbursts, but she had her own agenda. If there was one thing Stacy was, it was focused. She left to go inside and refresh her cocktail.

Stacy walked back to the deck on the spacious north Scottsdale house, carrying the iced vodka. The views were spectacular, not as great as they used to be when more buildings were lit up at night, but still, quite acceptable. Fleeting bits of light from the house danced across the negative edge of the pool, reminding her of a long-ago trip to Portofino, where she met Curt and his portfolio. He was appallingly tight-fisted when it came to money, but he personified conspicuous consumption and kept her in a lifestyle that she'd always envisioned, so even the rigid prenuptial agreement was tolerable. Curt had no other family. He lived in a paranoid world where he was certain that a divorce would cut him off at the knees, delivering unearned wealth to some gold digger. That was the downside. The upside was that the agreement would become null upon his death, some amount of cold logic taking over: if he couldn't take it with him, he'd rather anyone but the government take it. But then again, Stacy could be a very patient woman when it was in her interest. Fortunately, she wouldn't have to be patient much longer.

Given Curt's net worth and extravagant surroundings, most outsiders wouldn't imagine that $450,000 was enough to even get his attention. But for him, it was the principle. He didn't like losing at anything, and he didn't like Claire, either.

Stacy sat on the chaise lounge, snuggled up in her black cashmere wrap, and sipped, savoring the olive when she reached the halfway point of her cocktail.

CHAPTER 7

Claire and Robert turned into the alleyway but halted as they took in the small SUV parked behind Claire's house, on the right side of the gravelly alley. The car was dark and appeared to be empty, although it was impossible to tell looking through the back window of the vehicle.

"That's strange. I rarely see any cars back here." They moved out of the ambient light from neighboring houses and into the cover of the old oleander trees lining the alleyway. Claire's back gate rattled as the latch was lifted; the old wooden gate creaked open. They stayed in the shadows as two men moved as quickly and as quietly as possible, got into the SUV, and started the engine. The car remained dark, devoid of any interior lights that might illuminate its occupants. The car's rear light blinked once, and the SUV began to crawl down the alley, pulling away to the west.

Claire and Robert watched the car until it reached the end of the block, then saw the headlights engage as it turned onto the regular side street, just a normal car out on a normal night, probably heading home. They exchanged a worried glance and walked the remaining steps to Claire's back alley gate.

"Who were those guys? They were in my *yard*." Even though she whispered, Claire's agitation was palpable.

Claire's bungalow was built in the '60s, when it was common practice to build guesthouses or freestanding garages in the backyards throughout central Phoenix. Her property hosted a freestanding building—which might be more accurately described as a garage-sized shed with a light switch, an unused washer-dryer hookup, and a garage door. Claire rarely used the garage door since she didn't own a car and could access the garage through the small side door just to the east of her kitchen entrance. She put her key into the back door's locking mechanism, relieved to see that that the door was still locked. The back door to the bungalow opened directly into Claire's kitchen. The kitchen was small, arranged in a galley-type design, but the last owner had upgraded the counters and appliances to high-tech, top-of-the-line models. The little night-light in the range's hood was off. "That's odd," said Claire. Claire left the light on all the time, but maybe it had just burned out. She moved the toggle, and the light sprang to life. Very odd indeed.

She looked at the kitchen table and at the coffeemaker on the counter. She could see the slight dust-free outline next to the left side of the coffee machine. It was just a narrow band, but it looked like the machine had been moved and put back almost exactly right. Almost.

"Robert, I think someone was in here. In my house. Not just my yard. My *house*."

He moved beside her. "Let's look around to see if you were robbed or…or something. Before, you know, you decide whether to call the police." No one wanted to involve the authorities in anything anymore than was absolutely necessary, a decision that required much more prudence while the Brigade was on patrol—which would start in about twenty minutes or so and remain that way until the Monday morning police shift resumed its efforts to "restore law and order!" Even when there was no order to restore.

She turned on the lights and moved through the house, Robert right behind. The great room —not all that great, actually quite modest—was easy to see at a single glance, two small white leather love seats, a pretty white marble coffee table, and an antique dining table that was covered with books, a coffee mug, and Claire's reading tablet. Just as it was when she had turned to get her now missing deposition and laptop out of the tote, hours ago, ready to settle in to do a disagreeable task. She stared at the scene, feeling a bit uneasy, without really knowing why. Something was, well, off.

Moving into the main bedroom, Claire could tell that everything looked just as she'd left it. White duvet pulled up to the headboard, two king-sized pillows propped nicely at the top. Perfectly made. Her second bedroom didn't really function as much of anything except a place to put her rowing machine and a few free weights and a corner to stack off-season clothing. Against one wall were a few paintings she hadn't gotten around to hanging. And a bookcase filled to capacity with books, board games and random stuff. It was such a disorganized mess she wouldn't have the slightest clue whether anything was disturbed.

Claire checked the front door, still locked and chained. She felt a little more settled, and her breathing started to return to normal.

Robert began to get edgy. He really needed to leave immediately if he was to get back home before curfew. It was only about a mile and a half, which he could make with a slow jog. But he had to leave now.

"Claire, I need to talk to you about what I found at work, and I'm kind of concerned about leaving you here alone, but it's coming up on ten…"

She was standing at the dining room table, bending over to pick up the coffee cup to take it to the kitchen. She froze.

"Someone's been all through here, trying to make everything look undisturbed." She showed him the oversized coffee cup, holding it by the bowl in her right hand, the handle on the left. She looked at him. "I'm right-handed."

"Let's get out of here," Robert said, understanding dawning. "If we hurry, we can make it to my house by ten."

Claire turned off the lights and locked the back door. They dashed through the alley gate and jogged off into the night, without a word between them.

The main challenge they had with the alleyway designs in the older part of Phoenix was that they ran east-west. Robert's rental house was on Clarendon, a little over a mile north but only four blocks east, at Third Avenue, so they'd be unable to stay off the paved streets for very long. He led them over to Third Avenue, then headed north for the mile-plus trip, avoiding the more heavily traveled Seventh Avenue. They ran.

They didn't quite make it before ten, but luck was on their side, and they arrived at his house without incident. Robert's front door was set inside a small covered porch and flanked by narrow vertical windows on either side. What little street light shone on the lawn was shrouded by an enormous pecan tree, branches bare. Despite his occasional efforts at yard maintenance, what was at one time a charming little piece of lawn was still littered with thousands of crunchy little pecan shells, leftover from seasons long past. Robert entered his combination on the door's keypad and led the way inside.

"All right," said Claire. "Let's regroup for minute and try to figure out what the hell is going on. Why don't you start at the beginning?" Robert grabbed two cold beers from the fridge and motioned for her to sit on one of the two chairs at his desk, having dedicated what was certainly designed to be a dining nook as his home office.

He pulled out Owen Block's laptop from his backpack. He looked at the red label affixed to the front of the device.

Warning: police identifiable. This equipment is protected by the International Theft Prevention Registration System, which makes resale of stolen equipment impossible. To return to the rightful owner, please call toll-free...

Robert leaned back in his chair and closed his eyes, thinking back to his limited pre-Lucident job as a low-level information tech. *What does that warning really mean?*

"Robert, what are you thinking? Let's look at the files."

"I don't know, Claire. Look at this label. Could Lucident track the machine, or did the warning pertain only to attempts to resell stolen devices?"

"How the hell would I know?"

"I don't think we should open it without trying to disable anything that would make the computer's location available to Lucident."

"Do you know how to do that?"

"I'm not sure, but I'll try." He retrieved a small set of tools from a kitchen cabinet and carefully opened the hard case from the underside of the machine. He had no idea what he was looking at but saw a single red wire separated from the other components. He used a wire cutter and snipped the red line. Nothing happened. He closed the case again.

"What did you see?"

"I can't tell. I just made a guess and cut a wire. I mean, how much more trouble could we get in?"

Claire gave him a withering look.

If Block's computer was like all the other company-provided laptops, it would have an unchangeable, company-selected password consisting of last name, middle name, ampersand, and that Monday's date. Automatically refreshed every Monday morning. It was laughably insecure in a company that seemed obsessed with security; Robert guessed that it was more important that employees be unable to hide their activity from top management than to offer privacy to the individual. In any case, it didn't matter, since every new hire was well warned not to use the company computers for anything personal. Period.

Robert closed his eyes again and thought back to the termination report he'd seen on Block's computer, trying to tease Owen's middle name from his memory. Bingo. Everett. It was Everett. Mentally crossing his fingers, he entered: BlockEverett&01012024. Robert let out a rush of breath he'd been holding as the screen leapt to life. He saw the message pop up: *Device shut down improperly. Restore screen?* Robert practically slammed the enter button and watched as several windows opened simultaneously. He glanced at Claire, sitting to his left, untouched beer in her hand, intensely focused.

"Okay, okay. This is what I saw when I first looked at the screen." He slid the screen toward her slightly as she nodded.

"That's all right, I can see fine from here."

He slid it back. "Block was typing my patient visit reports into the main summary form when he got a text, and he told me to sit and wait for him, mumbling something about a quick trip to the men's room.

"When I looked at the discharge summary, it was completely wrong. Block's form read, 'Intake treatment plan: Admit to inpatient psych. Revised diagnosis: Malignant PTSD.'

"That patient left my office at 3:20 this afternoon, and not only was he not on death's doorstep, he actually seemed to be doing a lot better, especially with the new meds he was taking."

Claire stared at the screen. "I thought you said he left your office at 3:20."

"Right. His appointment was from three to three-twenty."

"Then how could he have been admitted at 3:00?"

Robert didn't have an answer to that.

"Keep going," said Claire.

Robert continued to scroll, highlighting each patient's discharge disposition as he went. "Deceased." "Referred to inpatient psych." "Deceased." On and on, form after form. Patient names familiar, summaries foreign.

"The next therapist's forms after mine happened to belong to you."

Claire leaned forward, energy rolling off her in waves.

"They're pretty much the same as mine, but three of yours read 'deceased,' and only a couple of your patients were referred to inpatient psych. I didn't recognize your name, so that's when I clicked on the link to your HR file…here…"

Her one-page Human Resources employment summary opened, along with her small mug shot, address, and, oddly, a note about family status: unmarried, lives alone, no children, no pets. Parents deceased. No immediate family.

"…So, I wasn't actually, well, stalking you. I just couldn't make sense of anything I was seeing. That's how I knew your name when I recognized you outside the corporate office building."

Claire could see how that would make sense, at least in the context of the rabbit hole whose entrance she was just beginning to glimpse.

"That seems odd, don't you think? Why would my family status be on my personnel sheet? And anyway, it's not correct. I have a sister. What did yours say?"

Robert looked blankly at her. Even if it had occurred to him to look, events had spun much too quickly to have done much beyond his perfunctory review. He moved the cursor back to his patient files and clicked on the HR link. His file popped up. He looked at the entry right under his photo. *Family Status: unmarried, lives alone, no children, no pets. Parents deceased. No immediate family.* He turned and stared back at Claire, whose eyes were riveted upon his. Neither spoke.

CHAPTER 8

Curt's phone buzzed, and he pulled it from his pocket as he remained seated. Tango's voice came through, calm and focused. "All went well. We had a very short window to get in and out without incident. We searched as much as we could, given the time and the fact we needed to get the transmitters and cameras in place as quickly as possible. We can listen in and find out where she is with the deposition, who she talks to over the next twelve hours. If we don't figure out where the policy is, we'll at least know if we have to go back for an escalated search and hope we can get in and out again just as easily. Powering up the computer link to you now. I'll wait while you open the link."

Curt Atkins looked at his laptop. He reversed the feed to just after Tango's men had left Claire's house. He fast-forwarded the video until he saw Claire enter the house with a male companion, images clear as day. Curt could see her walk to the kitchen stove and flick on the light under the hood. The sudden change in illumination caused the image to bleach for a couple of seconds before adjusting to the new lighting conditions. He could see her look at the counter tops and then begin to move throughout the house, followed by her companion. He checked the volume control on his laptop. On. Highest level. There was no sound. He continued to watch as she eventually stood in front of her dining room table, coffee cup in hand. She set it down slowly, and they both turned and left the house just the way they'd come in.

"The fucking sound isn't working," Curt hissed.

"I can reactivate the transmitter from the back alley, but I'm out of town

36

and can't get there until late tomorrow." Tango breathed softly into the phone, waiting for a reply.

"Can't you hear me? You only had *two* things to get right. You incompetent piece of shit!"

Tango smiled to himself as Atkins disconnected the call. Tango began to type a new text. *All okay, will wait for your go-ahead.* Curt was right. Tango did have only two things to get right, and they were both perfectly executed. Curt just didn't realize that his orders had been overridden by a higher bidder.

CHAPTER 9

Dr. Stephen Chen's phone vibrated in the pocket of his lab coat. He opened it immediately upon seeing a number he recognized well, despite it being used infrequently. "Mr. Parker."

AllMed was a holding company that included several subsidiary corporations, including Lucident, its main patient care delivery provider. AllMed's president and CEO, Stephen Chen, MD, PhD, exercised a vision that was as restrained as it was wide-reaching. Lucident was part of the fastest growing group of private providers of mental health services throughout the United States. AllMed gained both prominence and political power when American Veterans' Services, the privatized for-profit that took over the VA a number of years ago, itself outsourced mental health care for veterans. While the outsourced contracts made the entire federal budget look so much leaner, in truth, it only constituted a very costly shell in the game of shells that had become the US health care system.

"Dr. Chen." Chen's silent partner, billionaire Michael Parker, spoke, as always, in a confident, unhurried fashion. "I'm just calling for a status update. Where are we with the public announcement schedule?"

"Thanks to your work with Congress, we are right on schedule. In fact, I'd say that our early results are staggering—in the best way. We've concluded all of the pre-announcement tasks, and I think we can move the announcement up by at least ten days, unless you see some reason to delay. Are we on schedule with the FDA?"

"Of course, Dr. Chen. The expedited approval is already underway. As you know, I have invested painstakingly in many political campaigns over many years to, shall we say, *encourage* preferred outcomes."

Thanks to years of dark money donations to so many of their reelection coffers, Parker's efforts provided wide-open access to members of Congress. In turn, access flowed readily to the various agencies it funded, key among which were the Food and Drug Administration and the Department of Defense. Just as crucial, though, was Congress's dedication to the continuing escalation of the country's military budget and its ever-growing commitment to perpetual ground wars around the world.

"Mr. Parker, I expect that Lucident's federal contract, which is lucrative even now, will become a loss leader once AllMed's pharmaceutical division becomes fully operational.

"As you know, we've summarized and followed up on patient outcomes for our sample group. A1A has been developed in both an intravenous and oral form; both appear to be equally effective. Ultimately, I expect the pill form to be far more versatile, since transport and administration are far simpler. In its pill form, the drug could actually be used right on the battlefield, allowing traumatized soldiers to return to fighting."

Frankly, the form the medication took didn't matter a whit to AllMed, since it could manage its profits unilaterally, should one form prove to be more advantageous.

Having watched scores of big service providers go belly-up trying to be all things to all people, Chen made a strategic decision early on to narrow Lucident's focus to delivering mental health services to military veterans of the United States. For now, the civilian population would have to wait.

Chen patterned AllMed's research and development labs after several of the highly successful, efficient Asian research centers that could bring new drugs to market in a fraction of the amount of time required in the US. While the FDA still classified the research as having "Alpha test" status, AllMed's research had quietly moved into full-blown clinical testing with subjects currently enrolled in Lucident's PTSD clinical programs. Parker's reassurances about the FDA approval eased but did not erase Chen's concerns about violating the FDA classification.

Early results were staggering indeed. Internally, the signature drug in AllMed's repertoire was simply referred to as A1A, but that would change to the more 'marketable' Lucidaire with the rollout of the approved drug. Both oral and IV forms had been tested and patents sought on each.

"Are the patents ready to go as well?" asked Chen.

"Yes."

Drug patents, which until recently lasted only twenty years, had become problematic in terms of the pharmaceutical industry's insatiable greed, where profits were "averaged down" during the early years as they were forced to jump through countless hoops to gain FDA approval. Congress had moved just last year to make significant changes to patent laws. First, it extended the patent protection to thirty years, thanks in no small part to the paid lobbyists, including Parker's associates, whose collective budgets now exceeded $5 billion per year. Second, Congress passed laws that made it nearly impossible for new drugs to enter the marketplace unless they were developed and tested by US companies in US markets. It already took over $2B to bring a new drug to market, and that was *before* the last wave of protectionism was made into law. Gone were the days of drugs intended for sale in the US being initially tested in overseas markets, where the costs were far more manageable. Anti-regulation and anti–federal agency public sentiment, fomented largely through the shift in attitude following the 2016 election cycle continued to add grease to the already racing skids.

"Have you finalized all of the announcement proceedings, Dr. Chen?"

"Yes, of course. The only detail not yet determined is exactly who will participate in the Congressional press conference." Chen thought he detected a slight chuckle from Mr. Parker.

"Of no relevance to us, though, is it?" asked Parker.

"None whatsoever. Who decides to take political credit for the approval and implementation has no bearing on either our production or our economic projections."

Chen's abhorrence to public braggadocio and personal publicity were not only well known to Parker but were key personal characteristics that made Chen a perfect investment partner.

"What about performance compensation bonuses?"

"All research employees received a generous year-end package, with one more large package going to my research director upon the announcement."

"Would that be Dr. Jaffe?"

"Yes. She has been tireless in overseeing—and, in fact, directing—all the bench and clinical studies up to this point. Her work has been impeccable."

After only the slightest hesitation, Parker continued. "You have no disinclination, then, to having her continue in a key ongoing role in future drug research and development?"

"Most certainly not."

"Then an extremely lucrative bonus will serve her well. Very good, then, Dr. Chen. We'll talk soon."

Chen gazed down at the now disconnected line. *That was rather an odd thing for Parker to say*, he thought briefly. But he had too many other irons in the fire at the moment to dwell upon it.

AllMed had fully expected A1A to be market-ready in two years from drug development to complete FDA approval. The timeline was right on schedule. They were almost there.

CHAPTER 10

Setting down the half-empty beer bottle, Robert rummaged in his desk drawer until he found a large-capacity flash drive. He slid the drive into the port on Block's computer, preparing to clone its contents. He smiled over at Claire.

"Hey, if NASA can have redundant systems, we can too." The soft hum let him know the flash drive was taking on data. "Claire, you can use my computer and I'll clone the data onto my tablet, so we can both work."

Claire and Robert immersed themselves in the patient files, trying to make sense of what they were seeing. Claire spoke first.

"Let's start by sorting the database for the patients first entering treatment with each of us, maybe beginning with July 1, when Lucident's current funding cycle began."

There were fifty-one patients in all. The patients in the files all carried an intake diagnosis of PTSD. Some patients needed as many as four sessions per week in the beginning, with the treatment goal to move to one appointment per week, assuming appropriate progress. Talk therapy was adjunctive to medication protocols, in that it supported and made more effective the primary treatment – drugs. The medication protocols were managed exclusively by the full-time AllMed psychiatrists on the PTSD inpatient service at the AVS hospital.

Patients who were severely compromised upon return from the field most often were assigned a diagnosis of "malignant PTSD," a relatively new diagnostic category developed primarily as a way to enable increased reimbursement for inpatient care, as well as entry into the company's pharmaceutical testing program. Occasionally patients admitted with the simpler "transitional PTSD" diagnosis did not respond well to outpatient therapy and were subsequently admitted to the inpatient service under the revised "malignant PTSD" label. The program's express goal was to move patients from a critical, often suicidal condition to that of transitional PTSD, which was likewise a newly created diagnostic category, paving the way for open-ended treatment via both talk and drug therapies. Also quite generously reimbursed.

The two therapists each began to construct tables, listing their respective patients by admission date, intake diagnosis, discharge diagnosis, and discharge disposition, noting the date of any official diagnostic change and hoping to see some kind of pattern. They switched from beer to coffee.

"So, Robert, do you know many of the other therapists at work?" Claire stood to stretch, giving her eyes a break from the computer monitor. She took off her glasses and noticed a tiny speck of paint on the earpiece. She flicked it off with a short, unmanicured fingernail.

"Not really. I guess I kind of keep to myself, but I've met a few other, well, mostly guys over the years. The company work is so regimented, and between the timetables for patient appointments and wasting time at Block's office twice a week, there just hasn't been an occasion to get to know anyone more than to give a passing nod."

"Seeing as how we have the proverbial keys to the kingdom," said Claire, "let's pull up a couple of other therapists' files and add them to our tables."

"Excellent idea."

While Robert took over entering the patient information, Claire picked out three other therapists at random. She focused on their personnel files, which now safely resided in the cloned machine.

Strange. None of the three remained employed at Lucident. Their files all indicated termination during the past seven months or so, all signed by none other than Owen Everett Block. She opened an Internet search engine on her smart phone and typed in the first therapist's name, Melanie Overstreet.

It was on the third page of the search results that she located an article from the *Albuquerque Journal*:

"Services were held for Melanie Overstreet, aged 37, on Thursday, August 8, following a fatal hit-and-run accident on Albuquerque's near north side. No next of kin were located. Investigators continue to search for the driver, asking any witnesses to call the Albuquerque Police Department."

Claire turned the monitor to Robert and nudged his arm to have him look at her screen. She clicked on Overstreet's linked HR screen and spoke softly. "Unmarried, lives alone, no children, no pets. Parents deceased."

CHAPTER 11

Curt Atkins was in an ugly mood. With what he was paying Tango, he couldn't believe the man's stupidity. Although Curt would have preferred the entire $900,000 policy, half of that would be enough to get him through the next payment to his creditors, and after that, well, he'd just figure something out. He always had before, and he could do it again. Cat landing on its feet and all that. Stacy was none the wiser, and he planned to keep it that way. Opening the closet in the guest suite, he hunted through to the area that held his ski clothes, pulling out his black pants, black turtleneck silk sweater, and neck gaiter. They would work just fine. Curt dressed quickly and slipped back downstairs to the kitchen. *That bungling fuck*, he thought. *If you want something done right…*

Stacy looked up from the chaise lounge as he approached her. "Hey, babe, we really can't figure out what to do before Monday if I can't get audio from your sister's place. I'm going to have to reset the transmitters myself." *Tango's a fool if he thinks I'll pay him for a half-done job*, he thought.

Curt would need about an hour to get to Claire's neighborhood; he'd be fine on the freeways, but once he got to surface streets, he'd have to be careful to avoid the Brigade. And that would eat up a lot of time. He wanted to get there and back before daylight and estimated that leaving Scottsdale at about 1:30 a.m. would do it, with plenty of time to spare. Tango had told him the audio transmitters had been placed in Claire's house but required reactivation, something that could be accomplished from about twenty yards away. He wouldn't even have to go inside, which was a good thing, since startling a sleeping woman in the middle of the night promised all kinds of problems.

"Just be careful, Curt. Wake me when you get back."

Stacy returned to her view and the last of her drink. *God*, she thought, smiling. *That man is nothing if not predictable.* She thought of him as an actor following a script written by a malevolent playwright, unaware of the tale's approaching climax. He may have the trappings of a gentleman, but he still had the heart of a thug. And, oh, that ego. Totally predictable.

She listened for his little black Audi to leave the garage and waited until she could see the taillights winking away through the dark desert night. She picked up her phone and began to type.

CHAPTER 12

Mack was a little stiff from sitting in the locked men's room and was glad to finally be out. Stretching his 6'2" frame, he extended his arms, checking the time on his watch. He walked down one floor to the third-floor men's room, listening at the door before removing the tiny piece of hardware that let him lock the room from the outside, too unobtrusive to be noticed by anyone not knowing what to look for.

He stepped in and turned on his flashlight. The body of a small man, slightly overweight, was slumped against the wall behind the door. Nobody home, no lights on, either, but he was breathing. Perfect. He returned the locking hardware to the door, just to be extra careful, and climbed the short flight of stairs to Block's office. He no longer noticed the slight hitch in his step, a parting gift from his stint in Afghanistan.

At 1:45 a.m., Smith used his key to return the elevator to service, pressing the button for level three. He held the door open as he watched Mack and his partner, Green, maneuver the unconcious Owen Block into a janitor's trolley and enter the empty elevator compartment. "Wait until 0200 hours before exiting the emergency door. Mack has arranged to have the van there waiting. The driver will take the package to the warehouse, and at that point, it is no longer your concern. One of you needs to stop the door from closing so you can get back up to level four as soon as the vehicle leaves."

Geez, thought Smith, *where did I ever pick up that corny dialogue?* No matter, his men felt more at ease with military-sounding chat than with normal conversation. The janitor's trolley looked just like the one that had been rolled out of the clinic shortly after closing time earlier tonight with the contents of the office whose slide-in nameplate read, "Claire Wilheit, MSW."

A few minutes later, Smith's small tablet lit up with AllMed's security screen. While he wasn't sure whether Kingston had been in Block's office, the security record showed Wilheit at the clinic at 8:28 p.m. The information Smith had was limited but suggested that at least one of the people he'd seen leaving the grounds was Wilheit. At the moment, the only logical assumption he could make was that her companion was Kingston, since his was the last open file Block had.

Smith's fingers began to fly over the keyboard, his inquiry reaching deep into the bowels of HR.

Fifteen minutes later, Smith opened his phone, punching in his boss's number. He'd never met him in person, just knew that he went by the moniker Noble. This wasn't the kind of business where people used their real names. "Package extracted without issue. Expanding search for Block's laptop."

"Very good. Keep me in the loop."

Claire Wilheit's Encanto address was familiar enough to Smith that he could visualize the neighborhood. At one time, all the homes and neighborhoods surrounding Encanto Park exuded charm and quiet, making the area among the most desirable in midtown Phoenix. Budgetary crises had left the city no choice but to sell the park, and the perimeter chain-link fence had gradually been replaced with block wall. Kingston, on the other hand, lived in a tired enclave, a small, run-down group of blocks that had somehow seen what could only be described as reverse gentrification.

The building's silent alarm had been tripped just before nine o'clock. Smith wasn't certain that Kingston had set it off, but it was a reasonable working assumption. Working on the theory that Wilheit had left with Kingston, Smith reasoned his way through the puzzle. They could be colleagues or friends, or they could be lovers. The latter represented the greatest risk to the company, since intimacy could undermine Lucident's efforts to keep employees compartmentalized, thereby stifling communication. *So*, Smith thought, *let's deal with the assumption that they're a couple, and rule that out first.*

It was a weekend. If they were a couple, it was far more likely that they would spend time at her place, since it was no doubt a whole lot nicer than his.

At 2:12 a.m., Smith's employees returned to Block's office, task completed without any problems. He handed Green, the shorter man, a slip of paper with 730 West Wilshire written in pencil. Green quickly looked at the address and then crushed the paper with his left hand.

"I'll need a thorough search—unknown whether the destination is occupied. You'll have to figure it out once you arrive. Try to minimize collateral damage, but the laptop is the priority." Smith added, "Just keep me up to date." He wondered absently what Olivia was up to right now. He'd interacted with a lot of operatives in his line of work, and she was one of the best. He'd connect with her tomorrow to conclude their transaction.

Mack and Green exited through the ground-level emergency door. Green dashed to the parking structure to get the car while his partner kept watch at the Lucident door. As soon as Green was out of sight, Mack opened his phone to send a message.

CHAPTER 13

Curt's mood lifted slightly as he kept his speed at ten miles over the limit, confident that he wouldn't stand out from the few other vehicles on the road at this time of night. Driving had become his preferred method of relieving stress. He loved a high-performance vehicle, even though he had to travel well outside the city limits to test its chops. He drove like a slalom skier, weaving in and out of traffic, leaving as little room as possible to slide back into the driving lane, imagining strategically placed cones even when he had the road to himself. And while he liked having the road to himself, it was a lot more fun when he could scare an actual driver.

He felt the small box on the seat next to him for the tenth time, safeguarding it like the precious totem it was. Tango had supplied two sets and had given one to Atkins, who congratulated himself on his foresight to keep it. Contingency planning. The only way to go. When he exited the freeway at Indian School Road, it was just after 2:00 a.m.

Tango sat in his car, engine off, parked just at the end of the alley behind Claire's house. He watched the GPS screen tracking Atkins's car. He smiled. Actually, it was really just tracking the audio activation device. Even better. He didn't expect to see Curt's car for another thirty minutes or so. He cracked open the window enough to let the soft chill of the night do its part in helping him stay alert.

As he prepared to settle in for the wait, Tango thought back over the past twenty-four hours—the lucrative contract for the search and recovery of insurance policy documents that Curt was convinced were secreted somewhere in Claire's home. He didn't know and didn't want to know how this rock-solid conviction came about, but he suspected it was more Stacy's doing than the other way around. It didn't matter anyway, because he had a job to do, plain and simple. If he needed detailed information that was relevant to the job's successful execution, he wanted every bit of it. If it wasn't directly related to the job of the hour, then it could only create potential distractions. He'd collected half of Curt Atkins's contract amount up front, and even after paying his men and acquiring the materials and supplies he needed, his bank account was $65,000 fatter today than it was last week. The superseding contract, however, dwarfed the remaining sixty-five grand by a factor of ten.

Planting the cameras had been child's play, carried out by men he'd used several times before, reliably discreet, reliably greedy. They'd left the audio transmitters as well, just to ensure the plausibility of the plant, but Tango knew full well they'd never be activated. The real treasure had been hidden in the little guesthouse between the alley and Claire's back door.

CHAPTER 14

In the small rental house on Clarendon, the charts and tables that Robert and Claire had begun to assemble were looking disjointed. The timelines for patient progress, charted by changing diagnoses, didn't seem to correlate with either the other therapists' records or with their own. Robert added the remaining five active therapists' files to the database, still searching for commonalities. Claire focused on Internet searches for names of the other former employees she'd initially identified. Overstreet had died in a car accident. People died in car accidents every day. But, statistically, they were unlikely to die in unsolved hit-and-run crimes.

She ran general internet searches for news articles about the other therapists going back a year. Nothing came up. She searched the Maricopa County recorder's office for property records, divorce decrees, and everything else she could imagine. Nothing. Claire could envision someone deciding to move out of Arizona—frankly, it was pretty easy to imagine herself moving out of state—but she expected to find something on the web, regardless of geography.

"Claire, add these names to your search, just to see if you can find out anything." Robert handed her the worksheet with the names of the other therapists formerly employed by Lucident.

Her fingertips danced across the keyboard, the powerful search engine digging deep into the World Wide Web.

Claire was unable to locate even a small bit of information on the first four of the six names Robert had given her. The fifth therapist, Jacob Morgan, was a different story. She let out a quiet "Yes" when the initial search page yielded over twenty results. She clicked on the first link, to an article that appeared in last month's digital version of the *Arizona Republic*, Phoenix's once respected newspaper.

Not my first choice for investigative journalism, but sometimes, she thought, *you just gotta play the hand you're dealt.*

"The body of Phoenix therapist Jacob Morgan was found in a Tempe hotel room Tuesday, after housekeeping was unable to enter the room. Morgan, 51, was the victim of an apparent suicide. Investigators estimated the time of death to be sometime Saturday. Toxicology results will be released by the medical examiner once tests have been completed. Sources in the examiner's office indicate that prescription narcotics and alcohol present in the room are likely to be confirmed as the cause of death."

A small photograph of Morgan accompanied the article.

"I remember hearing about this," said Robert. "The Arizona Psychology Association had an online fundraiser for his burial expenses, because…"

"He had no known family." Claire completed Robert's sentence. They looked at the family status in Morgan's personnel file. It read just like theirs.

"I don't know what the hell is going on, but there's something terribly wrong here. I've got a really, really bad feeling about this." Claire combed her fingers through her unruly hair, cupping her hands around the back of her neck to knead out the little knot that had begun to form.

"What do you want to do?" Concern lined Robert's face. Neither of them, apparently, had jobs to return to on Monday.

"I'm exhausted, and I'm afraid to go home, but I don't really want to get a hotel room in Tempe." Her halfhearted attempt at humor fell flat. "I need to get some things from home and go somewhere safe to try to figure out what's happening."

"Claire, it could be dangerous for you to go back there."

"Well, I'm not exactly going for a new outfit and my makeup, Robert. I have some allergy meds I need to get. It won't take long."

"Claire! Someone broke into your house!"

"Right. And they were gone when we were there earlier. Look, you can drive me if you want—or not. I can just jog back home."

"No, you can't get there and back without risking running into the Brigade."

Claire just stared at him. She waited for him to speak again.

"All right. Let's take my car and drive over to your house, grab what you need, and come back here, where it's safe." The expression on his face made her question his assumption.

CHAPTER 15

Stephen Chen's concern had risen by the hour since his first conversation with Noble earlier Friday evening, after Block's laptop was reported missing. He wasn't willing to wait until Noble felt he had an update worthy of sharing, so he picked up the phone to call Noble once more.

"Chen here. Do you have any updated information on our situation?"

"Yes, sir. We have two new Lucident hires set to begin first thing Monday. One new therapist and one new managing director of clinic operations. The new therapist will be assuming patient care duties immediately after Monday morning's orientation and will be able to assume her full quotient of patients by the end of the week."

Noble's speech was clipped and a little more rapid than Chen was accustomed to hearing.

"That's not the situation I'm talking about. What about the missing laptop?"

"Well…"

"You do realize that this thing needs to be resolved, and I need you to get this thing under control—completely under control—before the offices open on Monday morning. Can you wipe the computer clean remotely?"

"We never thought any of the computers would leave the premises but I'm working on a system that will enable us to do that."

Chen paced the length of his darkened living room, waiting for the coffee machine to beep, signaling that the brew was ready. The room's full-length glass windows revealed a spattering of lights below in the mostly dark vista. As he thought about his security director's response, Chen moved easily through the darkened apartment, its minimalist décor lit only by the motion-activated lighting under the cabinets. Clearly, Noble should have considered the possibility that a computer could fall into unauthorized hands.

Upper level personnel issues were strictly within the purview of the director's oversight, and while there hadn't been any glaring problems to date, the missing laptop might well constitute one. He was much too close to the goal posts to tolerate any rocking of the boat.

"Dr. Chen, I am working diligently on a plan to address the logistics required to repair any possible problems created by Block and his missing computer. Kingston's patient load will have to wait until Tuesday, the earliest I can bring a new therapist on board. As you may know, Kingston's departure from Lucident was unanticipated, at least this month."

While Noble didn't involve Chen in any of the day-to-day security or management issues of the company, he had been conscientious in letting him know anytime there might be a problem. But the unfortunate events in Block's office threatened to preempt the painstaking plans Chen had been executing flawlessly for the past year. Chen didn't like threats.

"I need a definitive report on the status of the missing laptop and the whereabouts of Mr. Kingston before Monday morning." If any of Kingston's patients were left hanging within the Lucident outpatient function, Chen would need to reassign them a malignant PTSD diagnosis and arrange for their admission to the inpatient service until they received the A1A protocol. Involuntary commitment was an easily implemented arrangement, particularly given the medically fragile state of the PTSD patient cohort. Chen wanted the new managing director to begin without the complications that abandoned patients would no doubt create.

"Yes, Dr. Chen, I'll take care of it and will stay in touch."

"Very good."

Chen, despite his role as Lucident's CEO, still retained much of the discipline he'd developed as a chemist, even though he'd left that work behind long ago. Rolling out A1A would be the culmination of almost a decade of tedious work, but the recent easing of drug patent laws would send the company's expected profits to a near stratospheric level—a trajectory to be followed closely by his own net worth. The shortcuts he'd had to introduce into the research methodology were less than ideal, from a scientific point of view. There was a time when such methods would have been untenable to Chen. It wasn't the way he'd prefer to do things, but, he thought, it could be managed.

Once the clinical trial results and FDA approval were made public, Lucident would be positioned to implement its Arizona model nationwide and to secure a no-bid contract with the US Department of Defense. All due to AllMed's wealthy, greedy patron. Michael Parker was a cold silent partner, but he was unwavering in his pursuit of the big goal, never losing sight of the end game. And he didn't interfere with operations.

There were just a few loose ends that needed to be tidied up. Chen strode back to the kitchen to pour a cup of fresh coffee. He checked his email and set up a notification in the event that a message came in from his security director. This could be a long night.

CHAPTER 16

Curt Atkins drove slowly through side streets, passing Wilshire at Seventh Avenue. He quickly glanced down the short street between his route and the walled-off park. He had made good time; he would circle the park once to make sure no one was out and about and would find a parking spot a few blocks away, just in case.

While Tango would have appeared supremely relaxed to anyone who observed him, his attention to movement and sound in the alleyway was intense—and rewarded as he saw Curt's car cruise past the alley opening. *Perfect.* Though he could have tracked Curt's movement from a remote location, direct verification was a redundant but important part of the way he worked. It was time to get into position so that he'd be able to leave the area unnoticed as soon as his job was complete. When his men had been at Claire's earlier, they'd left a small motion detector along the walkway in the backyard. Another redundancy. At this late hour he knew there was only one person who was likely to trip it, and he'd just watched him drive past the alley opening. Tango put his car into drive and cruised north on Sixth Avenue toward Osborn Road, where he could park and wait for the devices to signal Curt's arrival.

Tango watched until the GPS locater stopped moving, signaling that Curt's car was being parked. He clicked and copied the coordinates and forwarded them to two other men in his employ.

Curt grabbed the small electronic box from the passenger seat and exited the car, walking with a stride that was neither hurried nor slow. He had a heightened awareness of his surroundings, listening for any unexpected sounds that might signal he'd been noticed. The long midnight drive had calmed him somewhat, but his anger at Tango's incompetence grew with each step as he walked the three blocks north to Wilshire. *I'm so fucking done with this cops-and-robbers shit,* he thought. At this point in his life, he just didn't do this kind of crap anymore; that's why he'd hired it out in the first place.

Curt felt the box through the front pocket of his pants, tapping it lightly with each step as if to reassure himself that it was still there. Twenty yards away, that's what Tango had told him. He wouldn't have to risk going into Claire's house in the dead of night. He could probably activate the transmitters from the alley, soundless and unexposed.

Smith's men waited on the small side street just to the south of Wilheit's address. Mack nodded to his partner, watching Green holster the small handgun as he stepped out into the night.

"Just go in quietly and look in the main areas first—you might get lucky and not have to go into the bedroom."

"Yeah, but if I was really gonna get lucky, that's where I'd start." The smaller man smirked. "She'd be handing me that computer with a smile on her face."

Last job I do with this guy, the tall man thought. *Green was sounding reckless, and reckless gets you caught. I'll have a word with Smith when I see him next.*

CHAPTER 17

Robert and Claire quickly stuffed Block's laptop and Robert's personal computer and tablet with the cloned files into his backpack. They left through the back door of Robert's place and ducked into the old carport, which was shielded from the house by a dense hedge of old oleander bushes. Robert Kingston drove an old dark blue Toyota RAV4. The odometer had nearly 180,000 miles on it, but it still ran just fine, at least most of the time. Living so close to work, Robert preferred to walk during the cooler weather, so he didn't put on the kind of mileage he once did. Unhampered by street traffic, it wouldn't take them more than five or six minutes to get to Claire's Encanto neighborhood. They climbed into the vehicle for the short ride.

He pressed the ignition. Nothing happened.

"What the fuck?" Claire was otherwise speechless at yet another turn of very bad luck.

"Sometimes this happens. My car's kind of old." He climbed out of the driver's seat, grabbed a towel from the back seat, and popped the hood. He quickly cleaned the battery terminals and closed the hood gently, not wanting to attract attention by slamming it shut.

As he approached the driver's side door, Robert heard a scraping sound. He froze. Claire looked at him through the driver's side window, cocking her head as if in question. He raised a finger to his lips and pointed behind them. Robert could hear two male voices low in conversation, just murmurs, and their approaching footsteps. Their pace quickened, and he watched two figures dressed in Brigade uniforms jog past the end of his driveway.

"Oh my God, Claire, that was the Brigade." They sat in the darkened car for a full five minutes, waiting to be sure that the Brigade patrol wasn't returning. Five minutes whose value was yet unknown to them.

His next try worked. The engine clunked once and then hummed to life.

Robert eased out of the driveway, wondering if he should drive without headlights too. *Maybe*, he thought, *I'm just getting a little paranoid*. Then again, maybe it was warranted.

The RAV4 pulled to a stop on Wilshire, six houses east of Claire's bungalow. Better to walk quietly up to the house than to pull into the driveway with a car that might be heard or seen. Everything was quiet, neighbors sleeping, blissfully unaware of their arrival. The trip had taken less than ten minutes. Both passengers rolled down the windows, looking out for any activity, and especially alert to any sign of the Brigade patrol. Robert turned off the engine, and the therapists waited for a few moments to double-check their surroundings for noise or lights. It was quiet and dark. They stepped out of the car.

CHAPTER 18

Curt stopped in the alleyway just outside the gate to Claire's backyard. No one had followed him, no one had noticed him, and he was beginning to feel more confident. Despite resenting that he had to do this job himself, the little kick of adrenaline returned, like an alcoholic taking his first drink after years of sobriety.

Three blocks south, two men also dressed in black approached the little black sports car. They double checked the coordinates Tango had sent. It was the right car. With practiced efficiency, one touched the electronic skeleton key to the door handle, and the vehicle opened to them. As the second man climbed into the passenger's seat, he touched the electronic key to the start button. The sleek little ride purred to life as the men drove slowly away, heading northeast toward Scottsdale.

Green entered the living room of Claire's house through the west-facing casement window. He moved silently into the great room, finding his way with the red beam of his flashlight. It was bright enough to illuminate the space in front of him but wouldn't be noticed by a casual observer on the street. He began a systematic search for Block's laptop. It would be bad enough if Wilheit was sleeping in the other room, but a lot worse if she had male company. He touched the holstered weapon, reassuring himself that he had a solid backup plan.

He was completely unaware of the man who stood in the alley just outside Claire's backyard gate.

Curt pressed the button on the small handheld device that would activate the audio transmitter. The little indicator light came on but remained red. The lots in this neighborhood were narrow but somewhat deep. He must still be out of range. *Goddammit.* Very slowly, he lifted the latch and eased open the backyard gate. He stepped into the yard and edged toward the bungalow's back door.

Senses alert, Curt paused to listen but heard nothing. He turned toward the kitchen door and noticed a dim reddish light, visible only because his eyes had thoroughly adjusted to the dark. It was moving. *Shit. Claire must be up and about, in the middle of the goddamn night. What a clusterfuck.*

The side door to the freestanding garage was immediately to his left. As he turned the knob, the unlocked door opened without a sound. He slipped inside. He was at least ten yards closer to the house—most likely now within range.

Tango smiled as the motion detector in Claire's yard vibrated in the pocket on his left hip. With his right hand, he withdrew the other device, smiled, and flipped the toggle. Tango put his car into drive and turned left onto Osborn, away from the city's center.

CHAPTER 19

The fireball shattered the night sky and rose, vomiting flames and thick black smoke nearly a hundred feet into the air. Enormous chunks of debris were carried by the fire on its upward trajectory and then roared back to earth. The massive explosion was as loud as it was bright, turning the entire neighborhood into day.

Robert and Claire fell against the side of the car, stupefied by the sight just a short distance to the west. They simply stared, too shocked to process the scene in front of them.

"Move away from the vehicle." The voice came from behind them; they turned to see a figure in what looked like a uniform pointing what looked like an automatic weapon right at them. "Bring the backpack. Now, please."

Robert did exactly as ordered. Claire was frozen, her open eyes and gaping mouth lit by the raging fire. The patrolman kept his weapon trained on Claire, who was still too stunned to move, fright and confusion battling for control of her reeling thoughts. Her eyes darted between the man holding the gun and the inferno that had been her home and her sanctuary, symbolizing everything she had built in finally getting her life under her own control. Sirens warbled from the direction of downtown, the increasing pitch signaling their rapid approach. Robert was transfixed by the man's dark gray uniform sporting the Brigade insignia.

"Move. Now. We're running out of time." He pointed the gun toward a darkened house on the south side of Wilshire. "Inside."

It was as if Claire hadn't heard a word. Robert grasped her upper arm and pulled her along with him toward the open door, the Brigade agent on their heels, gun still ushering them forward. Claire watched as her neighbors raced into the street, shouting and shielding their faces from the blinding light and deafening noise. Robert's whisper was urgent. "Claire. Come on!"

The three of them entered the silent house, aware that now most of the occupants of the other houses on the street had awakened and were turning on lights. The neighbors, just like Robert and Claire, had no idea what was happening, just that it was big and very, very bad.

The Brigade man took them directly to the back of the house, pausing in the kitchen. "Open the backpack."

Robert complied, and the patrolman felt inside the backpack and pulled out both laptops and Robert's tablet. He took the computer with the Lucident logo and returned Robert's personal items to the bag. "Take your backpack, and give me your phones," he said as he handed them two replacement phones. "Use these instead. And only in an emergency." The patrolman led them into the backyard and to the alleyway behind it to the south, a mirror to Claire's property on the north side of the street. He held out a set of car keys. "Which of you is in better shape to drive?"

Claire was now visibly shaking, a predictable result of adrenaline running headlong into panic. Robert took the keys from the man's hand.

"Look, I know this doesn't make any sense to you right now, but just be glad that you didn't arrive a few minutes earlier or you'd be in the center of that ball of fire."

"What's going on?" Claire's speech was little more than a whisper. "My house is gone. Gone! What are you doing here? Are we under arrest? Someone broke into my house tonight—was it you? Were you following us?"

"We really don't have time for a detailed explanation. I wasn't following you. I was following the guy who broke into your house just before the explosion." He handed Robert a small GPS device. "Take this car and follow the GPS to the destination. Leave your car here. It will buy you some precious time. Do not go to your house," he said, looking at Robert. "It'll be in just as much danger as that one." He nodded toward the direction of the firestorm.

"You have a full tank of gas and won't need to stop until you get into

Colorado. There's an envelope with cash in the glove compartment. Do not use your credit cards."

Claire and Robert looked at each other. They talked over one another.

"How do you know who we are?"

"Colorado?"

"Just get going," the patrolman said. "Right now. South to McDowell, then west. The GPS will take over from there."

They didn't move.

"Now!"

Claire and Robert jumped and scrambled to get into the car. Robert started the engine as Claire opened the GPS device as quickly as she could with badly shaking hands.

They drove south, Robert struggling to control his urge to flatten the gas pedal. The now lit-up neighborhood filled the rearview mirror. Claire wanted nothing more than to be swallowed by the dark, silent desert night.

It was true, thought Aaron Davis, that he wasn't actually following Claire at that moment: he was waiting for the Lucident men. But he had rented the Wilshire property, just as he had several others around town, where he and his team could observe Lucident's therapists on their home turf. And what did she mean, someone broke into her house? Davis had been in the Wilshire area since about ten o'clock tonight and hadn't noticed anything amiss at Wilheit's house. He had placed only passive surveillance cameras directed at the therapists' houses throughout town, designed to see anyone who approaches from the front. That was a serious flaw, and one that he would remedy immediately. But the question neither therapist thought to ask was: "Why are you in *this* house?"

CHAPTER 20

Twenty-some miles to the north, Stacy smiled as she read Tango's text. She closed her phone and hummed to herself as she pulled back the soft sheets, welcoming a good night's sleep. She had no reason to get up early tomorrow. Tomorrow morning, once she independently verified the night's event, she'd send the final payment to Tango's account. Other than that, she didn't have anything pressing to do until Monday morning. Not one damn thing. She used the remote on her nightstand to close the blackout blinds. Snuggling under the down comforter, Stacy closed her eyes. Things were working out exactly according to plan. She'd just executed the last of many complex steps to secure a financially sound future without any of the marital baggage that might have otherwise been required. *Life is good*, she thought.

Thirty-five minutes after leaving the Encanto neighborhood, the little Audi pulled into the parking lot of the casino situated on the Pima reservation two miles east of Scottsdale Road. The passenger exited the car and quickly opened the door to his own car, which occupied one of the few spaces in the blind spot of the casino's security cameras. He backed out, and the Audi pulled in. Without looking back, the two men left the parking lot and the reservation and headed home.

CHAPTER 21

Aaron Davis inserted the external hard drive into the port on Block's computer, waited for the drive to flash green, and then wiped the Lucident machine of all its files. He opened the small mechanical room that held the furnace and water softener. He opened the water softener's lid and submerged the machine. It would be safely concealed in its salty lair, to be retrieved at a later time.

Intensely aware of the minutes passing, Davis stopped long enough to place a quick phone call.

"Yes, I got the laptop, and our two subjects are on their way...okay, understood, but I'm short on time and will follow up later."

He dashed down the alley toward the sirens and first responders, joining the other Brigade members as they jogged toward the flames.

"Anyone know what happened?" Davis asked, feigning being out of breath.

"No. And we won't have much time to figure it out, since you can be sure the Phoenix PD's gonna snap up jurisdiction on this just like they do with every high-profile crime."

The rivalry between the Phoenix Police Department and the Brigade first began with the privatization of "off-hours" and had grown into outright resentment, if not hostility. Major shootings, drug busts, and the like remained the province of the Phoenix PD, who swept in to investigate and take credit for arrests. While it pissed off members of the Brigade to be treated as the lesser of the two forces, it made the brass look good. That, in turn, made the elected officials look even better. By the time the small group had jogged up and onto Wilshire, fire and police vehicles were pulling up Seventh Avenue.

A Phoenix police captain had taken control of the scene, holding up an arm to stop the Brigade. "We'll take it from here, guys. You can go back to your posts."

"That sure as hell didn't take long," muttered a Brigade member. "Might even be a record. Assholes."

CHAPTER 22

Saturday, January 6

Aaron Davis opened his eyes after the three hours of sleep he'd finally managed to get. His eyes couldn't have felt worse if he had poured gravel into them. He got out of bed and went straight to the kitchen of his apartment, starting some coffee and clicking on the television. He opened the police scanner on the counter.

Wilheit and Kingston should be near Flagstaff by now. Maybe farther, if they hadn't run into bad weather or snow. Davis opened the GPS tracker on one of the phones he'd given to the therapists. Knowing they'd have to sleep and probably pick up some warm clothes, he didn't expect them to arrive at their final destination until later tonight, possibly even tomorrow. There was only one major road to Flagstaff, and delays were frequent. He checked their position. They were very close to Flag, as he'd expected. As long as he knew where they were, he wouldn't worry. If needed, he could remotely eavesdrop on their conversations. He'd prefer not to have to call them, since he didn't have the time to engage in a protracted question-and-answer session. There would be plenty of time later for dialogue. Right now, he needed to think.

What the hell had happened last night? He'd watched the Lucident men approach Wilheit's address and then observed the shorter man climb in through her side window. And he already knew when the Lucident guys would arrive, so they couldn't have been who broke into Wilheit's house earlier. What in the world had caused the explosion? Realizing the Lucident break-in would likely never be discovered gave him a small sense of relief. He wondered if there was anything left of the body that had most certainly blown up with the rest of 730 West Wilshire.

Every news station carried some variation of the same story. "Investigation is ongoing, but at a brief press conference ending just a few minutes ago, the governor and chief of police indicated that although the fire has been extinguished, the area would remain too hot for on-site forensics teams to evaluate the event until tomorrow at the earliest."

Well, that was worthless, Davis thought. He turned the volume up on the scanner and listened, grateful that the caffeine was beginning to kick in. He caught bits and pieces of conversation. "…RAV4 on the street was abandoned…registered to a Robert Kingston, 302 West Clarendon. Officers en route now."

Davis opened his phone and punched in a saved number. He began to type.

CHAPTER 23

Smith faced his employee as they sat across from each other at a small conference table. "Mack, let's go over everything, and I mean everything, that happened." Mack recounted the events of the night. He thanked his good fortune that Smith had directed Green, and not him, to search the Wilshire house.

"Green entered the premises, all according to plan, then *boom*. He was gone. So was the whole fucking house. I got out of there immediately and headed straight to Kingston's apartment. It was empty. Kingston wasn't there, his bed hadn't been slept in, and there was no laptop. Anywhere."

Smith's assumption that Kingston had gone to Claire Wilheit's place was beginning to gain traction. Not certainty—that would have to wait—but for now it looked like a reasonable working hypothesis. If he was right, Kingston had likely perished along with Wilheit and Green. This was far from the way Smith operated. Too many unknowns made for a sloppy operation, and sloppy operations could be fatal. Mack was meticulous and had carried out his mission expertly. Smith didn't feel any real emotion over losing Green, but had it been Mack instead, he might have had a few regrets. Mack was the consummate, loyal professional he'd come to expect.

The newscaster continued; both men looked at the screen. Smith turned up the volume a notch.

"Police are seeking a person of interest in the case, Robert Kingston, forty-two, of Phoenix, whose car was found in the area. Please call Silent Witness with any information on Kingston's whereabouts." A toll-free number appeared across the television screen, along with Kingston's photograph.

A wave of relief passed over Smith, as physical as a warm shower. "Looks like our boy was a tragic victim of an explosion." The feeling of relief was short-lived. Explosions don't just happen. Aging gas lines and leaking seals were common in some of the older Phoenix homes, so that was most likely the cause. But until they knew for sure, all it meant was another loose end. A worrisome one at that.

CHAPTER 24

Stacy Atkins poured herself a second espresso and sat at her computer. The local news had confirmed the explosion. Stacy retrieved Curt's password list— the little yellow sticky-note under the desk—to check to see if Curt had changed the password to open the machine. He hadn't. She accessed her private online folder. Its label read: "Favorite make-up tips" and held only one file: her money market account. Click. Three hundred and twenty-five thousand dollars flew through cyberspace, landing in Tango's offshore account. Balance due, now paid in full. That pretty much wiped out her money market fund. A solid investment, given the small fortune she would inherit in her new role as a widow. It had taken nearly nine of the ten years they'd been married for her to slowly bleed off funds from Curt's accounts. A thousand here, three thousand there. She didn't think it was enough for Curt to notice and she was right. It didn't matter now. Curt could reimburse her for the expense. Posthumously.

She'd wait another hour or so to make a police report, concerned that her husband had not returned last night. What if something dreadful had happened to him? The absurdity of the thought made her actually laugh out loud. She spread a little cream cheese on her bagel, enjoying her simple breakfast and marveling at what could be accomplished with a little cash and a lot of will. This whole series of events couldn't have been packaged up any more neatly. Her sister gone, Curt along with her. She didn't really mean to have her sister killed, but it wasn't her fault that Claire was in the wrong place at the wrong time. Now the nonexistent insurance policy charade could finally be put to rest. It had accomplished its goal: pissing off a greedy, mean-spirited spouse just enough to get him to Claire's house. Stacy hadn't been entirely sure that Curt would take the bait, but the promise of nearly half a million dollars combined with the pressure of a short time frame and a predictably domineering temperament produced an absolutely perfect storm.

She could picture the conversation with her lawyers as they notified her of their intention to withdraw the pending suit. "We're terribly sorry, Mrs. Atkins, but there is, of course, no way to proceed without a bona fide policy, and of course, given the tragedy that took your sister's life..." Blah, blah, blah. Of course, they would send her a final bill. Of course, she would not hesitate to call should she ever require their legal services in the future. Of course.

She would have to wait for confirmation of Curt's disappearance to take control of most of his liquid assets. It would take a while longer to assume control over the longer-term investments and retirement accounts, which she, as the surviving spouse, would gratefully receive. But she wasn't really in that much of a hurry. After all, it was literally, and figuratively, money in the bank. First things first. She was, after all, a very patient woman.

An hour later, Stacy Atkins disconnected the phone, having reported her concerns about her missing husband to the Scottsdale Police Department. As recently as three years ago, she would have been asked to wait an additional twenty-four hours before a person could be considered missing. But now, frequent kidnappings and gang violence had virtually eliminated the waiting period. Ironically, the arrogant campaign pledges after the 2016 election to eliminate gangs by deporting undocumented criminals was a joke. Subsequent research had shown that most of the gang members in the southwest were US citizens. She knew that one of the greatest advantages to living in her wealthy zip code was having residents' concerns elevated and prioritized.

The report went smoothly. Stacy spoke with just enough tremor in her voice to be convincing. No, she didn't have any idea where he had gone, just that the car was gone when she woke at 5:00 a.m., wondering why Curt wasn't asleep next to her. She described him as having been distracted of late, often pacing until the early morning hours, his sleep fitful. Yes, she was very worried. Yes, officer, thank you for looking in to his whereabouts.

CHAPTER 25

Stephen Chen returned to the expansive glass desk in his apartment office. His penthouse was owned by an investment company that was part of another AllMed subsidiary. The entire high-rise apartment project was high-end, offering commuters and executives an impressive array of amenities and a spectacular view of the old Margaret Hance Park. Chen's rent, paid to the investment company, was itself subsidized by AllMed as an executive perk. Although the developers pressured city officials to retain water conservation waivers for the park property, the public outcry was just too much in a state cursed with endless drought. As a result, the apartment project didn't appreciate at the rate projected when it broke ground, since its proximity to one of the few remaining public parks ranked among its chief selling points. Still, it was a luxurious place, and its central corridor location gave Chen easy light rail access to the clinics and to his offices and labs in the old VA hospital.

Chen gazed out to the north, considering how he had come to this point. His mother, an Army surgeon, had been deployed to the Middle East a number of years ago; one tour morphed into the next. Chen had been largely raised by his father, who was devoted to both Stephen and his wife. When Stephen's mother, Susan Masterson, MD, had returned to Phoenix after the last tour, she was broken and severely depressed. She rarely came out of her room, and her grip on reality was evaporating. One day she just hit bottom. Stephen remembered that morning as if it had happened yesterday. Susan was hysterical, incoherent, and armed with a kitchen knife when she rushed her husband, threatening to kill him. Stephen had to physically restrain her while his father called 911.

In retrospect, it was foolish for Stephen and his dad to think that they could manage Susan's PTSD on their own. Dr. Susan Masterson, along with her once brilliant mind, now remained locked away in the long-term psychiatric unit of the old VA hospital. Precious little had been done for her, since the VA budget had been decimated after Congress had tired of the scandals and complaints that dogged the system, eventually leading to its privatization. Stephen was on his own and had been for some time; his father had been permanently felled by a lurking, fatal bulge in an artery in his head that had, without warning, finally decided to burst.

Upon graduating with honors and dual doctoral degrees in organic chemistry and neurophysiology, Stephen Chen, PhD, went on to complete his medical degree. After medical school, he directed his energy into clinical research and worked tirelessly at several of the most prestigious labs in the country. Stephen loved his chosen field, not just because of its intellectual challenges but because he loved the discipline and unemotional aspect of the work.

Most of the big pharmaceutical research labs had tremendous talent on staff, but years of regulations, cronyism, and distorted funding cycles left the best among them frustrated and cynical. Worse, the big research and development labs were in fierce competition, each employing scores of lobbyists who canceled out each other's well-funded efforts. The escalating cost of maintaining armies of paid lobbyists took precious resources from the actual work the labs were intended to do. Delays in getting new drugs to market worsened every year.

Chen's only logical decision was to start his own lab, and he began to search out an investment partner willing to risk the necessary capital to develop it. Chen would assume all executive and strategic management functions and would have free rein to develop new treatment therapies as he saw fit. Chen's quietly placed feelers found their way to billionaire Michael Parker, and the rest, as they say, was history.

In the beginning, Stephen's intentions were good. However, operating in a cutthroat industry eventually required him to cut throats, too. Over time, cynicism emerged victorious, albeit salved by his flourishing net worth. In due course, his intentions became little more than dilapidated pavement on the golden road to hell. AllMed had become an enormous machine that ran with speed and efficiency and nearly immeasurable profits, thanks to its governmental contract.

Chen kept the management and research staff sleek and well compensated. After bonuses and an incredible array of benefits, remaining profits were devoted to securing top-notch researchers and lab workers and providing them with state-of-the-art facilities and equipment. Lucident was skirting the edges of legality—well, to be honest, had trampled right over them—with its unapproved clinical trials, having long since passed the ethical boundaries inherent in the field. *Just another month or so,* Chen thought, *and this will all be wrapped up.* Profits would be assured into infinity with the release of a revolutionary, privately developed psychoactive drug that was nearly perfect.

It was obvious to Stephen Chen that A1A would save lives. Veterans suffering from PTSD committed suicide to the tune of some eight hundred per year. And those were just the vets who had been formally diagnosed. The actual number was certainly higher, but no one knew just how much. Living with a family member with severe PTSD had untold consequences in terms of divorce, broken families, unemployment, and national productivity, all of which came with enormous social and economic costs. He could easily foresee the US military dumping billions of budgeted dollars into Lucident. The fact that A1A could be administered to soldiers in the field, allowing them to return to the battlefield in a matter of days, meant greatly improved economic and war zone performance. Not to mention that once the drug was formally approved, Chen was confident that the US would go to any and every length to prevent hostile nations from getting their hands on it. Chen had no expertise or any relevant experience in the machinations of US military policy, but Michael Parker did. Their complementary areas of expertise made them well-suited partners.

A1A's treatment protocol required three days of extremely high initializing doses in order to establish therapeutic levels of the drug in the patient's system. After that time, regular daily doses would maintain the proper level of drugs in the patient's body. In turn, the "nearly perfect" A1A came with its own internal police force: without their daily A1A maintenance, even captured prisoners of war would quickly cease to be a security threat. Dangerously high blood pressure, psychosis, and suicide became high probabilities within forty-eight hours after the drug was stopped. A1A had proved effective in about ninety percent of the patients so far. An excellent result, except, of course, for the other ten percent. The unfortunate patients for whom A1A failed would develop life-threatening side effects. Research suggested that there was a "silent" backlog of between twelve and twenty percent of veterans who remained undiagnosed. Veterans of wars that had been continuing nonstop for nearly three decades.

One of many problems in assessing the incidence, as well as the prevalence, of PTSD in the veteran population was that it wasn't always evident immediately—some conditions took years to develop or even be recognized. There was, in the military alone, an estimated pent-up demand of nearly eight million potential patients. From a profit standpoint, there was also an enormous volume of nonmilitary PTSD in the general population that would dwarf the military stats. But that, as far as Chen was concerned, was a secondary, future market. First things first. Once A1A was on the market, the profits would allow research and development into additional medications that might assist those who fared poorly on the medication. In the meantime, those patients who did not respond to A1A were being safely cared for as Lucident inpatients until such future time and circumstances offered an option.

A1A, reasoned Chen, was no different from insulin. Both would be needed throughout patients' lives. Diabetics without insulin would face certain death from kidney failure. However, diabetes wasn't a by-product of US military and foreign policy that spent billions of tax dollars to create generations of addicts. A1A was brilliant in its design and development. It was unfortunate that bringing it to market had required unsavory scientific practices and a few necessary human casualties, which even a few years ago would have appalled him. Now they were simply collateral—a cost of doing business. If nothing else, Dr. Stephen Chen had developed exquisite skills in compartmentalizing unpleasant information.

CHAPTER 26

Sunday, January 7

Exhausted to the bone and frustrated with the many lane closures on I-17 north out of Phoenix, Claire and Robert had finally stopped at a small roadside motel near the New Mexico-Colorado border outside Farmington. Despite taking turns driving throughout the day and into last night, eventually they had no sensible choice but to stop and get a few hours of sleep. Their tired little motel had seen better days, or more likely, better decades. The sign looked as if it had once read "Motel 6" and had been painted over to read, "Motel—clean beds, free Wi-Fi." The sign didn't even name the place. The half-asleep night clerk informed them that yes, cash would be fine, but sorry, the Wi-Fi was out of order.

They'd driven into biting winter-cold weather once they passed Flagstaff. The vehicle had a good heater, and although it got excellent mileage, they'd filled up at three-quarters of a tank an hour before pulling into the motel lot, not wanting the tank to get anywhere close to empty. Claire had used her phone to search for a used clothing store or something similar. Her navy sweatshirt did little to warm her, and honestly, it was starting to stink. She had no idea whether a larger anchor like Target (assuming there even was one on their route) would have surveillance cameras; better to try Goodwill or some other thrift shop first, where using cash was probably much more common. They needed to get warm clothes and food for the drive as soon as possible. It would only get colder as they moved farther north. The GPS was programmed to take them somewhere north of Montrose. They should be able to make the remaining drive in under five hours, unless, of course, the roads were bad.

Robert stirred on the double bed next to hers, blankets wrapped around him and the clothes he wore to work on Friday. Claire walked over to the window and peered through the room's slightly greasy polyester curtains. The early morning light was dim, and the sky was filled with dark fast-moving clouds. Snow clouds.

Claire shivered as she walked to the lobby for coffees while Robert showered. *Who the hell was that Brigade guy? And why the hell was he helping them?* She took the two covered Styrofoam cups back to the room, having jammed sugars and a few little packets of instant creamer into her sweatshirt pocket. She couldn't remember how or whether Robert had doctored his coffee Friday night. The temperature was dropping, and quickly.

Both hands occupied, she kicked the door to the room gently to let Robert know she was back. He opened the door with a shell-shocked expression. His hair was wet, his bearded face now replaced with a younger, clean-shaved version. He was dressed in the only clothes he had. The television was on. Robert's photo was on the screen, overlaid with an 800 number.

"…a person of interest, Robert Kingston. Please call Silent Witness…"

"What the fuck?"

"Guess they found my car."

"Was I on the news, too?"

"I don't know. I just tuned in."

"Give me five minutes to shower, and we're out of here." Claire stepped into the shower, little areas of black mold populating the chipped and broken grout. The towels were nearly threadbare. *Oh, perfect,* she thought. *Just perfect.* The only thing this place was missing was Norman Bates.

By 11:00 a.m., they had crossed into Colorado, having stopped at a Salvation Army thrift shop in a strip center just north of their motel. Fortified with down parkas, cold weather hiking boots, fresh clothes, and food and drinks for the road, they'd stopped to change at a gas station with an outdoor entrance to the restrooms. Claire was trapped between panic and numbness, neither of which would be helpful at the moment. She decided on conversation as good a distraction as any.

"So, Robert. Where did you grow up?"

"New Mexico, but I went to college in Philly, then came to Arizona for grad school."

"What made you go into social work?"

"Well, it wasn't my first choice." Claire raised her eyebrows in encouragement, waiting for him to continue. "If I'd had the money or resources to add a lot more years to my formal education, I would have liked going into math, or maybe engineering. But either would have required at least a PhD, and then possibly even more post-doc work. I could manage loans for the two years it takes to get a graduate degree in social work, but that tapped me out financially."

"So you prefer a field loaded with precision and logic, and yet here you are, a social worker? Working with PTSD vets, no less?"

"Yeah. Go figure. Well, with social work I still get to try to solve puzzles, just human ones." Robert continued talking. "It's not like I was driven by compassion for my fellow human beings, or some altruistic dream. It just seemed practical at the time. I was tired of the weather back east and decided to relocate somewhere with a better climate. And now here we are. In retrospect, a job at an engineering firm would have been a better choice. In fact, taking a job as a janitor in an engineering firm would have been a better choice."

The miles rolled away behind them. The skies ahead were threatening, but at least the insanity of the previous night was behind them, too. Claire focused on the barren landscape ahead, hands on the wheel.

"I can't for the life of me understand what that Brigade guy was doing on my street to begin with. And why was he in that house? Do you think the Lucident guy was the same guy who broke into my house earlier?"

"I don't know. Maybe, because how likely is it that someone's home gets broken into twice in one night by two different people? Anyway, the Brigade guy said he was following the person who had just broken into your house."

"Yeah, I heard that. But you don't *follow* someone from inside a house."

He had no response to that.

"What were you doing at the clinic Friday night, anyway? Did you say you forgot something in your office?"

"I have a sister named Stacy." Claire began the long, convoluted story about the looming lawsuit, the deadline to review the deposition, and how it had all come about.

"I've never understood her. Stacy went to college—she was always smart. Well, we both were. But she just never wanted to work. She's a lot more attractive than I am, so I think it was just easier for her to pick up well-heeled men along the way. A quick marriage and divorce in her early twenties—she would always laugh and describe it as a really long, bad first date. She's now on her second husband, Curt, who is a flaming asshole, but he's rich."

Robert pulled a Pepsi from the bag behind the driver's seat and offered it to Claire. She shook her head, focused on the highway. He opened it for himself.

"She's always resented me, at least that's what it seemed like to me, growing up. But even though she lives in a beautiful place, travels when and wherever she pleases, and has no financial worries at all, it's never been enough. After doing this therapy stuff for long enough, I'd have to say that she was jealous of me—why, I don't know. I've never purposely done anything unkind to her. It's pretty textbook stuff, if you think about it. I mean, jealousy is based much more on perception than fact, right? We haven't really spoken since our parents died, which is fine by me. I've seen the trail of human debris she's left in her wake. Frankly, interacting with her always made me feel like I was dancing with a rattlesnake."

"So what's with the lawsuit?"

"God only knows. I never heard anyone else mention a life insurance policy, but she seems to believe I have it, or I've cashed it, or some other scenario where I've screwed her over. It's not like she needs the money, but once she gets something into her head, she clamps onto it like a starving wolf with a chunk of fresh meat."

"It would be natural for you to feel some anger or resentment toward her."

Claire was aware that Robert was slipping into full-blown therapist mode, but she didn't care. "Well, maybe, but I put those feelings behind years ago. She can do whatever she wants with her life. I just don't want to be a part of it."

Driving was beginning to calm Claire. She couldn't even absorb the impact the explosion had on her world, so she swept it to the back of her mind, at least for a little while. She was beyond angry at the course of events, angry that her sister had figured out yet one more way to wrest control from a life Claire had spent her entire adulthood putting in place. The miles continued to move them closer to their destination, although neither of them had a clue what that might hold.

"What about you, Claire? How did you become a therapist?"

"My brother died after he got back from the war, and my parents never got over it. I wanted to help other vets, and it meant the world to my folks that I decided to go to grad school for my master's in social work."

He continued to gaze at her. She knew he was waiting for her to go on, but the whole story was profoundly personal to her, and she wasn't one to share intimate details of her life, especially with a stranger.

Claire looked ahead, unaware of the landscape rushing by. She was lost in thought as she considered how different his story was from her own. This was the lifework she'd chosen. Her much older brother, Sam, returned from the war in Iraq damaged beyond repair. For years, he drank to excess and eventually developed an opiate addiction that resulted in a couple of two-week stints in rehab, short-lived recoveries, and a repeated process. Sam was one of the vets caught up in the scandals that had plagued the Phoenix VA for decades. Investigations had been intense and public. Administrators were replaced and politicians elected and reelected on promises of change. But things never really changed. Although it was never legally proven, Claire was convinced that Sam was one of the uncounted victims of the alleged "secret" wait lists designed to make the "time before service" statistics look good—great, even.

Eventually, one blistering summer day, Sam just ended it all with his service weapon, parked in a car on a deserted road twenty-some miles west of the Phoenix city limits. It took an unknown number of days before his putrefying body was found. The scene was so horrific that his body couldn't be removed from the vehicle intact, so the car was towed to the medical examiner's office, along with its sad, unrecognizable cargo. No one really thinks about stuff like this, because, really, who wants to? There were people whose job it was to deal with the dead—some of whom had suffered unspeakably heartbreaking endings.

It was no wonder that politicians were able to persuade the Department of Veterans Affairs to outsource veterans' health care.

So, yes, Claire had intensely personal reasons for going into social work, and she'd done so for all the right reasons. That was not to say that her job at Lucident was satisfactory. Far from it. She'd had to report to people who had no clinical background or no real orientation to patient care or even basic well-being. Hapless, but not malicious. Others ranged from penny-pinching budget managers without a grasp of the human impact of their decisions to marginally competent supervisors devoid of even the most rudimentary social skills—case in point, Owen Block. But to be fair, they were probably just following company policy.

"You know, Robert, there's always been something that seemed off to me about the way Lucident sets up our schedules."

"What do you mean?"

"Well, Lucident's patients are among the most seriously compromised—many both physically and emotionally—in any outpatient practice anywhere. Yet the company limits each patient visit to twenty minutes—twenty minutes!"

"Claire, the only way therapy goes the traditional fifty to sixty minutes anymore is when private-pay patients are involved."

"No doubt. I figure that the twenty-minute sessions are in place because Lucident probably gets reimbursed on the number of sessions, not the total treatment time spent with patients. What we were taught in grad school is that traumatized patients need *more* time than others, simply because there are so many emotions to process."

"I was taught the same thing, Claire."

"And does it strike you as odd that the clinic has employed minimally-prepared staff providing therapy to such a fragile group of patients? I mean master's prepared therapists like us, are really the right fit for our PTSD patients. But when we were at your house there were two in the group we reviewed that were working on their bachelor's degrees. *Working on them.*"

"I didn't notice that," said Robert. "I guess I was focused on too many other things."

"It doesn't sound like patient care is the pivotal factor here—it all just sounds like profit margin to me."

"I can't argue with that."

"And another thing. Don't you think it's strange that we never find out anything about our patients if they become hospitalized?"

"Yes, I do." said Robert.

"We aren't even told if they had any medications during their stay—or if they take any meds after their discharge. 'Proprietary research' we're told. I once tried to find one of my patient's hospital charts."

"What did you find out?"

"I didn't find out anything. But I got caught snooping and got a written warning for it."

"Wow. I guess they really mean it about following the rules."

"Well, there are plenty of rules for people like us. I have to wonder, though, who sets the rules for them?"

At Lucident, the psychiatrists handled all the inpatient care, plus pharmaceutical management of patients, both inpatient and outpatient. They communicated with the clinic therapists mainly via email memos, which predictably resulted in badly fragmented care. The medication regimens were classified, so the clinic staff had no idea what prescriptions their patients were taking. Nonetheless, Claire was acutely aware that quite a few of her patients had improved through the drug protocols. Now that she thought about it, most of them seemed to improve. She wasn't narcissistic enough to believe it was due to her intervention. So, more likely, they'd improved due to the medications they took.

She looked over at Robert, who had closed his eyes, no doubt hoping to drift off for a while until it was his turn to drive again.

Millions of tiny snowflakes melted into wet pinpricks as soon as they touched the windshield. Claire and Robert drove over the highway crest and immediately saw the traffic delay ahead, some dozen or so cars at a complete stop in front of a constellation of flashing lights. Two tow trucks were slowly righting the jackknifed trailer blocking cars in both directions. Claire pulled to a stop at the end of the line of vehicles as a bundled-up uniformed figure moved toward them.

"Oh my God, it's a cop. Stay down. Act like you're asleep," Claire whispered as she grabbed one of the warm woolen hats from the Salvation Army bag behind the front seat. She pulled the hat's brim down as far as it would go and opened the window a few inches. The frigid air nipped at her face. The police officer stepped up to Claire's window. She opened it halfway.

"We're almost done here," the officer said. "We should have the road cleared within an hour or so. We've been turning back traffic since the accident happened earlier this morning. You can wait in your car if you have enough gas to stay warm, or you can cross the median just up ahead"—he indicated a flat spot between the northbound and southbound lanes another car length in front of them—"and head back in the direction you were coming from." He leaned toward the slightly opened driver's side window and turned his flashlight into the cab, noticing Robert's sleeping form. Claire tensed. Had he seen the news flash with Robert's face and name?

"Thanks, officer, we'll give it some thought." Claire nodded to the cop, who walked back toward the motorist now stopped behind Robert and Claire's car. She rolled up the window to contain the vehicle's warm air and watched him in the rearview mirror, trying not to look obvious. He paused behind their car and looked back. She couldn't tell if he was looking at her or at their license plate or simply surveying the scene ahead, but she didn't like it. He turned and walked up to the car behind theirs.

"I say we wait." Claire's tone was firm. "There's nothing behind us but danger and the possibility you might be recognized. I'm sure shaving helped, but it's not a very sophisticated disguise."

"I agree. If we don't see any progress in the next hour, we can reconsider our options. Going back would be a terrible idea, and if the snow continues, we could be delayed indefinitely getting to the camp." As if in answer, the tiny flakes turned into larger flakes, and a lot more of them were falling. The wind had picked up.

CHAPTER 27

Aaron Davis sat with three other Arizona Freedom Brigade members in his apartment on the near east side of Phoenix. Together they constituted half of the group of operatives who had infiltrated the Brigade nearly a year ago, after patient care improprieties in AllMed had come to light. The Congressional Oversight Committee on American Veterans' Services was more or less impotent, populated by politicians who were not terribly interested in finding fault with their own creation. Fortunately, the same could not be said for the private sector contractors staffing the committee. Leading the staffing team was Anna Dixon, whose face was now on the computer screen in front of the four Brigade moles.

Dixon was smart and tough. Born to Mexican immigrants, she'd had a long and successful investigative career with the Chicago Police Department, until the political infighting and innuendos among her superiors had forced her out along with a number of other seasoned detectives. She was offered early retirement and a reasonable settlement package and was thrilled to snap up both. Shortly afterward, she formed her own consulting firm. Landing this federal contract was a plum. Given her experience with Chicago politics, she was patently unsurprised at the committee members' apathy with the oversight function. Congress might not care about "improprieties," but she did, and her efforts were supported, although privately, by a senior-ranking senator. There would be other future contracts with entities who actually wanted solid, objective work done. But right now, she and her team would follow this thread to wherever it led.

Aaron Davis had been with her group since its inception. As a retired US deputy marshal, his years of tenure included investigation, witness protection, and management of seized assets—and a host of other experiences. Davis and Dixon had known each other for many years, and he'd been invaluable to her on quite a few occasions.

Dixon spoke, brushing her short salt-and-pepper hair back from her face. "Are the other therapists accounted for?"

"Yes, they're all under continuing surveillance." Davis checked his watch. "Clinic operations are set to continue without interruption on Monday morning. There will be one new therapist on staff, reporting to a new managing director, per AllMed's directives. We expect that Kingston's position will be filled quickly, within the coming week."

Dixon's informant, Perry MacRae, had infiltrated the bowels of AllMed's security nearly twelve months ago. His credentials were impeccable because they were real. He'd emerged from two tours in Afghanistan as a cyber specialist with special forces during the occupation in the early teens. Discharged with a leg injury that nearly left him permanently disabled, he'd acquired a skill set that underscored his value to the private contractor now taking over veterans' health care in the United States. Perry's monitoring of the enormous government contract had led to a string of investigative avenues that Dixon's team continued to pursue, despite the indifference of the Congressional Oversight Committee. After a while, the committee no longer asked for reports. Dixon, however, was another story. She was anything but indifferent, and the reason both Perry and Davis found themselves in Phoenix.

It was through Perry's patient, careful mining into the workings of AllMed and its subsidiaries that two suspicious deaths were finally connected to the Lucident program. Perry's position in the company's security division allowed Dixon's team the ability to monitor most of AllMed's outpatient activity in real time.

Perry discovered that the company routinely identified therapists who maybe asked too many questions, who maybe seemed like less than team players, or who broke with company policy. Employees had been told during their orientations and again in writing when they signed their employment agreements that Lucident computers were to be used for company business only.

Internal security monitoring of all the Lucident computers made it immediately obvious if one of the employees was using a machine inappropriately or attempting to access information other than his or her own patient charts. Once an employee was identified as a potential problem, Lucident's Human Resources department would schedule a staff meeting, reminding everyone once again about company policy and computer security. A second infraction resulted in a "trigger" in the form of a postdated entry into the individual's record, indicating "employment termination" for the following Friday afternoon at the close of day. It also notified HR to activate the hiring of a new therapist to take the place of the person who would be fired. The new hires would be notified by Wednesday of that week to report for orientation the following Monday.

Up until the past month or so, none of the different managing directors had been a problem. Owen Block hadn't quite figured it out, but he'd recently become suspicious. Block's computer usage patterns had changed rather suddenly. He'd started looking into old HR files of former therapists and other managing directors.

That, in turn, put him firmly in the path of danger. Thanks to Perry's monitoring, Block's progress on that path had been identified when Block's own employment record tripped the trigger. Block's extraction was dangerous and very risky, but it had been successful.

"Where are our two subjects now?" asked Anna Dixon.

One of the other men at Davis's table spoke up. "Right now, they're in Colorado about forty miles north of the New Mexico border. They've been stopped for a while now, waiting for a disabled vehicle to be cleared from the highway."

"When do you expect them at the camp?"

"It's impossible to say. It depends on the traffic cleanup and the weather. I'd estimate they'll arrive sometime between four and seven hours from now. But we know where they are, and they appear to be safe and following directions."

"What do we know about the explosion?"

"Precious little," replied Davis. "With any luck, our friends will be assumed dead and off AllMed's radar."

But even as he spoke, Davis did not feel particularly lucky.

CHAPTER 28

It was after 3:00 p.m. when Scottsdale police officers received notice of a late-model Audi matching the description of the car owned by Curt Atkins. Security personnel staffing the second shift at the Pima Casino identified the car after it, along with its owner, was reported missing. It was parked, unfortunately, in one of the security camera's few blind spots, so there was no way to go back to find out how long it had been there. Sitting with the casino manager, the officers showed him Atkins's photo.

"He's been a regular here for a while, at least since I've been here, which has been six months," the casino manager explained. "We've had a couple of incidents where we've had to ask him to leave—mainly because of shouting arguments and other patrons feeling threatened. He won a lot, but he lost a lot, too, and couldn't tolerate the failures at the tables. Haven't seen him for the last month or so, though."

"Are there other regulars who might have known him?"

"There could be, but I wouldn't have any way to identify them since we don't keep surveillance camera data for more than three weeks—we're on a twenty-one day overwrite protocol. I'll have my security people look at tapes from the past twenty-four hours and see if we can find him entering the casino or being in any of the gambling areas, either public or VIP spaces. But I will say I've heard rumors of his connections to lenders who are, shall we say, less than upstanding citizens."

The cops looked at each other. This wouldn't be the first time unpaid debts had resulted in deadly outcomes. If there was a suspected mob or gang connection, the feds would take over.

"We'll need a copy of the surveillance videos for the last twenty-four hours as soon as possible. Then we'll also want to take a look at the past three weeks, just in case we see him on the premises."

"Glad to be of help. What about the car?"

"We have a tow truck on the way, and it'll be impounded pending resolution of the investigation. Thanks for your help, sir."

"Sure thing."

CHAPTER 29

Smith refreshed his coffee, looking up as Olivia entered the hotel suite. He smiled and nodded a hello, indicating the coffee pot in the small kitchenette. She shook her head slightly, saying, "I'm way over my caffeine limit for the day, probably for the whole month, but thanks anyway."

She placed a large envelope on the table. "My report. This should conclude our business to date."

"Excellent work, Olivia."

"Yes, as a matter of fact, it was damned excellent." Olivia waited for Smith to speak.

"Our contract is now concluded, so I don't think we'll need you as the rest of this plays out." Smith brought her up to date on the explosion and its involvement with Wilheit, Kingston, and Green. "We still haven't located Block's computer and don't know if it was with Kingston when the explosion happened. The down payment is already in your offshore account, as is the balance." He handed her a smaller sealed envelope. "This is just a small bonus for work well done."

She slipped the envelope into her handbag without opening it. "How long until you get a forensic report?"

"Hopefully by tomorrow. Initially, the site was too hot for investigators to get in there to look for causes and whether anyone was inside—other than Green, of course."

Olivia nodded and stood to leave. She turned to Smith at the door. "Just let me know the status and whether you'll need me. I'll be here in Arizona for another couple of days, then I'm heading east for another job."

"Travel safely, Olivia. I'll be in touch next time we need your services."

They shook hands. Once Block's problematic cyber curiosity was identified, Smith had sent Olivia in to investigate. When she reported back that Block was a whistle-blower just waiting to go public, Smith was left with only one option. He thought again how fortunate he was to have such professionals working for him, and she did indeed do damned excellent work.

CHAPTER 30

It had been almost two hours since the highway patrolman had first spoken to Robert and Claire. The softly falling flakes had turned into dense, angry, driven snow. The therapists were staving off the cold, running the car only periodically to warm themselves and run the windshield wipers enough to brush the mounting snow off the glass. In order to conserve gasoline, Claire kept the car off until they could no longer tolerate the chilled interior. The snow increased in depth, night had fallen, and the wind was now howling. They could see the cop's flashlight moving through the densely falling snow as he plodded back down the row of stopped cars. It was much too cold for anyone to be without heat in a car, and the billowing exhaust from the cars in front of them was whipped away by the wind the moment it left the tailpipes. The officer slowly made his way back toward them, slipping frequently. He stopped at each car to speak to its passengers.

"Robert, climb over the back seat into the cargo area and cover yourself up with all of our stuff the back. We can't risk him getting a second look at you. Please trust me on this. Go!"

Six minutes later, Claire rolled her window down a few inches to greet the approaching figure.

"We're having a lot more difficulty clearing the road—it could well take us all night. We're recommending that people turn around and head back toward Montrose for the night. Then check back in the morning for a highway traffic report." He trained his flashlight into the cab. "Where's your friend?"

"He went back with the people in the car that was behind us. They decided to take your advice and turn back." She couldn't tell if his eyes had narrowed at her statement or because of the biting wind.

"Well, everyone has to turn back now, as it's too dangerous to continue to wait here. At the rate this snow's coming down, we're approaching blizzard conditions, and we need every possible bit of road cleared so the snowplows can get through in the morning." He kept his flashlight pointing into the front cab of the vehicle.

"Thanks, officer. I'll turn around right now." Claire rolled the window back up and watched as the officer continued his journey to the vehicles behind her.

"What a damn waste of time. Stay hidden until I get this car turned around." She backed up just enough to move around the car in front of them, then rolled far enough forward to cross the median. The snow was now a good six inches deep, but at least the wind had blown some of the fluffier stuff off the more level areas of the median.

Claire edged onto the median, holding the wheel in a death grip. It was impossible to tell where the highway stopped and the median began, and the driving snow obliterated much of what the headlights would have otherwise illuminated. While the wind had blown off some of the softer powdery snow from the surface, it left behind its treacherous icy cousin.

Despite the two or so miles per hour Claire was driving, she sensed the slick carpet lurking just below the freshly blowing snow. The car began to move in a direction other than where the wheels were pointed. She braked hard.

"Claire!" Robert shouted from the back. "What's going on?"

Claire glanced quickly to her left, straining to see if the cop had noticed the difficulty she was having with the car. He hadn't.

"Do you want me to drive? You seem apprehensive driving in the snow," he asked from the back of the car.

"No. If we get stopped again, we can't risk anyone identifying you. We're sitting ducks here. And of course I'm nervous driving in the snow—I grew up in Phoenix, for God's sake, not Alaska."

Their car inched forward toward the southbound lanes, its four-wheel drive doing its job. In the rearview mirror, Claire could see the officer's bobbing flashlight as he continued to talk to the drivers of the other cars that had stopped behind them. She slowly stopped the vehicle. "It's okay. Come on out."

No sooner had she spoken when the car began to slip ever so slightly again sideways. Claire instinctively slammed on the brakes. The car slid another yard before stopping completely. Breathing hard, she let her forehead drop to the steering wheel.

"Let's change places for a while, Claire. I have plenty of experience driving in snow, and if we end up in a ditch, we'll end up being identified for sure."

After they quickly changed places, Claire picked up her phone and searched the map for a hotel on the northern outskirts of Montrose. It took three calls to find one that had a vacancy. It took them another hour to make the slow, painstaking drive to shelter. Robert looked every bit as strained as Claire by the time they pulled into the hotel's parking lot.

Stiff and tired and stressed, they opened the door to their room and deposited their small cache of possessions from the car onto the desk next to a dresser holding an older model television.

"We passed a pizza place about a block back. I'll call for carryout." Robert checked his own phone for the restaurant name and phone number. "You okay with mushrooms and onions?"

"Sounds like heaven. You order, I'll go in to get it. Your face has already been seen too many times." She hoped her face hadn't been seen, at least not yet.

CHAPTER 31

Chen called Noble for the second time on Sunday.

"What is the status on the laptop?" Chen didn't bother to keep the annoyance out of his voice.

"Smith won't know much more about Block's laptop until the Phoenix PD is able to get into the Wilshire house. But he's wired into the department, so he'll know what, if anything, they found in real time." Noble continued, "If the laptop was in the explosion, we may never get a final answer."

Chen listened and waited for him to go on.

"There's nothing we can do but wait right now."

"Understood," Chen said. "Keep me informed, regardless of the hour. I'd like you to meet me in my apartment lobby at 7:00 a.m. tomorrow for an update."

"Will do." Noble had been to Chen's apartment building only once before, for his final job interview.

Noble hoped he sounded calm and in control. But his concern had ratcheted up, bumping up against the edge of panic. He knew that Smith was a professional, but Smith's clearance in the security division didn't include the "need to know" that the simple, automatic Monday morning password reassignment was not enough to keep a skilled computer analyst from accessing the full patient and HR database—if the machine fell into the wrong hands. Not nearly enough. It was Noble's responsibility to have made certain that every contingency was covered, even in the extremely unlikely event that something like the Friday night theft of the laptop occurred. He didn't make mistakes often, and this one was serious.

Chen had hired Noble shortly after he'd taken early retirement from the FBI's Chicago office. Of course, then he was John Ricker, an eighteen-year veteran in the Facilities and Logistics Division, working in the construction management and acquisition department. It was hardly a flashy James Bond-ish role, but it was good, solid work, and it went well for a number of years. But fourteen years into his career at the FBI, Ricker made a mistake. The architectural plans for the renovation of not only the Chicago office annex but also the New York office were highly confidential documents. Ricker's ill-fated affair with a woman he only knew as Nancy came to an abrupt halt when, one freezing morning in December, she left his apartment with the hard copy schematics and, as he discovered later, an external drive containing the contents of his computer. He wouldn't have known the latter, except that she made sure to tell him.

Ricker's nerves were on edge after Nancy's call. His vacillation between reporting the theft or staying silent took an enormous emotional toll on him. Eventually Ricker's own procrastination made the decision for him—disclosing the theft, and by default his own poor judgment, was one thing. But trying to explain why he waited fourteen months to report it? Forget that. Despite the intervening years, his fear of being discovered dogged him every single day. Nothing had ever come of the theft, and he hoped against hope that nothing ever would. Until one day, it did.

Almost three years to the day of the document theft, the Chicago FBI headquarters was on the front page of every news outlet in the country: *Fire Rips Through Chicago's FBI Headquarters; One Agent Dead, Four Others Hospitalized.*

There were hundreds of stories with similar headlines covering the subsequent investigation, but the long and the short of it was this: terrorism was suspected, but no organization or individual took credit for the blast. Every avenue into the investigation came up empty. All that was ever discovered was that the fire had started in long-forgotten passageways beneath the lowest level of the building, areas that had been blocked off and unused for years.

No other terrorist attack or any other adverse event had happened since. Ricker honestly had no idea if his careless actions contributed to the disaster, but he prayed they had not. As time went by, he had all but convinced himself that the two were unrelated.

Seventeen years into Ricker's career, one of his employees was arrested for taking a bribe to plant a recording device in the campaign headquarters of an incumbent state senator. Before the field agent went to trial, he was found dead of an apparent self-inflicted gunshot wound. The Bureau had handled the incident discreetly, but despite its forward face of fairness and independence, it was subject to the same political pressures and turf battles that were inherent in every bureaucracy since the beginning of time. The state senator was reelected, so no apparent harm had been done. Unless, of course, you counted the agent who blew his own brains out. Nonetheless, the internal speculation was ugly. Ricker's boss had no intention of taking the fall, so it landed squarely on Ricker's own shoulders.

The Bureau allowed Ricker to take early retirement with a reduced pension and positive employment references after signing a nondisclosure agreement that was an inch thick. He couldn't have been more grateful for a quiet way out of the Bureau. All that was ever mentioned was a tiny article along with a small photo in the FBI newsletter, thanking him for his many years of service and wishing him the best in his future endeavors.

Eight months later, thanks to the network of agents he'd known, he found himself interviewing with AllMed for the position of director of security. His credentials, of course, looked impeccable, and Chen offered him the position at a generous salary. Ricker didn't mention that his career in facilities and logistics didn't provide him with the complete skill set needed to manage the full range of AllMed's security needs, especially the highly specialized cybersecurity functions. And he most certainly didn't mention his nagging worry that he had been responsible for leaking the architectural plans.

"Mr. Ricker? John? Are you still there?"

Jarred from his wretched stroll through memory lane, Noble responded. "Yes, yes, Dr. Chen, sorry."

"Did you hear me?"

"Yes, Monday morning at seven, I'll be there."

Ricker's own plan was to simply hire the talent that was needed, and that came in the form of Smith. The other unknown—the one that really worried him—was finding out what had happened to six of the other therapists who'd been discharged. They just, well, vanished, each of them within thirty-six hours of their respective planned Friday afternoon terminations. Smith had assured him that they wouldn't be a problem in the future, and Ricker took him at his word. Mainly because he just didn't want to know. But the loose ends still troubled Ricker. He'd just have to tie up those ends before Chen even realized they existed. But Ricker, known to Smith only as Noble, was out of his depth. And he knew it.

CHAPTER 32

Anna Dixon nodded as she listened to Davis's update.

"I agree. We have to leave the other therapists in place until we build the rest of the case's foundation."

"Anna, look, I'm concerned that things are escalating at Lucident. We have the remaining residences under passive surveillance, but there just isn't enough manpower to watch them all twenty-four hours a day."

"I've got people looking at the cloned security information now, and we know what to look for in the HR trigger, so the clinic staff is being well monitored. Perry's on top of that. I can't do anything to immediately add surveillance manpower, but I've already authorized additional surveillance cameras on the other therapists' residences, as you suggested. I'm concerned, too, but it's what it is. Right now, I want us to concentrate on tracking down the patient group on A1A, not just those who are actively under treatment but also those who appear to have left the treatment protocol."

Aaron agreed. He'd been working that part of the puzzle on his own end for weeks. How forty patients just seemed to have vanished from the face of the earth remained an unknown, although not an entirely unexpected one. The patients in the clinical trials, like the therapists, were single and had no living relatives, so no one in the outside world was looking for them or even knew they were missing. The only way Dixon's group had identified the unaccounted-for patients was by comparing data on the paramedic and first responder reports, one of the few databases that remained public, if you knew how to dissect the data. Dixon didn't know how, but Perry MacRae did. Still, neither Dixon nor MacRae had been able to locate them in the Lucident computer base. At least not yet.

With mounting frustration, both Davis and Dixon had found dead ends in trying to follow patients through the system. They were beginning to build a pretty solid set of theories regarding the former therapists, but neither the Tempe suicide nor the Albuquerque hit-and-run offered fruitful leads. The other therapists they'd been able to intercept after Friday afternoon "employment terminations" seemed to be in the dark with respect to anything outside their immediate patient interactions. No surprises there, since the inpatient and outpatient functions were completely compartmentalized. All but one had been placed in a specialized type of witness protection program. The last person was scheduled for processing within the week. Next, they'd need to deal with Kingston and Wilheit. And now, of course, Block.

The information and entry into the HR files that Perry had been able to access dealt with outpatient clinic personnel only. Davis hoped that Dixon's people would be able to follow the cyber path into the inpatient personnel records so that the full complement of patient care providers could be analyzed. He knew they'd be the people who would have direct knowledge of the treatment protocols and disposition of the A1A patients.

Anna spoke again. "We're still monitoring our daily video feeds on Chen's activities. He rarely interacts with anyone outside of the labs. Seems to be an all-work-and-no-play kind of guy. Regardless, we'll still watch him coming and going from his apartment as well as the veterans' hospital."

Davis and Dixon hoped that they'd be able to get a handle on enough evidence to prove, at the very least, malfeasance at AllMed. If not, the only way to get at it was to do it from the other direction, which meant that someone from one of their teams would need to go in from the front end. As a PTSD patient.

That was a risk neither was anxious to take.

CHAPTER 33

Monday, January 8

The scanner in Aaron Davis's apartment beeped twice. He looked at the clock. Five a.m. He leaned over and turned up the volume.

"...at least one victim. No complete skeletons, cadaver dogs still on premises awaiting access."

Shit. What did he miss? Aaron turned on the television, and a gaggle of local reporters could be seen talking to their off-screen cameramen behind the attractive Hispanic woman now conducting an on-camera interview.

"As of this morning, we don't know the cause of the explosion, but we are investigating all possibilities. We have cadaver dogs on site, and they should be able to enter the area early this afternoon once the debris has cooled enough to allow them to do so safely." The spokesperson for the Phoenix Police Department continued, "Initially, we expect to have them identify whether the site contains human remains, and if so, how many."

The reporter asked, "How will you be able to identify them?"

"Once we determine—and I stress, *if* we determine—someone was killed in the fire, we'll have the dogs search out scents for a particular individual."

"And whom would that be?"

"If we do find remains, we'd start with the home's resident or residents, of course, and then branch out from there as appropriate."

"What can you tell us about the homeowner?"

"Her name is Claire Wilheit."

A photo of a slender blonde woman in a black evening gown flashed on the screen. She was standing next to a man in a tuxedo whose face had been blurred out, an obligatory photo obviously taken at a formal gala of some kind.

"All we know about her at the moment is what one of her neighbors was able to tell us—that she was employed as a therapist somewhere in Phoenix. At this time, we are hoping to hear from her. Let me repeat: at this time, we don't know whether anyone was in the home when the explosion occurred."

"Do you think she was killed in the explosion?"

"As I said, we don't know right now. As soon as we have additional information, we will make an announcement."

"What about the person of interest, Robert Kingston, whom you identified last night?"

"The investigation may take us in that direction, but I remind the public that a person of interest is just that. It does not mean a suspect or perpetrator, just someone we need to talk to."

"What else can you share with us here at KABC?"

"We also have specialized cadaver, or victim recovery, canines arriving today from New Mexico. These dogs are cross-trained as arson dogs and are specially trained to detect scents of various explosive materials, so they'll help us narrow down whether this explosion was likely to have come from a gas leak or other substance."

"Will you ask for assistance from the ATF?"

"We don't yet know if this case might fall under its jurisdiction. That's all I have to share at this time, and when additional information is available, we will call another press conference."

The reporter turned to face the camera. "Thanks for joining us at KABC, this is Christina Ramirez. Tune in again for the news at six, followed by a fascinating report on the history of canine investigation beginning in the fourteenth century." She flashed a perfect white smile at the camera and signed off.

Aaron Davis groaned. He, along with many other law enforcement professionals, pinned little hope on help from the Feds. The Department of Justice had just begun to recover from the damage it had suffered after the

FBI's alleged influence in the 2016 elections when it was besieged by even more scandals. The FBI found itself the perpetual Congressional scapegoat for all things nefarious. Nothing was ever proven, nor were charges ever brought, but public confidence in the Bureau had plummeted and had yet to recover all of the ground that had been lost. The political infighting remained intense and resulted in political and operational gridlock, even after so many years. There were still a lot of ethical, excellent agents in the Bureau, but they were too often stymied in their efforts to buck any corner of the bureaucracy. Lots of other superb agents had resigned in frustration over the years and moved on to other jobs. Fortunately, Davis and Dixon both knew some of the best investigators the Bureau had employed. In fact, it was better all around that they no longer worked for the FBI, because several had become available to work for Dixon's consulting firm.

Davis expected the later report to show that one unknown victim would be discovered in the aftermath. It was unlikely that he'd ever be identified, since even Perry had only known him as Green. Perry was aware that it would be vital to the case they were developing if he could obtain some of Green's DNA, but even he doubted that was possible; they had always been meticulous about wearing gloves when working for Smith. Smith had insisted on it.

Davis muted the television and went back to his computer to continue his work. He was scheduled for another conference call with Dixon later today and wanted to complete his summary on the status of the surveillance teams watching the remaining therapists. He was also keeping tabs on Kingston and Wilheit. Given the vehicle wreck and bad weather, he'd watched them reverse to the south to stay in a hotel out of Montrose. They'd no doubt be on the road again soon, as the traffic had cleared. Barring any other problems, they'd arrive at the Meyer fishing camp by dinnertime.

There might be more information on the local investigation by then.

CHAPTER 34

Stacy Atkins considered her calendar for the week. She would have to cancel both tennis lessons—just for appearance's sake—but would keep Friday's envelope-addressing luncheon for the Scottsdale Friends of Children with Disabilities. By then she would be so overwrought about Curt's disappearance she could put on the bravest of faces and be showered with the greatest of sympathies by the other women at the annual event. She had a new Armani dress suit to wear. In fact, it still had the Neiman's tag on the sleeve, and she looked like a million bucks in it. *Now I'll actually be worth it*, she thought, chuckling to herself. *And quite a few times that.*

Her smile faded as she recalled the fight they'd had over that purchase. Yes, it was pricey, but she explained for the hundredth time to him, they had images to maintain, and this was a relatively cheap way to do it.

"Goddammit, Stacy! Do you think I'm made out of money?" He'd actually had the nerve to scream his recriminations at her.

"Quit being such a prick. We have plenty of money, and besides, I'm sure your accountant can find a way to write this off along with all of your other dubious deductions." He glowered at her and stomped out of the room.

She was impaled on the horns of a dilemma of her own making. While she couldn't imagine having to tolerate living one more day with him, she most certainly couldn't imagine living a day without his money. She was glad to be rid of him. Months of planning had been necessary to set all of this in motion—the attorneys, the bullshit insurance policy, her asshole sister, and, most importantly, maneuvering her way into the hungry pockets of the man named Tango.

She went downstairs for a good, long workout in the home gym, looking forward to the sauna afterward and a lovely dinner of chilled salmon salad.

CHAPTER 35

Smith's Monday morning was far busier than usual. He'd arranged for Block's replacement as Lucident's managing director of clinical operations to hit the ground running in order to minimize disruption of patient care activities. The therapist who had been hired two weeks ago to fill Claire's expected departure had completed her orientation and was in her new office, reviewing case files for her first day's patient load. Because he wanted to be sure she had most of the week to acclimate to the standard complement of fourteen patients per day, the remaining therapists needed to share most of Kingston's load until he could be replaced. Smith was a security expert, not an administrator. Although he understood the need to act as one right now, he really wanted to just get through the unwelcome management demands of the week.

Despite Smith's temporary foray into middle management, he was unconcerned about the ongoing general security of the company. Mack could handle the day-to-day issues, and if something needed Smith's attention, he'd escalate as necessary. It was the issue of Block's missing laptop that concerned him the most. Smith's concern was slightly lessened since the password—and all passwords on the intranet system—had been automatically reset as of 12:01 a.m. Monday, as it did every week. The fact that Mack was watching to see if anyone would attempt to access the intranet after the reset was reassuring, but only to a degree. It was unlikely that anyone, even other staff, would be able to access Block's laptop since his middle name, part of the company's password algorithm, was unknown to anyone else. Block's middle name appeared nowhere publicly, also part of company policy.

By now Smith had a fairly high confidence that Kingston was the thief, and he was awaiting, along with Noble, the forensic conclusion as to the body or bodies at the explosion scene on Wilshire. He'd feel a lot better if one of them was Kingston.

CHAPTER 36

The roads north of Montrose were in reasonably good shape. Although the snow was still falling, it wasn't as heavy; at least the wind had died down. The four-wheel-drive vehicle was performing beautifully. Armed with a full gas tank, the therapists headed north, Robert at the wheel.

Neither had slept very well the night before. They were exhausted in every way but glad to get back on the road.

"What do you think will happen when we get to the camp?"

Claire thought for a moment. "No way to know, but I have to believe the Brigade guy is on the right side of things, and the fact that we're still safe and not arrested is at least a little comforting."

"Don't you think it's suspicious that he happened to live in the house down the street from you?"

"Yeah, actually. More than a little. I know we weren't inside for more than a few minutes, but it looked kind of, well, empty."

"I thought so, too. It reminded me of a rental house with generic staged furnishings so that people could kind of imagine themselves living there, but not so much that it might turn them away."

"Why do you think he was following the person that he said broke in?"

"I have absolutely no idea, but he must know who the guy is—make that *was*—or how would he even have known to follow him? And what in the world is the Brigade doing mixed up in all of this, anyway?"

Claire spoke. "He must have been expecting us, or why would he have had this car there? With the money and the GPS already in it? And what the hell is he doing with that fucking gang of thugs to begin with? None of this makes sense, so…"

"Holy shit!" Robert's eyes were glued on the rearview mirror. Claire whirled around to see rapidly approaching flashing red and blue lights.

"Is that for us? Were we speeding?"

Robert put on the turn indicator and began to pull over to the side of the road. His grip on the steering wheel was so tight that his knuckles were actually white.

"Shitshitshit. What are we going to do?" Robert put the car into park.

"Just act calm. We don't even know what he wants. Maybe he's not even after us."

But the flashing lights slowed and stopped. Right behind their car. They waited, trying to appear composed.

"Oh my God." Robert's hands still clutched the wheel. "He's going to ask us for license and registration, and then he'll know who we are. We're screwed."

Claire yanked open the glove box, searching for the vehicle's registration and having no idea whose name might be on it. She pulled out a manual for the car, some napkins, and a small first aid kit. Underneath it all, she found a small plastic bag that held the papers indicating the car's registered owner and the proof of insurance. She nearly tore the papers as her shaking hands extracted the documents.

"He's getting out of the car." Robert's eyes had never left the rearview mirror.

Claire turned around, willing herself to breathe slowly and appear relaxed.

Claire rolled down the window when the officer approached the passenger side of the car.

"License and registration, please."

Claire handed him the registration and insurance documents. Robert made a show of attempting to pull out his wallet.

"Hello, officer, I didn't think we were speeding…"

"You weren't. But you have something caught in the tailgate, and it's dragging on the highway. That could be hazardous for you or for other drivers."

Claire reached for the door handle to see for herself, but the policeman held up his hand to stop her.

"Please remain in your vehicle until I can verify the registration information. Sir? Do you have your license available?"

"Um, I think it's in my backpack, so I'll need to get it from the back."

Claire spoke up. "I can find it. I think I saw it with our sleeping bags. I should also take a look at what's caught in the tailgate."

The officer moved aside as she grasped the door handle and stepped onto the snowy shoulder of the road. As she transferred her weight to the ground, she slipped, falling into the man as he tried to break her fall. She gasped with surprise and murmured an apology as she took the gloved hand he offered to help her up. Just when she grasped the outstretched hand, a blast of freezing-cold air bit into the exposed skin on her face. It also snatched the small white paper right out of the cop's hands, wafting it up and away from them, moving much too high and fast to be retrieved.

"Oh no! Now what?" Claire stared at the small bit of white flying away from her and the cop.

"Ma'am, I am so sorry! That was entirely my fault."

"No, it's okay, officer, you were just trying to stop me from falling."

"Look, you'll need to order a duplicate registration when you get to where you're going. Let's just get the driver's license and clear the debris from the tailgate, and you can be on your way. I'm really sorry for the inconvenience."

They took careful, measured steps to the back of the SUV and saw what had caught the cop's eye—Robert's long gray scarf, Salvation Army sales tag still attached. It looked like a long, frozen piece of gray lasagna. She quickly opened the back and stuffed the now filthy scarf into the rear compartment. She began rummaging around, making a show of trying to locate Robert's wallet.

The police officer's radio crackled to life, static followed by a call sign and series of numbers. The officer looked up at Claire.

"Rollover emergency south of us, this weather is really treacherous. I have to go. Just consider this a warning. Be careful and get that new registration as soon as you get the chance."

Claire brushed her windblown hair away from her face to say something, but the cop had already turned and was jogging back to his car. She braced herself on the side of the car as she made her way back to the passenger door, each step more perilous than the one before. It wouldn't do to twist an ankle. As it was, she already wanted to throw up.

"What happened, Claire?" Robert's voice shook.

"I dunno. I slipped, and I guess I knocked the registration out of the cop's hand. He was really apologetic and told us to get a duplicate and to be on our way."

"What if we had to give him my license? I'm a person of interest! I'll be arrested and detained. Then maybe end up with an accidental overdose in a seedy hotel. Or maybe step into the street and become a hit-and-run vic—"

"Stop. We didn't have to give him your license. We didn't get arrested. We didn't get detained. We're okay right now."

Robert's breathing slowed. He ran his hands through his hair. "I know, I know."

"I mean the worst thing that happened was losing the registration, which won't matter unless we get stopped again. And we won't get stopped again. We're not speeding, we're being very careful, and the car is in great shape. On the other hand, your new scarf is ruined."

He smiled at that. It was a shitty-looking scarf, anyway.

"Robert, do you want me to drive for a while?"

"No. Let's just go. Just give me a few minutes. I swear to God, if these roads don't kill us, the stress will, for sure."

They sat quietly for a good five minutes. Then Robert put the car into drive and pulled back onto the highway. They'd only been stopped about twenty minutes, but during that time the wind had become much worse, punctuated by powerful sudden gusts. They could feel the vehicle rock with every one of them. Still silent, Claire and Robert continued north, deeper into Colorado toward an uncertain destination.

CHAPTER 37

"Breaking news!" The headlines rolled across the television screen in Aaron Davis's apartment. Aaron turned up the volume and looked at the screen: 4:40 p.m.

"The Phoenix Police Department is now live with an update on the explosion Saturday in the Encanto district."

"Preliminary reports indicate that there were likely two victims in the explosion that took place in the early hours of Saturday, January 6. It is not known if they were male or female. We have not been able to locate Robert Kingston, identified yesterday as a person of interest. We will pursue all avenues of inquiry, including the investigation of whether we're able to recover any DNA at the scene. At the moment, we are working on the assumption that one of the victims was owner Claire Wilheit." The same formal photograph of Claire showed on screen, this time cropped to exclude her tuxedoed partner.

"Again, if anyone knows the whereabouts of Mr. Kingston, please contact..."

Aaron stared at the screen, the remainder of the PPD statement fading out. Two victims? *Two?* He knew Green was killed because he'd watched him enter Wilheit's house, and he'd been there watching all night. Someone else had been on the premises in the middle of the night. How? Why?

Working backward, Davis started to reconstruct the puzzle. The only other way to access Claire's house was through the alleyway directly on the north side. Whoever was in the house had to have come through the back. Claire and Robert said they were both in the house earlier that evening and

117

that there'd been a break-in, but that's all he knew. Even if the second victim's DNA could be recovered, it only had value if it belonged to someone already in the system. He was flying up to the cabin himself tomorrow morning and would head up the debriefing personally. He added to his list the importance of deeper investigation into that part of the enigma when they were all at the camp.

He wasn't sure why the only photo of Claire that seemed to be publicly available to the police depicted her as a socialite but was glad it looked so much different from the Claire he'd met on Wilshire just a number of hours before. It wasn't much, but he thought it would be enough to buy a little time, and perhaps a little anonymity for her. It wouldn't last forever, but he'd take whatever he could get.

CHAPTER 38

Stacy stared at the computer screen. She rebooted the machine twice and triple-checked the account numbers. Curt was always the one who reconciled the checking account balance. What the fuck?

She accessed the transaction details.

With the exception of three hundred dollars, the checking account had been drained with a single withdrawal dated three weeks ago.

She opened a new window on her computer, now looking at their retirement account. Her hands shook. She expected to find the $4 million and change that Curt had told her they had. One thousand dollars remained.

Next, the money market accounts. She expected to see almost two million dollars in the combined money market and stock portfolios. Ten thousand dollars remained.

"Wrong! Wrong!" She was alone in the den at Curt's desk, shrieking at the computer. "You fucking asshole!"

She checked and double-checked every account, checking, savings, stocks, retirement. Same result.

She stood abruptly at her desk, sending the chair flying backward, nearly tripping on it. She hurled her glass against the wall, the sound of the shattering Waterford drowned out by her scream.

The combined balance of all their accounts was $17,360.

CHAPTER 39

Tired beyond words, Robert and Claire pulled into a long, narrow gravel lane covered with several inches of fresh snow. Night was encroaching, darkening even more quickly as they were swallowed by the forested woods. The GPS had guided them through winding, forked routes, frequently "recalculating." They were so turned around it would have been impossible to find their way back to the two-lane paved road they'd left almost an hour and a half ago, even if they'd arrived in daylight. There was a small wooden sign at the lane's entrance, partially obscured by wet snow, now iced over. It read: *Meyer's ... ish ...p ...lcome.*

"Finally, thank God." Robert drove on, grateful for the tiny posts which held red reflectors at eye level. Without them it would have been treacherous going, since there was no way to tell where the sides of the graveled surface fell away on either side of the lane. As it was, he could no longer sense the pair of ruts tracing the center of road beneath the wheels.

After ten additional, very stressful minutes, they pulled into a small parking area in front of an old one-story lodge boasting a wide porch covered with drifting snow. The GPS announced, "You have arrived at your destination." The lodge's curtains were drawn, but several rooms were lit, and a bit of white smoke wafted from the central chimney. Robert pulled in next to one of two cars in the lot and turned off the ignition.

Claire looked at Robert. "Are we supposed to go in?"

Before he could answer, two figures approached them from the side of the lodge, addressing them by name.

"Ms. Wilheit, Mr. Kingston, please follow us. This way, please."

The foursome stepped into the warm lobby of the lodge and were assaulted by smells of cumin and coffee.

"We know you're tired and have a whole lot of questions." The taller figure spoke, pulling off a thick scarf and woolen hat. He looked to be in his midfifties, with a short, graying beard and shoulder-length hair. "I'm John. Please put your belongings on any of the tables. I have some hot chili and fresh coffee, if you'd like."

Claire didn't move. She crossed her arms. "I'm not putting anything anywhere until you tell me what the hell is going on." Her gaze was fixed on him.

"We will tell you everything that we're authorized to say. What you need to understand is that we have gone to tremendous effort and risk to get you safely out of Arizona. No one outside of a few people know you are here, and that is how it needs to stay, at least for the immediate future."

The second figure stepped forward, extending her right hand. "Please call me Kate." Robert leaned forward to return the handshake. Claire did not move. Instead she turned her glare on Kate.

"Look," said John, "it's very late, and you've had a very long couple of days. Tomorrow our coordinator from Arizona will be here, and he's asked us to let you know that he'll try to answer every question you have. Please have something to eat, and then you can get some sleep—there are two adjoining rooms down the hall to the left. You'll be comfortable and warm there. And you will be safe."

The chili was spicy and hot. They both ate two bowls, mopping the last with chunks of sourdough bread. Exhaustion settled in on full stomachs. Claire and Robert took their things and found the adjoining rooms. Each room had its own bath and was furnished functionally with two double beds, a dresser, nightstand, and comfortable reading chair. The beds were piled high with pillowy down comforters. Without speaking, they each took a bed, but in the same room. Their agreement was unspoken but clear. This wasn't a good time to be separated.

Despite their fear, mental and physical depletion won out. They fell asleep, only to toss and turn with troubling dreams that would be unremembered in the morning, replaced by a vague echo of unease.

CHAPTER 40

Tuesday, January 9

Claire and Robert awoke to the sound of an engine. They moved quickly to their room's window at the back of the lodge. A single engine seaplane with enormous skis where the wheels would have been landed smoothly on the wide, empty expanse. A single bundled-up figure emerged from the plane's cabin carrying the handle of an oddly shaped box. As soon as the passenger neared the short pier that was frozen into the icy lake, the plane rolled away and lifted into a gray sky, veering right as it passed the tree line on the opposite side of the lake. The pitch of the engine lowered as it moved out of sight, until it could no longer be heard.

"Well." Claire spoke in a quiet tone. "As Dorothy Parker once said, 'What fresh hell is this?' Let's go find out."

As Claire and Robert entered the main lodge area, the figure from the plane pulled off his parka and looked at them. "Good to know you arrived safely." He extended a hand in greeting. "Aaron Davis."

The two therapists looked at each other, instantly recognizing him, then back at Davis. "You?"

Davis ran his hand over his short, sandy hair. "Let's sit down. We've got a lot of talking to do." They all took seats at the large community table, John and Kate setting cups of coffee and English muffins in front of each person in the small group. Claire sat directly across from Davis so she could observe his body language as well as hear what he had to say. He had wide-spaced eyes, some kind of nondescript hazel color, and directed his gaze at her as he started to speak. It was a little difficult for her to peg Davis's age, but based on the lines in his face and the gray starting at his temples, she guessed mid-forties. Claire was usually pretty good at detecting when someone was lying. She knew well, though, that the best liars forced themselves to use eye contact. She also noted that Davis was in bad need of a shave. Maybe he was as tired as she was.

It took just over an hour for Davis to provide an overview about his role with Dixon's group, his infiltration with the Arizona Freedom Brigade, and the covert surveillance into AllMed's web of corporations. He described Lucident's place in the network. Robert asked several questions as they came up. Claire just listened with the same intense expression she'd worn when they first sat in Kingston's dining nook what seemed like a month ago. Aaron answered each question as succinctly as he could without being dragged off topic.

"Why are you telling us all this?" Claire finally spoke.

"We've debated at length how much to share with you but agreed that this is the only way for you to really comprehend how grave the situation is and that your lives are literally in danger. Frankly, the stakes don't get a lot higher.

"We still don't know what caused the explosion, but reports during the night suggest that it may have been intentional, not the result of a random gas leak or the like. One of the possibilities we're looking at is that someone was trying to kill you." He looked directly at Claire. She blanched.

"You mentioned that there was a break-in at your house the same evening as the explosion. Can you tell me exactly what happened?"

Claire and Robert described their discovery at Claire's house with as much detail as they could. Periodically Davis interrupted with a question.

"I'm not challenging your recollection of events, but a bit of dust and a misplaced coffee cup aren't conclusive proof that someone was actually inside your house. I understand that you observed two intruders in your yard."

"Yes, you *are* challenging my recollection. I know my own house, and I know my own routines. So, you can believe me or not. Your call."

"I apologize. Of course you do."

"Why on earth would someone want to kill *me*? And who was the guy who broke into my house?"

"All we know is that the man I was following was called Green, but we don't know his real name. He worked for Lucident security. As to your other intruders, right now, we don't have any idea who they might be or why they were there. In fact, we aren't completely certain about the intent, either, but it's a prudent operating assumption."

"Do you think he set off a bomb?" Robert was confused, because this, like everything else that had happened over the past few days, didn't make any sense.

"No. There's no reason he would knowingly kill himself. He's been working for Lucident for a long time and has been smart enough not to get caught. He's neither incompetent nor is he—was he—stupid. We don't know who else was killed in your house, but our working assumption is that the unknown person was responsible for the explosion."

"And how do you know this Green person wasn't responsible? Maybe he was involved in the earlier break-in. And can you answer my other question—why would anyone want to kill me?"

"We have someone inside Lucident's security operation. It's the way that we've been able to be proactive in protecting the last number of therapists who were fired. We were, unfortunately, too late to help two others. We have no idea why someone would want you dead and have no real reason to think that's the case—we just want to investigate every possibility, no matter how remote." Davis avoided responding to Claire's suggestion that Green was part of the early break-in. He'd been aware of the Lucident men's movement the entire night, and Green hadn't been anywhere near Claire's house.

"Are you talking about the Albuquerque and Tempe therapists?"

"Yes." Aaron was somewhat surprised at how resourceful the two of them had been in such a few short hours. "As for the others, we've placed them in a specialized witness protection program we've developed, outside of official governmental channels. If we're successful in building a case against AllMed, they will be asked to testify if they're needed. We're prepared to offer you both the same protection. I advise you to take it."

"Will we need to testify?" Robert asked.

"Most likely. The other therapists don't seem to have much information, but you have both seen a number of different patient and HR files and are the only ones who can provide insight into the individual patients and their dispositions."

Although Robert had only known Claire Wilheit for a few days, he could tell by her body language and facial expression that she was ready to dig in for an argument.

"Are you seriously asking me—us—to give up our identities, our entire lives, and move to some place we don't know and never look back?"

"Yes."

"Fuck off."

Aaron looked at Claire with interest. He had no idea what to expect from her, but she was solid and exuded intelligence and more than a little stubbornness.

"Let's take a break for a few hours," said Davis. "I have to make a conference call and do a lot of research before that happens. We can discuss this as much as you would like, but right now there are some things we simply need to do."

As he spoke, Aaron Davis rose from his seat and opened the odd crate he'd carried from the plane.

"The latest reports from Phoenix have identified two distinct sets of human remains in the Wilshire site. We have a unique opportunity to secure your safety and anonymity." He handed each therapist a cotton swab. "Once we run DNA profiles on you, we'll be able to insert them into the investigation so that you are both identified. Proof of your 'deaths' will be ironclad, and no one will ever have a reason to try to find you. That is, of course, unless you give them some reason to."

Robert and Claire swabbed the insides of their cheeks and handed the cotton-tipped sticks to Davis.

"This shouldn't take too long. This is a fully mobile, state-of-the-art DNA processor. I'll have the results to our security guy in Phoenix within the hour so that he'll be able to enter them into the investigation's database at just the right time."

CHAPTER 41

Badly hungover, Stacy awoke to the sound of banging on her front door. The previous night had been a panic-filled nightmare. She really shouldn't have started in with the cocaine, but she was close to frantic and nearing the end of her rope. Her head felt like it was in a vise, and her gut threatened to contract into a full-on vomiting episode.

Detective Beverly Genn looked at her watch as she knocked once again, louder, on the front door of a gorgeous, sprawling home overlooking north Scottsdale and the more distant Phoenix beyond. She and her partner were getting ready to leave when the door opened. A wild-eyed woman with short platinum-blonde hair and bloodshot eyes stood there. Stacy had considered not answering the door, but when she saw the badges hanging from lanyards around their necks, she thought better of it. It wouldn't do to look unconcerned if they were here regarding Curt.

"Excuse me, ma'am, are you Stacy Atkins? Scottsdale Police Department here with a few questions. May we come in?"

Stacy opened the door. "Of course, officers. Do you have any word on my husband?"

They stepped inside and were immediately appalled by the appearance of the grand foyer. The floor was littered with broken glass, shards of what looked like once beautiful Chinese vases, and an empty McCallum's bottle that apparently had rolled into the corner.

"Is everything okay, Mrs. Atkins?"

Stacy looked around, hoping that the little white paper bindle holding the remaining half gram of white powder was out of sight.

"Uh, sure, you know, I'm just worried about my husband."

"I'm Detective Genn, and this is my partner, Detective Karen Martinez. Mrs. Atkins, we're actually here on another matter. We have some bad news regarding your sister. She was presumably killed in a random explosion early Saturday morning. Can we sit down?"

Looking appropriately stunned, Stacy motioned them to the small study off the foyer. "What are you talking about?"

The officers filled her in on the terrible explosion and fire, and Stacy told them she hadn't watched the news all weekend.

"Investigators have located what seem to be two sets of human remains, and we believe that one may be your sister, Claire Wilheit. We'd like to ask you to voluntarily provide a DNA sample as a possible match so we can try to determine if that's the case."

Stacy stared at them. Her mind, still foggy, was spinning with paranoia. She needed time to think.

"I'm not really comfortable doing that right now." She stood. "This is a shock, and I have a lot on my plate at the moment."

"We'd rather do this voluntarily, but if we need to, we'll come back with a warrant."

"Then go get your fucking warrant," Stacy hissed. "We're done here."

With the sound of door slamming behind them, the Scottsdale detectives didn't speak until they were back in their car.

"Something's really off here."

"No shit."

As they were putting on their seat belts, there was a tap on the passenger's side window.

"I'm a little overwrought, understandably. Of course I want to do everything I can to help you. I'll give you a sample." Stacy's hands were shaking. Not much, but not lost on the detectives, either.

Five minutes later, the detectives headed down the long, sloping highway toward Scottsdale, cotton swab in its properly labeled evidence envelope.

"What's that line from *Alice in Wonderland*?"

"Curiouser and curiouser?"
"Yeah, that's the one."

CHAPTER 42

Back at the Scottsdale Police headquarters, both detectives sat with their case supervisor, Ben Wolf. Stacy Atkins's DNA sample was now being processed and the detectives' role in collecting it done.

"So maybe it's just a hunch, Ben, but there was something seriously wrong with that woman and that scene. The Atkins woman looked as though she hadn't slept in a week and was made up of nothing but raw, exposed nerves."

"It's certainly possible that she is just worried about her husband," he replied, then waited for them to continue.

"Maybe, but we've been to enough places and delivered enough bad news to think that her response was, well, inappropriate. We only saw the front area of the home, but it was trashed—it looked vandalized. So, no, things didn't square."

He tended to agree. These were two of his best, most seasoned officers, and if they said something wasn't right, he'd let them pursue it. Wolf pressed the intercom on his desk. "Stan, can you please come in?"

Stan Deering was the lead detective on the Curt Atkins disappearance. He listened to the two detectives' stories and brought them up to date on his own case.

"Interesting. Let me show you what we've just pulled up on Curt Atkins." Stan opened his tablet and showed the other three a spreadsheet.

"We've been able to fast-track a search warrant and have been looking into Atkins's banking records and have found major withdrawals over the past twelve months."

Deering let out a soft whistle. "Six million dollars? In cash? In just twelve months? Where did it go?"

"Don't know yet. We can only go so far without another warrant, and there's no readily apparent information about where the money went. We're not even sure who or what to name in a subsequent warrant.

"But we can see that he liquidated all the assets he could during the first six months of the year, and then more as each group of bond holdings matured. He took an enormous penalty on the 401K. My people are going back another twelve months, because we think there's more."

"Looks like our multimillionaire disappeared leaving a net worth of less than twenty thousand bucks, in that range."

Wolf looked at his three detectives. "I want you all to drop everything else and follow these leads. I don't care where they take you. If you need to coordinate with the Phoenix PD, fine, but use your judgment." The Phoenix PD and its unholy relationship with the Arizona Freedom Brigade had cost the department most of its best cops. Corruption was rampant, and the overall skill level had plummeted. Confidential information had about a fifty percent chance of not being leaked. Scottsdale had declined offers of police privatization, preferring to maintain its relative independence. The city's budget was hit hard as a result, but the leadership remained convinced that the money was well spent.

"Oh, and there's one more very peculiar thing. The computer at the Atkins home has logged in to the accounts fourteen times in the past twenty-four hours. Even stranger, a money transfer of three hundred and twenty-five grand was made from the home computer several hours after the explosion."

"Well, Mrs. Atkins was overwrought all right. But maybe not about her husband's welfare."

CHAPTER 43

Michael Parker looked down thirty stories onto a wintry, picturesque Central Park. A light carpet of snow covered the grounds, still beautiful, still treasured by New Yorkers and the unending river of tourists. He marveled at the state of things, chief among which was his net worth. Born to a Russian oligarch, his father had gained his substantial wealth through the generations of corruption in the Russian ruling class, which despite cycles of political upheaval and waxing and waning of Cold War politics, hadn't changed all that much over the past hundred years. Power was still power, and money was still money.

Parker's Iranian-born mother fled her country in the early seventies with nearly a billion dollars, thanks to her distant relationship with the long-dead dictator. Parker's physical appearance was a blend of the two and, as it turned out, a lucky draw. While he had his father's stature, his mother's exotic, olive coloring and dark eyes allowed him to pass as a member of any number of Mediterranean gene pools. He liked his current name, Michael Parker. It was unmemorable, generic enough to avoid stereotyping, and one of several under which he held passports proving diverse citizenship.

Through his connections, he'd found his way to Stephen Chen and did nothing to dispel Chen's belief that it was he who had sought out Parker. Parker considered his capital investment in AllMed to be a potentially good one. In and of itself, he rated the downside risk associated with Chen's venture to be about average, with a fixed exposure. The upside, on the other hand, was enormous, and he felt comfortable with it in his investment portfolio.

Even if it went belly-up, it wouldn't do any real damage to his overall financial health.

Now fifty years of age, Parker had achieved doctorate-level expertise in both international politics and economic theory. As soon as the US Supreme Court passed Citizens United, he focused dark money contributions to enough Congressional lifers that he could basically pull a whole lot of strings without the people involved ever knowing they'd been played.

On the flip side, the Middle East ground and air wars following 9/11 provided him a beautifully useful private business template that needed only periodic tweaking. His ownership in both privatized military and personnel services was bolstered by silent partner arrangements with an array of corporations providing hardware, infrastructure, and weaponry of every kind. It was an unusual but effective vertical marketing structure.

Although the immigrant deportation effort was disastrous for families and the economy alike, it was a real jackpot for AllMed and A1A. Undocumented Latinos were offered the option of joining the US military and after four years of service could formally apply for citizenship. Another key part of the post-2020 jobs programs included hiring dispossessed coal and steel workers throughout the Rust Belt as soldiers. The ramping up of boots on the ground throughout the Middle East added to the avalanche of new PTSD patients in the military. Studies suggested that reluctant military conscripts developed PTSD at nearly twice the rate as their more enthusiastic counterparts.

Successful implementation of A1A in the market would provide the third leg that would guarantee long-term stability of his global wealth position. Simply put, he could influence, if not control, the policies that created continuing warfare, supply the execution of the war effort, and reap unending profit from the damaged goods returning home. Parker felt like the conductor of a great orchestra whose sections had no idea they were part of a larger symphony that only he could hear.

CHAPTER 44

Anna Dixon's demeanor on the screen changed little, but Aaron knew from his years of working with her that she was concerned yet resolute. Aaron faced the screen as he sat at the lodge's sturdy old table. They could both hear the soft murmur of the therapists' voices from their shared room. There were occasionally louder sounds, mostly argumentative, but then they resumed their quiet conversation.

Aaron brought Dixon up to date. "Kingston's and Wilheit's DNA profiles should be in the investigator's system now, replacing whatever DNA they recovered from the remains. Local investigators have already recovered Kingston's DNA from his apartment, so his DNA will be definitive. Final reports will conclusively show that they both died in the blast."

"What, if anything, do we know about the second body?" Anna Dixon's expression was tight. It was unlikely that she'd slept any better than anyone else on the team.

"Nothing right now," replied Aaron. "We have the individual's DNA, but there's nothing in any of our databases to allow a match. So all we can surmise is that he, or she, has never been arrested and never served in the military or police forces. If we had fingerprints, we'd have a lot of other databases to consider, like whether this person ever had a securities, teaching, or real estate license, that kind of thing."

"Any update from Perry?"

"No, he'll be pretty busy with all of the Lucident activity today, but if he gets any relevant information, he'll get in touch right away."

"What about our therapists?"

"We've shared what we agreed to with them and have told them about the protection program. Wilheit's pissed off, but Kingston seemed to take it all in. We'll have more discussion later today after we conclude this meeting."

"Where are you in terms of thinking we need to have someone enter the Lucident patient system?"

"Right now, I'd say the odds are pretty high that we won't get much further without it."

"Okay. Let's talk again tomorrow, and sooner, if necessary. Good work, everyone."

Dixon's image blinked off, leaving the screen saver to take its place.

Claire and Robert entered the lodge's lobby area to join the others.

"We've been talking about our situation." Robert took a seat at the table and continued. "Look, I don't have a job anymore, and as you are aware, I have no family to keep me in Phoenix. I'm leaning toward accepting your offer for protection but need to have a few questions answered."

Davis nodded at him to continue.

"First, I would need housing and work. This is all I'm really qualified to do. I don't have any other references and obviously can't use anything in my past. So how would this even work?"

"Successful relocation means that we develop, in conjunction with you, a new identity. We don't want to arbitrarily decide on something that won't be compatible with you—who you are, what you value, that type of parameter. Experience shows that doesn't work because it just isn't sustainable. That means we develop a comprehensive backstory, including job history, education, family, et cetera. It will involve placing information, backdated of course, into every search engine history. We don't just drop you into a strange setting. It will take some time for you to transition into your new identity. You'll be provided housing at our expense, a modest bank account to get you started, and a good job—with retraining, if that is in your best interest. After about a year or so, once we're sure no one is looking for you, you can begin to embellish your own new life, decide whether you want to change jobs or where you live.

"Like I said, no one should ever come looking for you unless you yourself provide a reason. Our results in the protection program have been excellent, and that's no doubt because our protectees prefer life over death. It's not something we offer lightly.

"In order to save your lives, we've already established incontrovertible proof that you died in the explosion. There was a very tight window within which to insert your DNA records into the investigation, and we took it. Right now, we think the best place for you, Robert, to begin your new life is in a small suburb of Portland, Oregon. You don't have to decide right this minute, but you do have to decide within a couple of days."

Robert looked at Aaron Davis for a long moment. "I won't need a couple of days. I'll accept the offer. Thank you."

"Ms. Wilheit?"

"I don't like the idea, and I resent being put in this situation. I need time to think and to get more information from you."

"Fair enough. Mr. Kingston, if you would please collect your things, Kate will take you to another location where you can begin your transition."

"Now? As in right now?"

"Do you see any reason to delay?"

He didn't.

Robert took his meager belongings from the bedroom and moved to Claire, giving her a hug. "Be safe and take care. I'm glad we could help each other get through this." Nodding, she returned the hug, albeit somewhat stiffly. Her emotions and nerves were on edge.

"You, too, Robert."

Davis shook Robert's hand. "Have a good, safe, long life, Mr. Kingston."

Claire poured herself a cup of tea and retreated to her room. She stared out the window toward the lake as she breathed deeply, calming herself to think through her situation. After twenty minutes of meditation, she stretched out on the bed, pillows propped against the wall. How in the world had she come to this place and this time in her life? She'd just extricated herself from a toxic romance that had taken its toll. Her boyfriend's constant, insidious fault-finding had successfully eaten away at her own self-confidence, resulting in erratic sleep, loss of appetite, and significant weight loss. After finally getting rid of him, she was able to restore some semblance of balance and physical health in her own life. She got rid of that ridiculous blonde hair color and donated six equally ridiculous ball gowns to charity. And then, just as she was beginning to feel comfortable again, she was broadsided by her sister's lawsuit. With the explosion, her house, the anchoring symbol of her self-reliance, was gone, along with every possession she owned. Now she was in a secluded mountain cabin, being told that she needed to abandon her entire identity and run from reality. She attempted to come to grips with it all and just couldn't.

You can't change the past, she thought, wondering how many times she'd told her patients the exact same thing. *Start where you are. You're alive. You can't put the house back together. You can't change your sister. What can you do?*

Claire closed her eyes. She felt pressure behind her eyes and a burning in her sinuses as she used every bit of discipline she could muster not to cry. It didn't work. She could feel the tears leaking from her closed eyes, warm wet patterns that flowed across the sides of her face and down the back of her jaw onto her neck. She wiped her face with her sleeve and then used the top edge of the sheet to blot her face dry. She'd developed one hell of a bad headache but was too depleted to care.

CHAPTER 45

"Dr. Chen, good afternoon." Chen's clinical director, Vivian Jaffe, greeted the CEO in her usual professional manner. "Would you like another update on your study results?"

"No, thank you, doctor, your reports are very thorough as always, and quite encouraging."

She nodded and left to see to her scientists' latest tabulations. She was quite optimistic herself, now that the results' stability had turned into predictability, the last hurdle before the announcement to come next month. She was confident that A1A's performance was solidly understood and found acceptable by AllMed. The work that remained before the formal event was basically developing a platform for the announcement, press releases, speakers, and the like. Administrative drivel didn't interest her in the slightest and would thankfully be handled by others. In her laboratories, she was in her element, and she wanted to keep it that way. Let the administrators do their job; she would do hers. She wanted to focus her time and energy in research and development for the next drug, one that would shrink the A1A risks and side effects to acceptable levels. She was aware that she defined "acceptable" quite a bit differently than did her boss.

Dr Jaffe's concern about the side effects, while there from the outset, had grown exponentially. Dealing with the forty inpatients now in a semipermanent holding state—quite literally—was more than troubling, but the idea of thousands more in a similar state—in the way too near future—crossed the line. At this point, all she could do was escalate the new drug's research and development timeline as much as humanly possible. As desperate as she viewed the situation, she was unwilling to cut corners in scientific research. It was not lost on her that AllMed's CEO failed to share the same commitment. She was angry at herself for going along all this time, ignoring the facts right in front of her face. Now she had no choice but to confront the reality, unpleasant as it was.

Stephen Chen used his passkey to enter two sequential locked areas of the veterans' hospital. It was an enormous sprawling monolith on Indian School Road, just over a mile north of Lucident's outpatient clinics and corporate building. Jury-rigged structural additions to the main inpatient hospital over the past decades left its condition similar to every other major medical center that still remained on its original campus. Wayfinding was challenging in the best of situations, but the renovation of the secured units resulted in illogical navigation patterns. Despite the state-of-the-art signage experts they'd brought in from northern California, there was only so much lipstick one could put on a pig, he thought. Still, they'd done a superb job with what they were given.

The final door had a small sign: "Long-Term Care Unit. Authorized Personnel Only." Chen used his passkey one more time. The units were modular in design, more spacious private rooms than a typical hospital intensive care unit. Because they were basically rehab patient rooms, they didn't require space in which to pack all the life-saving equipment and staff access their critical care cousins needed. There were sixty rooms in the unit. Forty were presently occupied. The number was close to what he'd expected, given the initial testing group of 430 patients. Beyond the first module were two identical units, both empty, awaiting an expected influx of patients over the next twelve months. Whether additional units or facilities beyond that were needed would depend entirely on the initial volume of new patients getting A1A after it was officially approved and how long they stayed in active treatment. And upon how quickly a second ameliorative drug could be developed and brought to market. If the second drug followed the path of

A1A, it should hopefully be completed in twenty-four months. If the new drug only required a modification of the existing A1A formula, the rollout could be considerably sooner. In any case, he'd done all he could to anticipate the volume, and if necessary, off-site facility arrangements could be made within the expected time frame.

Of his forty-one patients, seven were now in a persistent vegetative state. Brain dead. They would continue to be studied for another number of weeks, then would quietly be taken off life support. The other thirty-four were in medically induced comas. Their care requirements were fairly basic: routine nursing care, nutritional and respiratory support, and physical therapy to minimize muscle atrophy. It was particularly important for hospital staff to make sure that bed-bound patients were moved often enough to stop bedsores from becoming life-threatening problems. Keeping and caring for patients in such an extended state of induced coma was much more of an art than a science, and he'd been pushing the limits. But it was the only option he had to try to help them. He'd made sure that there were two full-time hospital-based rehab doctors on staff at all times. Their training and credentials were impeccable.

Stephen entered the third patient room on his left. The name on the door read simply: Susan.

Stephen never let more than three days pass between his visits, and when he could, he stopped in daily on his rounds through the laboratories. The soft music coming from the speakers in the room combined with the hum of the respirator and monitoring machines to create a hypnotic effect. He spoke in a soft voice. "Be patient, Mom, we're almost there." When Chen had admitted her to the inpatient service, she hadn't changed from the catatonic state she'd entered right after her psychotic break. Three months ago, he'd order her placed into a medically induced coma, joining the other patients in the unit. She would be the first to be brought out of the coma when A1A was approved in just a few short weeks. Unlike the other patients in the long-term care unit, he'd had her transferred to this unit for admission without the same problematic A1A protocol failure that brought the others here. Despite the fail rate, she still had nearly a ninety percent chance for success. Without A1A, she had none.

Stephen Chen believed this was the only chance for her recovery, given the poor prognosis of patients undergoing years of psychoactive IV drug therapies. Even those who eventually graduated from such extreme treatment protocols were often left with some level of diminished brain function. Which didn't really leave them much better off. It certainly never restored their original quality of life. Was Stephen playing God? He didn't know then and didn't know now. He'd eventually come to the realization that no amount of introspective thought would give him the answer.

Although Susan Masterson, MD, no longer physically resembled the vibrant woman he'd known during the first part of his life, at least she no longer looked like the crazed woman paramedics had taken from his father's kitchen nearly eleven years ago.

CHAPTER 46

Claire emerged from the bedroom with a freshly scrubbed face and slightly swollen eyes. The small group's dinner of sandwiches and soft drinks was light but enough for her. It was impossible for her to judge Aaron's mood, and she was usually quite good at nonverbal reads. *That kind of skill generally did go with therapist territory*, she thought wryly. But not with Davis.

"Can we talk now?"

"Absolutely, Ms. Wilheit."

"Look, you can quit with the formality. Claire is fine." She took a breath. "I trust you. You saved both of our lives. I think you're trying to do the right thing, but letting you make an independent decision to completely erase my life is beyond unacceptable."

Aaron nodded. "Claire, please believe me, I completely understand how you feel and how challenging—"

"No. No, you do *not* know how I feel, and knock off the patronizing shit."

"Point taken. Let me restate what I meant to say. I've worked with many people who have gone into witness protection, and while each situation is completely different, there are some responses that are fairly universal. Each person brings his or her unique temperament, skills, and strengths and fears to the situation. We would—I would—never suggest such an extreme solution if there was any other way to ensure your safety."

He could sense her tension begin to ease. Not much, but enough that he felt encouraged.

"Okay. I get the irony. If you hadn't acted when you did, I probably wouldn't even have a life decision to make at all. So now I'm officially dead, right? And so is Robert?"

He nodded again.

"So now we have a big problem to solve. Make that two big problems. Here's how I see it: the police and Lucident and everyone else in the public thinks that Robert and I are dead. But the people who sent Green now know he's dead, too. We know that because of your Lucident informant, right? They only know that another person—one other person—is dead. But because there are two official confirmations, Robert and me, the people who sent Green now have to understand that there's a problem with the information. They can only assume that either Robert or I were killed, but not both. But they have DNA proof that we both died. Are you following me here?"

Aaron's gaze intensified, focused directly on her. He nodded, immediately grasping her logic.

"So they have to assume that there's something wonky about the DNA evidence, right? Should they believe none of it, or part of it, and if so, which part? Which would mean that they won't stop looking for either of us since they don't know who really died and who didn't. If we assume that Green, or whatever his real name is, didn't set off the explosion, what else do we know, Aaron?"

Understanding lit up firing points in Aaron's brain. Claire continued, but he had the feeling she was reasoning this through as she went, talking to herself as much as to him.

"Let's assume that the unknown person, 'X', whose remains were discovered, knew of or set off the explosion. Is it possible he did this—I'm assuming a 'he' here—without anyone else in the world knowing? If so, why would he? Without being sure I was in the house? There isn't any reason I can possibly think of that someone would want to kill me, let alone risk his own life in the process. So where does that leave us?"

"Let's work through the assumption that someone wanted to kill you. That leaves us in one of only two places that I can think of," said Aaron. He was surprised by the speed and comprehensiveness of her logic, but he was right with her. "First, he was working alone and wanted to see you dead and was an incompetent killer. Which would be obvious, since he blew himself to smithereens. Possible? Maybe. Or second, he set some kind of alarm that would trigger the bomb when you entered the house, and something went wrong."

"When I entered the house? Through a side casement window? Who would enter their own house through a side casement window with a rusty old crank? And anyone could have entered the house—a housekeeper, a friend—plus, I had just entered and left the house with Robert a few hours earlier. And if he set an alarm to trigger the explosion, he sure as hell would have gotten away from the blast area. That scenario just doesn't hold water, either.

"And another thing. Green couldn't have been the target. The only other person who knew Green was going to enter the house at exactly that time was your informer. Plus, you said you were following Green when he broke in. How could the bomber have known that Green was going to be there?"

"Right."

"Do you have another hypothesis?"

"Someone hired the bomber to do it," Aaron said.

"Then you'd have to go back to the assumption that I was the target. There's another possibility out there. Someone wanted the hired bomber dead. Someone who didn't know or care that either Robert or I were killed and maybe didn't even know about Green."

The possibilities were numerous and complicated, and Aaron knew that no quick answer would be found. In fact, maybe no answer would ever be found. Period. Unlike the movies or crime novels he'd read, sometimes there just weren't answers to be had, just a series of blind alleys and dead ends. What he did know was that they were about out of time to rescue the situation.

"So, the only option we have to explain the situation to our unknown person—"

"Is to have the investigation discover a third victim of the explosion," Claire finished for him. "There's no other way for Robert and me to stay safely dead." She sat back from the table and looked at him with her arms crossed, as if finishing her closing argument to a jury and waiting for his rebuttal.

He stood up abruptly, grabbing his phone to text Perry: *Urgent you call immediately.*

"Let's see what can be done. It might already be too late. But if it can be done, Perry can do it."

Perry MacRae went to work with a vengeance. First, he needed to establish a reason to send the cadaver dogs back into the explosion site for a second look. An anonymous tip provided simultaneously to the mayor, the news, and the Phoenix PD got that ball moving. A small drone the size of a cicada had deposited a sample of "clean" DNA—that is, DNA not in any known database—into the charcoal-smelling rubble so the dogs would be certain to find it. All the canines had to do was sniff it out, which he felt confident would happen, and he wouldn't even need to reenter the investigation's database to tinker with the findings. If necessary, he could alter the data later, so, either way, he could ensure the result.

He reported back to Davis and Dixon and returned to finish out the rest of his day at Lucident's security office, while Smith was otherwise engaged in crisis management.

CHAPTER 47

"The number you have reached is no longer in service. Please check the number and try—"

"Fuck! Fuck!" Stacy threw the phone at the wall. She finally admitted to herself that Tango was gone and that he would never answer that goddamn phone.

She'd been able to hold her emotions in check during the unsurprising call from her lawyer. He explained that with the explosion unsolved, and the fact there was no deposition, combined with the fact that her husband had disappeared (thanks to the ever-prompt Scottsdale PD's announcement late last night that Curt was missing, and anyone knowing his whereabouts was asked to blah, blah, blah), her case would have to be placed on hold indefinitely. He asked if she would like her bill, which now totaled $7,500, sent to the house? Yes, she told him, that would be fine.

Nothing was fine, and Stacy had absolutely no idea what to do. She was keeping her free-wheeling panic under control with Valium, which helped a lot but did nothing to promote a solution. The $11,000 mortgage payment was due in two weeks. That's all the time she had to figure out a plan.

Stacy pulled herself together enough to sit down at a cleared table with a notepad, calendar, and calculator. She would be officially broke if she allowed the mortgage payment to go through and if she were to actually consider paying her attorney. Clearly, she could not do either. Yes, a plan was exactly what she needed. She began drawing out a timeline.

Flashbacks interrupted her tasks.

"Curt, why do we have to have so much money invested in this one house? The monthly payments are huge."

"First of all, Stace, it's not that much money. I've only made the minimum down payment, so it's really the bank that is making the investment for this place."

"But…"

"Second of all, we agreed that finances are my issue and my worry. I know you had concerns about our prenuptial agreement, but I think it's always been in your best interest not to have to worry. I know what I'm doing."

"I'm just saying that if there's an emergency, I need to be able to access all of our financial information."

"Look, Stacy, there's not going to be any fucking 'emergency.' Period."

They'd had the same argument countless times, and after Curt broke his arm in a ski accident, he eventually relented and took her through the various steps involved in accessing online the array of holdings they had, although he stopped short of adding her as a signatory to any of them. Stacy had her own credit cards, and he provided a monthly stipend for her to manage paying their balances. She was sick of feeling that she was on a leash, tethered to Curt's whims and moods. He didn't usually complain about her shopping or spending habits, so she didn't rock the boat any further. It didn't matter anyway, because she saw where he kept the passwords to all the financial accounts—stupidly written on a piece of paper taped under his desk. Curt changed passwords frequently, so knowing the names of the accounts didn't help since he never told her when he did. This she knew since she had tried to access all the accounts shortly after Curt's little tutorial. After her initial frustration she found the little sticky note under the desk, showing all the updated passwords. What an idiot.

She returned to her timeline.

CHAPTER 48

Wednesday, January 10

Ben Wolf and his three top detectives sat at the small round conference table in Wolf's office, drinking bad coffee from Styrofoam cups.

"We've got a DNA link confirmation between Stacy Atkins and one of the victims at the Wilshire scene in Phoenix. Just confirmed this morning. Claire Wilheit was killed in the explosion. The second victim has been positively identified as Robert Kingston." Beverly Genn added, "The updated report from Phoenix found evidence of a third body at the site, but so far there is no link to any DNA in our systems."

"Stan, what do you have on the Atkinses' financial situation?"

"Right now, we're working on two different assumptions. One assumption is that Curt Atkins bled out his accounts to an unknown location and planned to leave his wife once he'd finished plundering their fortunes. He's been systematically moving assets for at least the past year, so it's quite possible that he's been planning something. We don't have proof, but this kind of stuff does happen, and more often than you'd think. Husband figures it makes more sense to disappear with the money than to lose half of it in a divorce.

"The second assumption is that he possibly had gambling debts and got mixed up with organized crime or something similar. We don't have any proof of that, either, or even a good working hypothesis. While we do have a few confidential informants within the 'bad loan' industry, they haven't heard any rumors—which doesn't mean anything conclusive. Still, the casino manager identified him as a regular customer with both big wins and big losses. Rumors of connections with underground mobsters fly around casinos all the time and have become such favorites of urban legend that we tend to take them with a grain of salt."

Karen Martinez nodded. "Either scenario would fit with leaving his car at the casino, then disappearing. That way, if he'd taken the money and split, he'd still leave open the suggestion of foul play, hoping that in some short amount of time, any search for him would end. We don't have any record of him getting on a plane at Sky Harbor in Phoenix, but a guy with his kind of money could easily arrange private transportation out of Arizona. There are plenty of smaller private airports as well. It's been almost five days, and he could be anywhere in the world."

"Right now, I'd give more weight to the plundering husband theory."

"Why is that that, Stan?" asked Martinez.

"The reason that organized crime, especially in the bad debt department, has continued to thrive is that the people running the show are smart. It would be a seriously stupid move for them to leave Atkins's car in the casino parking lot," Deering said. "And to ignore a seventy grand asset when they're dealing with debt isn't just stupid, it's bad business."

Ben Wolf agreed. "Let's assign a status of closed with an option to reopen and leave this case on a back burner. All we really know is that a guy is not where his wife thinks he should be and that he's taken money out of his own account. Still, I think we should keep our options open to keep an eye on Mrs. Atkins. She's the only person who could have withdrawn that three hundred and twenty-five thousand on Saturday morning. We don't have any reason to pour more investigative resources into that, but let's just make one last casual inquiry before I close it up. Beverly and Karen, can you drive out to talk to her? Let her know what we think may have happened."

Karen answered for both of them. "Can't think of anything we'd rather do." Both detectives smiled a bit as they rose. "Let's go pay a visit to the lovely Mrs. Atkins."

Thirty minutes later, the Scottsdale detectives knocked on Stacy Atkins's door. They'd been patiently waiting on the front stepped entryway. They knocked again, announcing themselves.

Martinez looked at her partner. "You think she's here?"

"Don't know. We can try to find our way around to the back or somewhere with a window we can look through…"

They heard a click as the lock disengaged. Stacy Atkins looked a lot more composed than she had at their last visit.

"Hello, detectives. Do you have any news about my husband's whereabouts?"

"May we come in?"

"Yes, please."

The three women sat in the same seats they'd occupied during their last visit. The foyer was now spotless.

"We've been able to verify that your husband has withdrawn large amounts of cash from most of your financial accounts going back at least a year."

The color drained from Stacy's face, and she said, "I don't understand."

"As of today, we are suspending the investigation into your husband's disappearance. Initially we thought he may have had gambling debts, but we have no evidence to support that. Unless you have reason to believe otherwise, we believe that Mr. Atkins has most probably left the state of his own volition and may have left the country. I'm sorry, but sometimes an unhappy spouse would rather deplete or hide assets than to risk losing them in a divorce. That may be the case here."

"But we were happy! We were planning a future together…was there another woman?" Stacy managed to look simultaneously distressed and confused.

"I'm so sorry." Detective Genn continued, "It's always possible that he'll turn up at some future point, or perhaps it's all just a misunderstanding. We just don't have any basis upon which to continue the investigation."

"I see. Thank you for coming to tell me all of this." Stacy stood up, as did the two detectives.

"Please feel free to call at any time, if you have further concerns." Martinez turned to Stacy before leaving. "I do have one last question. We noticed that a large cash withdrawal, over three hundred thousand dollars, was made from your account on Saturday morning. Might you know anything about that?"

"No, of course not. Maybe it was some kind of automatic payment Curt set up."

"That's probably it."

Stacy held the front door open for them.

"Good-bye, Mrs. Atkins." Just before the door closed behind them, Karen turned toward the blonde woman with her hand on the jamb, ready to close the door. "Oh, we thought you would want to know that your DNA sample was most helpful. I'm sorry to say that your sister, Claire Wilheit, was killed in the Phoenix explosion this past weekend."

Stacy nodded and closed the door.

As they drove back to Scottsdale, Beverly looked at her partner. "Did you believe her?"

"Not a goddamned word. She wouldn't have even asked about her sister if we hadn't brought it up."

"My thoughts exactly."

Stacy locked the front door after the detectives left. Her shock at them telling her about Curt's withdrawals was real but not for the reason they thought. She'd realized that they'd accessed her banking transactions. But the fear that they might have been inside her computer unnerved her even more.

CHAPTER 49

Wednesday, January 10, and Thursday, January 11

Just before midnight Wednesday, Stacy finally shut down her computer. She had several credit cards in her own name, most of them carrying the names of high-end department stores, but because they were either Mastercard or Visa accounts, they were useful anywhere. The collective balances ran $6,022.00. She paid the Neiman Marcus and Nordstrom accounts in full because they had the largest available credit, which would give her a full thirty days to rack up more charges before being billed again. She paid the minimum balance on the remaining cards. Her available credit on the second group of cards wasn't all that high, and at this point, she didn't care about interest on unpaid balances. What Stacy needed right now was to maximize the amount of credit available so she could remain solvent for the greatest length of time. The payments took just over $3,500 out of the remaining $17,000 in the accounts she and Curt shared. Screw the mortgage payment.

Banked airline mileage would get her about three hundred thousand miles, enough to travel anywhere she wanted. Well, at least one way. First class wasn't an option this time.

She was surprised at how many cruises were designed for older singles. Even though Stacy was still quite a way south of forty, she figured that's where the odds favored her. She focused on cruises mainly designed for guests over sixty. She'd struck gold once before in Portofino, so why mess with a perfect record?

151

Stacy clicked "Purchase." She would be out of Phoenix tomorrow afternoon, connecting to a flight from JFK later that night. Her luxury cruise ship would depart from Cinque Terre Saturday night. She could get a new phone and tablet at the airport kiosk. This computer needed to die a quick death here in Phoenix.

CHAPTER 50

Thursday, January 11

Stacy Atkins picked up her espresso cup and headed to her closet to select an appropriate wardrobe for the Mediterranean venue. There were only two errands she needed to do later today. The first was to return the Armani suit to Neiman's, giving her a $2,600 (plus tax) credit balance. While it was a perfect choice for a charity luncheon, she had more suitable clothing selections for the kind of trip she had in mind. The second was to make a trip to her bank to cash out most of what remained in the shared account. She considered leaving a thousand dollars in the account, just for appearance's sake. Not that she cared about maintaining its "Platinum" status. On second thought, a thousand dollars was a thousand dollars. She could keep the account open with a hundred dollars. No way to know if she'd need the account at a future date.

Stacy went online to arrange for the post office to hold her mail for three weeks.

The last thing she did before leaving was to dash off a note to her housekeeper, who would be at the Scottsdale residence Friday afternoon. She would have to assume that Maria had seen the local news.

Dear Maria,
I've had a horrible family tragedy this last week and am very upset.
I'll be away for a couple of weeks. Here is payment for two weeks.
Please take next Friday off, with my thanks.

She slipped a check for four hundred dollars under the note and left them both on the kitchen counter. Maybe Maria would get to the bank while there was still enough left in the account to cover part of the check, but probably not. There were a few automatic payments that would be executed over the next number of days—her club membership, her monthly exterminator bill, things like that. Maria's check would sit in the bank all weekend, waiting to be returned for insufficient funds. By then, Stacy would be on the other side of the planet. And frankly, Maria's finances weren't Stacy's problem.

CHAPTER 51

After a lengthy discussion with Claire at the lodge, Aaron agreed to speak with Anna Dixon to see how she'd feel about Claire helping him and his team with the case.

Claire had made a well-considered and convincing argument that her background and inside knowledge of PTSD patients, treatment options, and the course and nature of the condition could be an asset. Davis's private conversation with Anna Dixon lasted only fifteen minutes, and she was in agreement with his assessment. For now, Wilheit could stay.

Davis and Claire sat with John at the lodge's central table and began to develop a plan for one member of the team to be admitted to Lucident's outpatient and, ultimately, inpatient service.

"Aaron, do we have any idea how much time we would have before AllMed's final FDA approval is granted?" asked John.

"No. But no doubt it will be followed quickly by federal hearings giving approval for the immediate delivery of A1A to patients in the state of Arizona, then launching of the treatment protocol to in-theater military members suffering from PTSD. I certainly expect the marketing department of AllMed has a sleek, state-of-the-art press conference ready to go at a moment's notice. Or at least to be released once committee members finish squabbling over who would get to take first credit on the national media stage."

Dixon would get advance notice through her committee, but whether that was an hour or three days remained to be seen. They knew, however, that the time frame would be greatly compressed in order to head off the inevitable leaks that would preempt the monumental announcement.

It would be Perry's job to identify who on Dixon's team could best carry off the most plausible profile and to then create a military backstory and enter the deployment history into the system. Davis's next Brigade shift was to begin Friday night. So, Aaron would have to be back in Phoenix by midday on Friday at the latest to monitor the pending PTSD patient's intake, which would occur sometime before the curfew ended Monday morning.

CHAPTER 52

Michael Parker stepped out of his glass-walled shower, wrapped himself in a luxurious navy cashmere bathrobe, and walked into his living room. He poured himself a short glass of bourbon, neat. Sitting in front of his computer screen, Parker opened an encrypted file.

In accordance with a tradition that began long ago, American Veterans' Service (formerly Veterans Health Administration) patients were handled in a trio of separate but related systems based on competing funding and insurance systems. Budget and appropriation battles were fought each year among the three massive departments: the American Veterans Department, the Department of Health and Human Services (which included health service allocations for the general public), and the Department of Health Services for Indigenous Peoples (DHSIP), formerly a division of the DHHS.

Back in the late '70s, federal law provided for the nationwide categorization of hospitals. Experience in the Korean War—and more definitively in the Vietnam War—showed the impact of solid, well-implemented patient triage in the battlefield. Patient survival hinged largely upon getting proper care during the "golden hour," the first sixty minutes after a traumatic injury. Hospitals throughout the country were assigned one of three categories depending upon the resources on hand to treat trauma patients. Not only were Level I, II, and III Trauma Centers established, the categorization was expanded for specialties including cardiac, high-risk obstetrical/neonatal care, and psychiatric care.

What set Arizona apart, though, was the medical insurance filter now in the emergency systems' protocols. Comprehensive insurance and medical history evaluations were instituted throughout first responder training statewide.

All in all, it did provide a more expedient process to determine what hospital was best for the patient, financially speaking. Again on the positive side, it reduced a lot of post-emergency patient transfers. Unfortunately, it also put patients at risk for longer transport times. The first responders were frustrated and continually complained to the governor about response protocols putting financial concerns ahead of patients' needs. The governor listened. But he did nothing to change it.

Nonetheless, the first responder system for psychiatric triage now in place provided for any patient exhibiting signs of PTSD, or suspected PTSD, to first be transported to the AVS emergency department for further triage. If suspected or confirmed PTSD patients were not AVS eligible, they would receive a secondary transport to a hospital that accepted their insurance.

The system, as it now stood, was incredibly advantageous for AllMed and Lucident. It virtually guaranteed that every potential veteran with PTSD found his or her way into the system. It also created a civilian PTSD database that could be mined at some future date, anticipating that A1A would find its way to becoming the preferred treatment for all patients with the condition, regardless of their insurers or ultimate hospital destination.

Parker opened a new document and began adding bullet points, things he'd need to do before he left New York.

1. AllMed personnel security issues:
   John Ricker, director of security. Background and qualifications for position—review and conduct secondary vetting.
   Vivian Jaffe, MD, director of clinical research. Surveillance of her private phone account indicates possible concerns with research methods and protocols. Conduct additional surveillance. Increase frequency of updates.

2. Stocks. Ready pharmaceuticals' buy and sell orders. Review investment levels in military ordnance manufacturers. Adjust as appropriate.

3. Contact Singapore. Finalize alternative pharmaceutical production contract.

Michael Parker smiled. He couldn't have designed this scenario better himself. Except that he had. Down to the last detail. He closed the computer screen, picked up his drink, and walked to the wall of glass that showcased the spectacular view of Central Park. He turned up the volume on his favorite opera. He could complete the list in the morning. While he acknowledged that his father would have been proud, the sentiment wasn't really relevant.

CHAPTER 53

Jason Kennedy spoke to Davis and Anna Dixon on the secure display screen while Claire looked on.

"It won't take any effort at all for me to infiltrate the PTSD group." Jason grinned. "Although from the outside it might look like I should have PTSD, I don't. But I have a pretty comprehensive idea of what it looks like."

There were several excellent candidates within the Phoenix group, but Jason's military background from his service in Iraq was made to order for his upcoming role as a PTSD patient. He had been injured by an IED along with several other soldiers on the same mission. He wouldn't have to memorize details because he'd already lived them. His overseas treatment was well documented, with three surgeries on his injured leg. His employment history wouldn't even have to be fabricated, since veterans frequently found their way into civilian law enforcement. Kennedy's roundish features and broad, open face reminded Claire of the actor John C. Reilly.

Claire would work with Kennedy every waking hour until the weekend event could be properly staged. She would return to Phoenix with Aaron Davis and remain in his secure apartment with Jason until he was in the AllMed system, and beyond as necessary. After that, her witness protection placement would be determined, as would any future role she might have with Dixon's consulting group. She placed her worries firmly into a compartmentalized pocket of her brain and focused on the demands of the situation.

CHAPTER 54

Friday, January 12

Jason Kennedy looked over the prehospital assessment guidelines for the third time.

"Placing a 911 call is the easy part. Aaron will arrange for one of our other Brigade members to be an additional witness to your actions so that the paramedics will have an objective report about your recent behavior. The more extensive the documentation of the events that preceded the emergency call, the better our chances of getting you identified as a critical psych patient." Claire placed several hard copy summaries in front of him. They described in detail the triage symptoms necessary to be triaged directly to the veteran's hospital emergency department.

"But all they can do is get you to the AVS emergency department. Whether you get admitted is up to the doctors on staff when you arrive and whether there are any major traumas ahead of you in the triage queue.

"So let's throw everything at the wall right from the get-go. You'll have an episode of bizarre, paranoid behavior as soon as you report for your shift on Sunday night. Adding both visual and auditory hallucinations will work in favor of your getting priority in both prehospital and emergency department triage systems."

In the other room, Davis was listening as Anna Dixon spoke in low tones.

"After all these months of nothing, Monday's video feed showed Chen leaving his apartment with another man at 7:34 a.m. They shook hands and then parted company. Our facial recognition program has a match. Guy's name is John Ricker."

Advanced facial recognition programs had been available to Homeland Security as well as the CIA and FBI for years. But as in all things dealing with technology, it was just a matter of time before once-proprietary technologies became commonly available commercial products.

John Ricker's face filled half of the split screen.

"We can't easily get into the FBI personnel files, but this photo showed up in a newsletter with a small note about his retirement. From the Chicago's FBI office," Anna said. "He was there at the same time I was a detective at the Chicago Police Department. There was a bad situation, a fire, at one of the FBI buildings at the time. One agent died.

"There was speculation—but then again, cops are always speculating about something—that the FBI fire was caused by an explosion or enabled by a mole in the Bureau. Or perhaps by a disgruntled former agent who had knowledge of the headquarters building. But this we do know for sure: Ricker left the FBI shortly after the fire occurred."

"So what is he doing in Phoenix with Stephen Chen?"

"Let's find out. Have one of the team follow him. Maybe we won't have to have Kennedy get into AllMed after all. But he still needs to be prepared for it."

CHAPTER 55

John Ricker sat at a small cafe table across from a woman from his long-ago past, listening to her speak quietly. He only knew her as Nancy. She, in turn, was watching the former FBI agent drain his martini. Her honey-colored hair was pulled back into a low ponytail.

"The answer to your question, John, is that we've always known where you were. From the moment you left Chicago."

He stared at her. "What happened back in Chicago? Did you have something to do with the fire?"

"No, John. It was you who had something to do with the fire. You leaked the plans, and for all anyone knows, you sold the plans to someone on the wrong side. Or someone not on your side, anyway. Your name has never, at least so far, been associated with the plans, the leak, alleged payoffs…"

"You stole those plans from me!"

"Or, as I was saying, what could easily be seen as treasonous acts resulting in the death of an FBI agent. That's the kind of investigation that never closes."

"What do you want?" John's complexion had turned a light gray.

"The exact date and timing of AllMed's announcement on A1A. And it needs to be at least one week in advance."

"Why? And how do you even know about A1A?"

"Seriously, John? Why? Money." She didn't answer his question about how she knew about the drug.

"You're going to blackmail me? That's ridiculous. I don't have enough in my 401K to cover even two years of retirement."

"We know, John. Did you hear me ask you for any money?"

She stood up from the little table. "Enjoy your lunch, John. I'll be in touch." She handed him a small piece of paper displaying a typed phone number. "Let me hear from you every day."

"Would you like to order, sir?" The waiter had been keeping an eye on the table, maintaining a discreet distance after delivering the martini. The couple had made it clear that they'd let him know when they were ready to place a lunch order.

"No, thank you. I've had a change in plans." He placed two tens and a five on the table. "Keep the change."

Ricker forced himself to walk at a normal pace as he left the restaurant, head down. It was all he could do to keep the nausea at bay, but honestly, he just wanted to throw up. Over and over again. He bumped into a petite, gray-haired woman as he stepped outside, nearly knocking her over. He muttered, "Pardon me," extending a hand to help her regain her balance before hurrying along his way.

He didn't notice the small piece of dark felt that she slipped into his pocket. He turned left as he exited and began a brisk walk, heading south.

The petite woman opened her phone. "You'll be able to monitor what he does as long as he's wearing the jacket—it's unlikely he'll notice the transmitter. It just looks like a little piece of fabric, some leftover lint from the dry cleaners. We'll need a more reliable way of tracking him, but for now, this will have to do. I'm following his lunch companion." A pause. "Yes, I know, getting a photo of her is my top priority."

She closed her phone and headed north on Central Avenue, staying a full block behind the blonde woman who'd been sitting with Ricker.

The younger woman crossed the street to wait for the next train.

The graying middle-aged woman approached her. "Excuse me, dear, would you mind taking a picture of me in front of the train stop? I promised my granddaughter I'd send her a photo from my vacation."

"Sure, no problem." She took the phone the older woman held out. "Is it set up?"

"Yes, dear, thanks so much. Could you take two, just to be sure?"

CHAPTER 56

Half an hour later, Marian Thomas joined the small group in Aaron Davis's living room. The phone had yielded a couple of good prints, but more importantly, it had captured the blonde woman's photograph.

Marian shook her head with a smile. "Never underestimate the power of us short, grandmotherly types."

The phone she had handed to the blonde at the station was nothing special, except that the screen and its little camera icon had been modified. The blonde woman had carefully framed the traveling grandmother on the screen and snapped two pictures. The viewfinder showed the subject on the other side of the camera but recorded images of both the subject and the photographer. If anyone thought to look, the image playback only showed the subject. The other images were stored wirelessly and were now being run through the same facial recognition program that had identified John Ricker as he shook hands with his boss five days ago.

So far, the few fingerprints the blonde subject deposited on the phone hadn't matched any of the databases Anna Dixon could access. They still might, but no one was holding out any real hope for an easy match. The photo, though, was a different story.

Fingerprints were of very limited use in most current-day investigations. Sure, sometimes a person's prints would be identified if they'd already been in the system, but the database of fingerprints was minuscule compared to the billions of surveillance photos generated over the past decade in every major airport and train depot in the world, even down to everyone who attended any kind of large sporting event, going back to the post-9/11 days.

Aaron's computer pinged. He opened the screen and nodded as Anna, still in Washington, DC, began to speak.

"Okay, we've got her. Ricker's lunch date is a woman known as Liz Malone. Full name, Belinda Elizabeth Malone. She's thirty-eight years old, graduated from Michigan State with a major in business administration. She's worked as a translator in the customer service department of the First Bank of Illinois and is fluent in Spanish and Mandarin Chinese."

"That makes sense, since so much of the US banking system now relies heavily on foreign investors and their movement of international funds," Aaron replied. He looked up from the Internet search he'd begun on a separate device. "What else?"

"She was working in Chicago when Ricker was there. When the fire happened. I guess we can safely assume that they knew each other there."

Marian spoke. "There's an awful lot of coincidences stacking up."

"Aren't there, now?" Anna's smile belied her sarcasm. "And what could she possibly have to do with AllMed?"

Liz Malone closed her phone and shook her hair out from the band holding her ponytail. Back in her hotel suite, she placed a conference call with her business partners. They discussed timing and tactics, but by this time tomorrow, they'd have put the finishing touches on several large anonymous investment accounts, each poised to make enormous market transactions during the seventy-two hours preceding AllMed's announcement of A1A's success.

"Are we ready with the accounts we need to make our stock purchases in companies supplying military ordnance?"

"Yes, Liz. We're also ready to begin our phased investments in the three largest manufacturers of military aircraft in the world."

Liz and her investors expected that the second group of stock purchases would be slower to increase in value, simply because of the time lapse between government appropriations and the actual manufacturing time frames. So the gains might be slow, but they would eventually be huge.

"What about the put options?"

"Also ready. We've identified the world's leading drug manufacturers—both Big Pharma and boutique firms—and will execute the puts as soon as the market opens in the morning."

The "put" options let the holders bet that certain stocks would decrease in value by locking in a transaction, or "strike" price, at a specific date. The holder of the put option would make more money as the value of the stock fell toward zero, as long as the stock value was in place at the expiration of the option. As soon as AllMed's announcement was made, the stocks of a great many other pharmaceutical companies would be expected to plunge, especially for companies that were heavily invested in older drugs used to treat PTSD patients—antidepressants, anti-psychotics, anti-anxiety medications, and similar drugs. Her timing was perfect. Years ago, put options expired only once each quarter, on the third Friday of the designated month. Predictably, the clustered timing created the potential for market chaos, so now options could be set to expire at the close of market on the third Friday of every month. She could arrange for all the options to expire this coming Friday, rather than having to divide the expiration dates among two or even three cycles.

Some pharmaceutical companies had drug portfolios that were very broad, patents spanning a wide range of treatment disciplines, and whose patients had vastly different demographics. Drug development decisions were incredibly complicated, trying to balance the demands generated by older retired patients with the younger, cosmetic-conscious consumers and everyone in between. Some knew how important it was to reduce their vulnerability in a market that was artificial in every way. They were all hedging against fiat.

Other companies chose to develop depth, rather than breadth, in their drug patent portfolios. Corporations like AllMed, which had closely related products, including outpatient mental health services, direct operational contracts (AVS) for a focused patient group—veterans—and now a complementary drug, were at greatest risk. The value of pharmaceutical companies that were structured in such a way could collapse if their competitive environment changed, and they'd find themselves in bankruptcy before they knew what hit them. There was a lot to be said for horizontal diversification, but not all pharmaceutical companies believed in it. And many didn't have the means even if they realized the idea was sound.

Speculation would no doubt go on and on. Analysts would wonder whether A1A would ever be taken public. Potential investors would drool, at least when they weren't wringing their hands asking for a Xanax refill. But none of that mattered to the investment strategy now being prepared for the days leading up to AllMed's big press conference. Liz and her group didn't gamble. They assessed risk, and they were conservative in their approach. In recent years, prosecution for insider trading had become so rare, it was laughable. The stock transactions now being set in motion had very little downside risk.

Malone's small investment group had spent years developing a cache of dangerous, compromising, blackmailable evidence against a score of well-chosen targets. They never knew how long it might take to make the call or whether any one setup would bear fruit at all. But this arrangement with Ricker would dwarf anything else they'd done to date or might even hope to do in the future. Liz thought it was a lot like buying a ton of fishing rods and just leaving them in the water, year after year, to see if anything nibbled. It was an original, if bizarre, business model.

Sometimes you had no idea where that path would lead. Even to something as seemingly random as a benign discussion about a guy wanting a job with a medical start-up company in Phoenix, Arizona. Although even that wasn't so random, since she'd been following Ricker from the day he first arranged an employment interview with Stephen Chen, PhD. The rest was just checking the fishing rods from time to time to see if the bait needed to be refreshed.

Malone thought back to the fire at the FBI building and how she'd gotten started in this line of work.

———————————————————

One of Malone's early clients was convinced that the FBI was building an investigation against him for interstate trafficking in stolen goods. She had advised him to stop his allegedly illegal activities at once and to leave the country. He refused and demanded that she find out for sure, not wanting to end a lucrative run. He upped his fee to persuade her to continue her investigation. So she did.

Since its opening in the early 1900s, the FBI's Chicago office had occupied several different buildings. Growth in its scope of responsibilities and the sheer number of personnel it employed resulted in its sections being spread out geographically. The section dealing with Organized Retail Theft was located in an annex near the Chicago Loop, in rented space in a beautiful, old historic structure. The building needed a lot of renovation, and the Facilities and Logistics Division was charged with planning structural and system updates. Liz tracked down the FBI agent in charge of facilities, one John Ricker, and inserted herself into his life.

One of Malone's people had entered the charming old building through long-forgotten underground tunnels that showed up nowhere except on the old documents Liz liberated from Ricker's apartment. He needed to place a bug in the office of the chief investigator working the client's case to see if the Bureau had anything solid. It did. Malone's client's suspicions were right, but he was about a month late in hiring Malone. Unfortunately for him, he was caught dead-to-rights and ultimately had to enter a plea agreement. It continued to amaze her how often clients hired experts whose advice they refused to take.

The fact that the fire was actually an accident wasn't relevant to anyone. The FBI agent's death was unfortunate but not intended. The fire had most likely resulted from older gas lines that Malone's man had unwittingly damaged on his way out of the building. Sloppy, but it was all in the past.

Ricker, she thought, *was a fool.* His carelessness with his work product made her job much easier than it would have been if she'd had to locate another entrance to the FBI's headquarter offices. When she left Ricker's apartment that cold pre-dawn morning, she had no idea how valuable her leverage would become years later. The hard copy architectural plans, along with Ricker's fingerprints, sat next to the duplicate hard drive from his computer in a safe deposit box at the First Bank of Illinois. *Poor sap*, she thought.

Liz walked into her bedroom to change for her workout, retying the ponytail. She looked at herself in the mirror before heading to the garage. She never thought she looked like a Nancy anyway.

CHAPTER 57

Nursing a coffee at a small café in Foggy Bottom, Anna spoke to the older gentleman across the table. In all of Washington, DC, there were a tiny handful of politicians that she trusted, and he was one of them. Will Stratton, the aging senator from Minnesota was a crusty old guy but was the man who had spearheaded the charge to establish the Congressional Oversight Committee, which now had Dixon's group under contract. While not an official member of the committee, he was in the heart of the loop, thanks to Anna Dixon and a number of his other sources on the Hill. He was just as convinced that something was wrong with the AllMed-Lucident pharmaceutical setup as Anna was.

"I'm concerned that we're running out of time, Will," Anna continued. "My man inside the Lucident security division is hearing rumblings about an announcement on the drug under development. And that it's likely to be soon, perhaps in the next couple of weeks. Right now, he's trying to mine information about outside PR or marketing firms that might be getting ready for something splashy. It's not the kind of thing that is likely to be done in house, but we're looking for that, too."

"Do you have anything more on the two deceased therapists?"

"No. It doesn't look like Albuquerque has the hit-and-run on its front burner anymore, and the Maricopa County medical examiner has closed the Tempe case as a suicide. We know they're connected, but we can't prove it. We don't even have enough information to go to a prosecutor at this point. We were able to divert the other therapists into a protection program, but they were so isolated from the rest of the AllMed activity, I don't think they'll be able to help much. They're more than willing to try, but I just don't think they have any useful information.

"We started more direct surveillance on Chen this past week and learned something interesting about one of his employees, John Ricker, who is referred to internally as 'Noble.' He seems to be the only interface between Chen and the rest of the security division. Perry has heard his boss, Smith, on the phone several times with Noble, but the conversations were brief and nonspecific."

"What else do we know about this Mr. Ricker?"

Anna filled him in on Ricker's role with the Chicago FBI and the timing of his departure shortly after the deadly fire.

"People leave employment all the time, Anna, so that, in and of itself, means nothing."

"I agree. But he met earlier today with a woman who used to work with the First Bank of Illinois and who was in Chicago at the same time. Her name is Belinda Elizabeth Malone."

"Still not enough."

"When we tried to follow her trail after leaving the bank, it just suddenly stopped. Poof."

Will Stratton raised both eyebrows, looking at her over the top of his reading glasses.

"Stopped. No record of her anywhere for seven years. And then she suddenly appears in a restaurant with John Ricker. Regular people don't know how to just vanish. People like us know, members of the law enforcement or intelligence services know, but it's not something a bank employee taking complaints in the customer service department would know."

"What about getting inside the AllMed research labs? And its inpatient services?"

"We have a cloned hard drive from the managing director of clinical operations, but his computer wasn't connected to anything outside of the Lucident outpatient employees and activities. My cyber guy is working at it but hasn't been able to access any of the inpatient data, the A1A research, or even any of the other employees in the company."

"Is that unusual?"

"It would be if anyone other than AllMed had this contract with AVS. The Oversight Committee, you recall, felt quite satisfied that AllMed had enough internal checks and balances to handle policing itself and declined to request funding for anything other than my contract. None of the members want to look too closely at their golden goose. I don't know of any other government contract that is so huge and has so little transparency."

The senator, however, had a pretty good idea about a few other such arrangements. They just weren't in DHHS.

"So. Let me see if I get this, Anna. One, we have no probable cause, nothing to support asking a prosecutor to convene a grand jury to investigate Stephen Chen or anyone else at AllMed. Two, we have no evidence tying the two employee deaths to AllMed. Three, we know nothing about patients being treated with A1A or anything else once they get admitted to the hospital. Four, we're being backed up against a wall with an uncertain time frame, which may or may not be in two weeks or so. Does that summarize things?"

"It does indeed."

"What do you want to do?"

"Go at this from two angles. I have one team member now being briefed on becoming a convincing PTSD veteran, and he will be ready to enter the AllMed system no later than 4:00 a.m. Monday. The exact time frame is uncertain, but we feel it can be done. The risk to him, though, is one I'd much prefer to avoid. Even if he gets admitted as a PTSD patient, we have no idea whether he'll get A1A, and if he does, what kind of impact it could have on his physical or mental health. No one knows anything about this drug."

"What's the second angle?"

"Go directly at John Ricker. Let's just start by telling him that the FBI has new information on the fire that killed the Chicago agent and is reopening the investigation. It's possible that he has no relationship to the events at the Chicago headquarters, but maybe we can throw him off his stride. Show him Malone's photo and ask him again. For all we know, Malone is just one of

Ricker's old friends from the Midwest enjoying a break from the ice and cold.

"The worst that can happen is that he knows nothing, and we leave it at that. We can play it by ear and ask him about his own background, his role at AllMed, and imply that we suspect some improprieties. I give it less than a fifty percent chance of yielding anything. It's probably more likely that he'll threaten to sue anyone suggesting a problem—and that we get a referral to the AllMed legal department."

"And how do you plan to approach him?"

"My team leader in Phoenix is a retired deputy US marshal, name of Aaron Davis. You met him once before, although briefly. If you can arrange a special reactivation for him, he'll be able to make our inquiry with Ricker official. That will pave the way for his testimony in front of a grand jury, should he have any to give. We just won't know until we get into it."

Will Stratton chuckled. Even five years ago, this would never have been possible, but Dixon knew her stuff. Terrorism fears had been stoked for so many years that the notion of due process had been greatly relaxed. So much so that what she was asking would take no more than a phone call and quick written memo. What might once have been considered a wildly speculative fishing expedition wouldn't even raise an eyebrow in today's justice system.

"That sounds like a good plan, Anna. I'll take care of authorizing an expanded role for Mr. Davis immediately. I'm concerned that if we don't stop this before the official announcement, we might not ever be able to. I have a couple of resources here that I can bring into play if we need them. But I'd prefer not to have to expose them because once that happens, they'll be burned as sources. Once the committee reports back to Congress and the president, the pressures to quash any untoward findings will be astronomical. It would take an act of God to reverse the momentum. Or an act of Congress, but I'd bet on God coming through first."

CHAPTER 58

Aaron Davis held up a small plastic bag containing one tiny white object. It looked like a large grain of rice.

"Here's your GPS tracker, Jason."

Kennedy nodded.

"I'm just going to place it under the wad of scar tissue on your right calf. Ready?"

"Yep." A swab of Lidocaine and a small scalpel made the insertion quick and easy. Kennedy noted a pinch and a brief sense of pressure inside the old wound. He watched Davis close the tiny opening with a dab of superglue, wiping away the excess with another swab.

Neither of them was sure how effectively it could track Kennedy once he was admitted to the AVS hospital, but it was unlikely to be noticed by the admission or intake staff. It was just a small bit of plastic, unnoticeable under the scarred flesh that twisted atop it.

Jason turned back to Claire, and they continued the preparation for his initial encounter.

"Initiate the PTSD crisis when you get to the Brigade office just before your shift begins. Aaron will be there with you. Start turning over furniture, throwing things, screaming. Everyone will be taken off guard. Try to back yourself against a wall, or into a corner if you're near one. Convince people you are paranoid and terrified. They're more likely to jump you if they think you have a weapon, so make sure they can see both of your hands. You need to appear to be listening just enough that your fellow Brigade members will try to calm you and reason with you. By shouting at someone invisible to everyone but you, you can lay the groundwork for auditory hallucinations. Once you see an unarmed person approach you, yell something like, 'Put the baby down!' That will help with the visual hallucination backstory."

Davis could picture the scenario. The small offices on Roosevelt and Fourth Avenue would be crowded with the last shift change before Monday morning. Brigade members would be grabbing their water bottles, checking their uniforms and gear, rechecking their assigned patrol areas. There would be about a dozen men in the office, animated conversation mixed with sounds of lockers opening and closing.

"As soon as I think the crowd has thinned enough to manage the scene, I'll give you the go ahead," Davis said. "I'll describe that you seemed to be seeing things that weren't there just before you had your breakdown. Then I'll be with you up until I see you in the ambulance. After that, we'll keep tabs on you via the tracker."

Jason Kennedy looked at his teammates and grinned. Both thumbs up in the air. He'd been in much worse situations than this.

CHAPTER 59

The digital clock read 4:15, and Aaron Davis was finishing up his conversation with his Arizona Freedom Brigade supervisor.

"Nah, we don't want you in here if you think you're getting the flu. Stephens and one of my other men have been asking for extra shifts, so I'm sure we'll be covered. Get some rest and check in with me Sunday, or sooner if you feel better."

"Thanks. I'll talk to you soon."

Davis hung up. He needed time to prepare for his encounter with John Ricker as a special deputy of the US Marshals Service. He knew from experience it was better to do something like this without sleep deprivation.

He looked at the freshly laminated ID card carrying his picture and title. He'd printed the card from Dixon's email, added his signature, and run the card through a small portable laminator he'd picked up from the children's craft department at the hobby store just a few blocks away. The card also contained a badge number that was completely legitimate. He'd left the card in the pocket of some jeans and run them through the dryer a few times to make it look a little more used. Not that it would matter, but it would lend a bit of authenticity to Ricker's unskilled eyes.

He was all ready to go and would head to Ricker's apartment once Marian verified that he was home.

Stephen Chen clicked "send," giving final approval for next week's final graphic design, press release, press conference schedules, and complete social media and online insertions. In just a few days, A1A would lose its internal nomenclature and henceforth be known as Lucidaire. The key marketing time slots had been purchased, commercials ready to go, and he expected Lucidaire to become a household name within a month's time.

The initial press release and announcement would be made by the chairman of the Congressional Oversight Committee. It would be up to him to determine who would join him, but Chen expected that it would include military brass and cabinet secretaries. Possibly someone from the White House. And anyone else the chairman wanted indebted to him. Stephen Chen hated the politics game and didn't really care who got to share the public glory.

Chen called AllMed's in-house PR director.

"Are we ready with the press conference plans?"

"Of course. I'll handle all interviews and public interfaces and continue to coordinate with the outside consultants working on their respective assignments. All the legal minutiae have been handled, and patent applications and protection are firmly in place. Contracts with production facilities and distribution networks are ready to be introduced."

It was hard to imagine any major laboratory taking a chance on losing out simply to try to negotiate to the last penny. If one did, there would be half a dozen lined up behind it to snap up the opportunity.

"I still think you should be the front man on this, Dr. Chen."

Chen had fiercely resisted his consultants' requests to be "The Man behind the Miracle," a ludicrous tag line floated by one of their focus groups.

"No. We've been through this. I want to stay completely out of the news cycles and unless something is really essential, remain so." He would grant only the most necessary interviews. Members of the Congressional Oversight Committee had their own marketing machines, and they'd each be more than happy to take credit for advancing the development of the amazing new drug. Once the US governmental engine got started, representatives from DHHS, the Pentagon, and the Joint Chiefs of Staff would move forward with their own considerable weight. AllMed could quickly become a background player. Chen could expand his research and stay out of the limelight. And, of course, revel in his newfound net worth. His business partner would be happy. The military would be happy. Congress would be thrilled. Veterans and their families would weep with joy. AllMed's profits would spin out at a rate he could only imagine.

He planned to make a visit to the hospital this Monday to see his mother, confident now that A1A was as ready as it could be; it represented her best, and probably last, chance. He would administer the medication and coordinate with her rehab doctors to bring her out of the medically induced coma. So, yes, a lot of people would be happy, but he'd be way ahead of them on the happiness scale if he could just see her awake and talking. Then he could deal with the other patients in the unit.

CHAPTER 60

Saturday, January 13

Detectives Genn and Martinez sat in Ben Wolf's office along with Stan Deering.

"We were a day late with our warrants. Records show Stacy Atkins left the country yesterday through New York, heading to Italy, per her credit cards." Deering spoke in a calm voice. "She booked a cruise that left Cinque Terre last night. Its next stop is Portofino, but the ship will be spending two full days at sea before it next docks."

"Can we get some help from Italian law enforcement?" asked Ben.

"Probably. Possibly. It's just a matter of how quickly we can get them to move, and if they feel like it." International cooperation with US domestic investigations was at its lowest point in ten years. The past administration's blatant disregard for diplomatic courtesy had soured relationships with the Far and Middle East regions and had finally roughened enough edges that even European cooperation was unpredictable.

"We don't have a warrant or even a credible investigation as a basis for asking for help. All we have is a woman whose husband is missing and who took money out of an account he owns. Not very convincing of anything," said Deering. "So basically, it depends on whether the Italians feel like cooperating."

"What about a search warrant for Atkins's home?"

Martinez answered. "We should get it early this afternoon, but it's going to be very limited—only for the computer or computers we can locate in the residence."

"Thanks, everyone, great work. Let's reconvene later after Karen and Beverly finish the search of the Atkins place."

CHAPTER 61

Stacy moved through the ship's casino, aware that nearly every eye in the room was watching her. She wore a red strapless, full-length stunner she'd bought for the Auxiliary Ball last spring. The only jewelry she wore were her favorite diamond and ruby drop earrings and a glittering diamond bracelet on one wrist.

The fact that she was the only cruise guest younger than sixty made her appearance all the more dramatic.

She nodded and smiled broadly as she approached the nice-looking man at the blackjack table. He smiled back, blue eyes crinkling atop a beautifully groomed white beard. She stood behind him as the dealer swept the table clean. He gathered his chips and turned to give her a brief hug, brushing her cheek with his lips.

"I'm glad you were able to come down before dinner, Stacy," he said.

"Oh, I only had a couple of business things to take care of in my room, and I finished sooner than I thought. I wouldn't have missed dinner, and it's fun to see you having such a successful night at the table. Well done, James."

She took his offered arm, being sure that her right breast touched his bicep, and they walked to the bar for a glass of champagne.

They'd met at the ship's pool shortly after leaving port last night. The captain hosted a welcome reception for the ship's newest batch of guests, with a spectacular array of fresh seafood hors d'oeuvres and cocktails.

Stacy noticed James Garrity right away and found herself accidentally bumping into him, sloshing just a bit of champagne on her white sundress.

They laughed easily and struck up a conversation that lasted until after midnight, at which point she excused herself, noting his expression of fleeting disappointment.

"Would you like to join me for dinner tomorrow night?" James looked directly at her with a warm, engaging smile.

"Yes, I'd love to. I have a few things scheduled tomorrow—I have some correspondence to deal with, a Pilates lesson in the women's gym, and then I really need to get my nails done. My manicurist was sick the day before I left home, and my hands look horrible."

He picked up her left hand and brushed it with his beard. "I think your hands look beautiful."

Stacy threw her head back and laughed. "What time would you like to eat?"

"How about eight? If you get done early, why don't you meet me in the casino for a drink before dinner?"

Man, I've still got it, Stacy thought. She'd been a little out of practice after being married to Curt, but honestly, it was just like riding a bike. She could spend more time perusing the offerings, but James was cute, and she'd learned enough about him last night to fill an encyclopedia. If you want to be the most interesting woman in the world, just ask a man about himself. He was widowed, not too recently, and had no children. He did, however, have a rather impressive portfolio. *So did Curt*, she thought, but Curt was never all that nice. James, though, appeared to be an entirely decent guy, lonelier than he probably realized. She had a lot of ground to cover, and the cruise only lasted another five days. She'd played this hand before, and there wasn't anyone better at it.

"See you tomorrow, then, and thanks for such a lovely evening. I hardly expected to be charmed on my first day at sea." Stacy blew him a kiss and headed off to her state room. He beamed back at her and watched every step until she disappeared into the ship's ostentatious interior. That was yesterday.

James had secured nightly assigned seating at one of only three two-tops in the entire dining room, right next to a large oval-shaped exterior window. Most of the other tables were four- and six-tops, designed to encourage social interactions among the cruise guests. This was, after all, a singles cruise. They both had the filet mignon paired with a terrific local Primativo. The food was wonderful and the wait staff amazing. The time flew by for them; they were engaged in lively conversation, punctuated by shared laughter. Stacy was aware that other diners were looking at them, and she suspected that many of the men and quite a few of the women were envious. She was amazed that most of them could even stay up this late.

"Would you like to get a giant cone at the gelato bar? We could take dessert out to the pool deck or, if you'd like, we could enjoy it on the balcony of my room."

She laughed in response and took his arm as they discussed their all-time favorite ice cream flavors. They were still debating the virtues of banana nut fudge and pineapple rum raisin when the elevator doors closed.

CHAPTER 62

Sunday, January 14

Jason Kennedy and Aaron Davis arrived at the Brigade station a little after 6:30 p.m. Davis's supervisor nodded to him, "Glad you're feeling better."

"Thanks. Must have just been one of those bugs."

The two Brigade members moved into the area where the day lockers were located. There were three other Brigade members there, replaying the afternoon's football game highlights while they got ready to start the last weekend shift at 7:00 p.m.

Aaron felt as good as he could about the weekend's preparation. Claire was patient, steady, and focused. She brought up a score of different scenarios, challenging Kennedy's responses to every "What if?" she threw at him. He could sense Kennedy's confidence grow as the hours went on and was pleased at the ease with which his team adjusted to its newest, albeit temporary, member in the form of one serious woman with tangled hair and glasses that didn't always sit straight on her head. He liked Claire's no-nonsense manner and flexible thought process. She wasn't a woman who was pretty in the traditional sense, but she had beautiful skin and striking natural coloring. Her unwavering, wide-set gaze suggested her intellectual gifts. Anna Dixon had given the final go-ahead during their midday teleconference. No one on the team had any doubt that Jason could play a convincing role. But they all had big concerns about subjecting him to an unknown drug whose side effects could be disastrous. And now, here they were.

Davis gave one short nod to Kennedy. Showtime.

Jason Kennedy stumbled slightly just outside the door to the locker area. He looked around, dazed. "Hey…" His voice was soft, but not so soft that the other men didn't hear him. Aaron could step in right away in an active role, but he waited. Better that another Brigade member took initial notice of Kennedy's approaching psychotic episode.

"Kennedy? You okay, man?" The oldest of the three men in the locker area interrupted his buddy's complaint about the referee's fourth-quarter penalty against the Ohio team. He stepped forward and into the main office area. Kennedy looked around, confused, then slowly backed away, knocking over a folding chair as he moved to the corner of the room opposite the front entry. He was mumbling to himself. He focused his gaze on a blank wall and began speaking in a louder voice.

Aaron stepped forward. "Jason? What's going on?" He touched Kennedy on the shoulder.

"Get the fuck away from me! Can't you see she has a gun?" By now all three Brigade members and their supervisor had joined the scene unfolding in the main office space. There was no "she" anywhere in the room, and no one had a gun. No one spoke. They stared.

Aaron spread his hands slowly, palms facing down. He motioned for his fellow team members to stay where they were. "Hey, buddy, it's me, Davis. Can you talk to me?"

"I don't know who the fuck you are. Can't you hear her screaming? What's wrong with you?" Kennedy moved behind the desk, looking frantically around the surface and underneath the knee hole. He continued to repeat himself, getting louder with each nonsensical outburst until his face turned red and spittle flew with every curse. He placed his hands over his ears and let out a long, bloodcurdling scream as he fell to the floor, sobbing. The Brigade supervisor was calling 911 before Aaron had a chance to tell someone else to do so.

Davis and another of the Brigade men crouched near Kennedy, speaking in soothing, quiet tones as they tried to calm him and convince him that everything was going to be all right.

I sure as shit hope so, Davis thought as he kept up the placating murmurs.

The paramedics arrived within five minutes, although to everyone at the station, it seemed to take far longer. One paramedic recorded Kennedy's vital signs. The other administered an IV while he was on the radio to the base hospital emergency coordinator.

"Got it." He added a dose of Valium to the IV solution. IV in place, the lead paramedic turned to the group. "What happened here?"

"I don't know. One minute he was in the locker room, then we heard a noise and we came out to see what was going on." The older Brigade member described the first few minutes of Kennedy's episode. Davis didn't need to add a word.

"By the time I got out here, Kennedy seemed to be having some kind of hallucination—he was shouting at a woman and was staring into space as if someone were there."

"Did he tell you he saw someone?"

"Yeah, he thought a woman was in the room and that she was carrying a gun. That's what he said," continued the supervisor. "He also said he could hear her screaming. He sounded paranoid and outright terrified. He wasn't making any sense."

"Any history of seizures or mental illness?"

"Not as far as I—"

Davis cut him off. "Kennedy has a history of struggling with PTSD from his tours overseas and the injuries he sustained." The others fixed their attention him. "I encouraged him to get some therapy, to talk to someone, but he insisted he could handle it himself. He didn't like to talk about it, which is not uncommon, as you guys all know."

"And did you suspect that his assumed PTSD would be a problem for him on the job, seeing as how you know him so well?" The supervisor's tone was verging on accusatory.

"No. Of course not," Aaron snapped. "He told me he was managing it, and that was good enough for me." He spoke almost as a challenge. "And I don't know him all that well, only from the shifts we've had together."

"Sorry, Davis. I'm just concerned and didn't mean anything by it."

"No problem. I'm alarmed, too."

The second paramedic interrupted. "We're good to go. We've got a veteran with suspected PTSD, and the AVS hospital is standing by to admit him. Does anyone here know if he has an emergency contact?"

Kennedy's supervisor said, "I'll check his employment records. In the meantime, just put 'supervisor in charge' as his contact information. I'll be sure we keep track of him."

They wheeled the narrow gurney though the front door. Davis watched as they placed Jason Kennedy into the ambulance and closed the back hatch.

Nothing more I can do until tomorrow, he thought. Perry will track him through the system. Even as he hoped that Kennedy's journey would be uneventful, he was extremely concerned.

The supervisor spoke up. "We've still got patrols to make. Davis, you want me to try to call in another partner for you?"

"No, I'm okay for this shift. Hopefully Kennedy will be ready for next Friday's weekend shift."

One glance at the faces of his fellow Brigade members told him all he needed to know. No one would agree to be partnered with an unstable and possibly psychotic partner. Kennedy's role in the Brigade was done. It was the inevitable outcome of the scheme they'd cooked up, and they all agreed that it was worth the price. Kennedy was a top-notch agent, and there would be many other opportunities for him in Dixon's world. He just needed to get through the AllMed maze and out the other side.

Davis grabbed his radio and stepped outside, heading out into the streets to start his regular rounds. It was going to be a long night.

Claire sat with Perry in Davis's living room, tracking Kennedy's movement in real time. They watched as the ambulance approached the emergency department entrance to the old VA hospital a few miles to the north. They settled in for a long vigil.

CHAPTER 63

Monday, January 15

Claire was watching the GPS signal and sipping her coffee when Aaron Davis rushed into his living room just before 7:30 a.m. Perry was napping on the sofa.

"Perry needed some sleep, so I told him I'd take over for a while. The chip hasn't moved since Jason arrived at the AVS emergency department."

"That was twelve hours ago!"

Perry stirred and sat upright, running his fingers through his hair.

"We know," said Claire. "It's pretty unusual for someone to stay in emergency holding that long, but I don't think we have cause to get too worried yet. If this goes on for another six hours, then we should start to get concerned."

Perry poured a cup of fresh coffee for himself. "Aaron, why don't you catch an hour or two of sleep? We'll wake you if there's any change in Kennedy's location. Marian will be in touch as soon as she locates Noble this morning. You'll need the rest before tackling his interview."

Aaron took a quick look at the small television screen. It was tuned to the local news station, volume on mute.

"Okay. See you in a few."

An hour later, Claire started. "Our boy's on the move." Perry joined her at the monitor and watched as the little dot moved forward, then back again, twice.

"I'm getting Aaron."

All three agents watched the screen as the dot moved in its odd dance and then just blinked out.

"Claire, Perry? What's going on?"

"Got it, Aaron. I'm on it." Perry rebooted the settings for the tracker. No light. He worked at the computer for nearly thirty minutes, but nothing he tried could reanimate the GPS tracker.

Claire stretched from her seat at the table and, turning, noticed the "breaking news" logo light up the television screen. She grabbed the remote and turned up the volume.

A young, dark-haired man was speaking to his cameraman. "I'm live at the American Veterans' Service Hospital in downtown Phoenix. We've just had reports that some kind of disturbance has taken place in the emergency department. Phoenix police are on site. Stay tuned for an official statement."

"What the fuck?" Claire stood to stare at the screen while the other two men watched silently.

The camera panned to the official police vehicles and ambulances in the background, then back to the reporter. Filler came on with reporters scrambling to occupy the next ten minutes, or however long it would take for someone from the Phoenix Police Department to speak.

"I'm Sergeant Logan with the Phoenix Police Rapid Response Unit. We received an emergency alert about thirty minutes ago from the emergency department at AVS. Let me start by saying there have been no injuries, and there is no cause for alarm. The security officer on duty at the hospital attempted to stop a belligerent visitor who was agitated at the long wait time for his son to be seen. He grappled with the guard and, in the confusion, seized the officer's taser and began firing it, striking three other patients waiting to be admitted. The distraught father was subdued and is being cared for by medical professionals on site. I repeat, no one was injured, and the individuals struck by the taser are doing well and are resting."

"Thank you for the update, Sergeant Logan. Kelly, back to you."

The screen image was replaced with a young blonde anchorwoman at the news desk. She was trying to look concerned, but it was nearly impossible when she couldn't move any of the muscles in her forehead. Her smile dazzled her viewers with a show of perfect teeth.

"Thanks, Eric. To our home audience, we'll break away if there are additional updates, so stay with us as we watch for more breaking news. In the meantime, please join me in welcoming Sam Miles, spokesman for SafeTase, the country's leading supplier of the new generation of electric shock weapons to law enforcement."

Claire was standing with both arms crossed in front. She shook her head in disbelief.

"Kelly, from preliminary reports, we have every reason to believe that the SafeTase gun used in this morning's disturbance performed exactly as it should." He droned on for another six minutes, touting the nonlethal advantages of his company's sentinel product and how its new technology allowed for repeat firing.

"Kennedy got zapped. That's the only explanation for the GPS shutting down," Perry said. "I can't reactivate a tracker that's been fried."

"Are you sure?"

"Positive."

Of all the scenarios any of them might have imagined, none included Jason getting tased on his way into the system. None.

CHAPTER 64

Stephen Chen looked at his director of security. "Thanks for the update, John. The sooner we're out of the news, the better."

Ricker looked exhausted. He should. Chen knew he'd been up all night Sunday reviewing procedures surrounding the upcoming press conference. Chen had moved the announcement up by two weeks. It was now scheduled for this coming Thursday. Then there was this morning's chaos at the emergency department. Chen would have to move back his mother's A1A medication to tomorrow. He wanted six straight hours to observe her immediately after administering the drug, and today wasn't going to give him the window he wanted.

"Look, it's 8:15, and this week is going to be extremely busy. I need to have you rested and fresh. Why don't you take the rest of the day off and catch some shut-eye?"

"Thanks, Dr. Chen. Call me if there's an emergency."

Ricker turned up his collar against the slight breeze as he headed to his apartment. He'd called Nancy late Sunday on the number she'd provided him.

"I'm sorry, John, was there something unclear about my requiring one week's notice?"

"Look," he hissed. "I didn't give you a week's notice because Chen just made the decision today."

"Let's just hope we can make do with five days' notice, John."

Liz Malone wasn't really annoyed but let the unspoken threat come through in her voice. She knew Ricker didn't control decisions that his boss made. Still, she liked keeping him off balance. As long as she'd gotten notice over the weekend, instead of on Monday or Tuesday, it wouldn't make any difference. She'd notified her partners to be ready to move as soon as the stock market opened Monday morning, and they had. The phased transactions began at 7:30 a.m., Phoenix time. They'd take place over three days and would be complete by the time the exchange closed on Wednesday, which would be 4:30 p.m., Eastern time. It was cutting it close, but she had never planned on the set of transactions taking more than four days anyway. She hung up.

That was last night. Ricker had returned to his office in the morning to check on whether Smith had made any progress on the laptop and to finish up a couple of pieces of correspondence before heading home.

Ricker was rattled to the core. It was her calm, steady voice that scared him most. He needed to get home, clear his mind, and try to get a few hours' rest. Chen had launched the announcement and Ricker knew the press conference gurus would be shaking things up in DC. Ricker let himself into his apartment duplex and closed the door. He needed a drink. Then some sleep.

Marian called Aaron Davis at 2:15 p.m. "He's at his apartment."

"On my way. Let me know if he leaves. I'll see you in about twenty minutes."

Claire pulled on her fleece jacket and stood. "Let's go."

"No."

"Yes." She had her arms crossed again.

"Perry's coming with me. You need to stay here. Ricker might recognize you, and I don't know how much resistance to expect from him. The situation is too volatile, and that means too much potential for danger."

"Aaron, that doesn't make any sense. How is he going to recognize me?

I've never met him. But he'll definitely recognize Perry. Perry works for him, for God's sake. And anyway, I can be very helpful—I've had years of experience reading body language and identifying stress points."

"Perry actually works for Smith, who works for Ricker—or as he's known, Noble. Perry's never met Noble."

"Seriously, do you think it's more likely that the director of security is going to recognize a staff social worker before recognizing one of his own security guys?"

"Actually, yeah, since he's been responsible for every single therapist who's gotten Friday afternoon walking papers. Two of them, you may recall, are dead."

Perry had been listening to the interchange and spoke up. "Aaron, I think she's right. You may get nowhere with him. If that's the case, even if he recognizes Claire, she can go into the protection program, and the investigation won't be any worse off." Claire was fuming at MacRae's assumption. "I think we'd be blowing it if I show up first thing. If he recognizes me, my days as Mack are done. And we have no other inside sources. Try this idea on for size. You and Claire go see Ricker at his apartment. You'll have to play it by ear, but I'll wire Claire so we have a record of what happens." Perry could see them both start to object. Holding up his hands, he said, "Stop. I know what you're thinking about legal or illegal recording. I'm telling you I don't think it will matter. Either John Ricker will dig in his heels, in which case you won't get anything useful at your visit anyway, or he won't. If things go right, he'll be unnerved enough that you can get him to start talking. If he's ready to talk, then I'll step in. Once he becomes aware that I'm the mole, and that I have firsthand knowledge of the company's inside workings, the ties to the two deaths, I think he'll cave.

"Aaron, let's all go down to Ricker's apartment. I'll have a nice casual cup of joe with Marian at the coffee shop across the street from Ricker's place and will be listening in through Claire's transmitter. All you have to say, Aaron, is, 'There's someone else I'd like you to meet.' I'll be at the door within two minutes. We're wasting time talking about this. We've lost touch with Kennedy, and I don't like it."

Davis said, "You're right. We can play it by ear, but it might be that you'll have to come in even if he refuses to talk. Let's get Claire set up and get out of here."

Claire stepped over to Perry. "Do you need me to take off my shirt or anything to wire me, like with a hidden microphone or something?"

Perry burst out laughing. "Not unless we're auditioning for a 1990's detective movie." She blushed. He handed her a small, generic-looking Band-Aid. "Just put this on your right shoulder and we're good to go."

Claire's irritation at Perry lifted, buoyed by his spontaneous laughter at a time when nothing was very funny at all.

Ricker's apartment was located near Fifth Street and Catalina. It was a convenient walk from the light rail on Central Avenue, just five blocks east. He rented the west end of a small duplex, kitty-corner from the little restaurant cluster that had sprung up over the past five years. There were several corners just like this scattered through central Phoenix, in response to the eight thousand or so newer luxury rentals that were built after 2015. The developers of some of the larger properties had dreams of fully occupied spaces, leases held by young professionals and university students, good cash cows. Their dreams, however, were basically pulverized when the economy tanked and occupancy rates fell to under thirty percent. Two of the larger corporations filed for bankruptcy.

John Ricker's single-story duplex was situated on a scant quarter acre of land owned by an older Tucson family who had hoped to cash out big with the anticipated real estate boom. Unfortunately, they waited just a bit too long. They watched the market soar and then crash. The small structure had been built in the '70s and looked south over a tiny graveled front yard. A three-foot high chain-link fence separated the property from the sidewalk, and a few of the chain panels needed repair. The property was in a valuable location, and once the economy returned, the owners might have another chance at a sale. Until then, they had no plans to spend any money on the rental units.

Aaron and Claire opened the little chain-link gate and walked up to the front door. Aaron knocked twice, as firmly as he could without banging. Thirty seconds later the door opened, security chain in place, as the man matching the picture in the FBI newsletter from long ago peeked out. He looked like he'd been sleeping.

"Can I help you?" He looked at the couple standing on his stoop.

Davis, holding out a laminated ID card, replied, "Aaron Davis, deputy US marshal. May we come in?"

CHAPTER 65

Jason Kennedy awoke slowly, the numbing fog clearing from his brain. He looked at his surroundings, immediately aware that he was in a hospital room with one other patient in the bed between his own and the door.

What happened? He concentrated. *I remember the ambulance ride, and being rolled into the emergency department, then...then what?* Overcome with exhaustion, he closed his eyes and drifted off to a dreamless sleep.

When he opened his eyes again, a young male nurse was standing next to his bed, adjusting the IV bag and taking a fresh blood pressure reading.

"Good afternoon, Mr. Kennedy. How are you feeling?"

"Tired, but otherwise okay. What happened? How long have I been here?"

"It's Monday afternoon. I'll ask your doctor to come in now that you're awake, and he'll be able to answer any questions you might have." He offered Jason a small, light blue plastic cup with a lid and bendable straw. "Please try to drink as much water as you feel comfortable doing."

A young doctor entered Jason's room shortly after the nurse left.

"Mr. Kennedy, I'm Dr. Morris, chief resident at the AVS inpatient psych unit. How are you feeling?"

Kennedy faced the cheerful young man standing at the right side of his bed. Dr. Morris looked twelve.

"Okay, I think, but I don't remember anything after I got to the emergency department. Wasn't that last night?"

"Yes, excellent, Mr. Kennedy. You were in ER holding early this morning when an incident occurred with a distraught family member. You were one of three people struck by a taser in the scuffle."

Kennedy's memory snapped back into place with startling clarity. *The shock, the intense pain and paralysis. Of course.* He thought back to his special ops military training, when each operator voluntarily submitted to being tased to understand what to expect should he be attacked with one in the field. Temporary memory loss was common.

"You had an episode at the Brigade headquarters Sunday night, and 911 was called. Do you remember anything about Sunday night?"

"Not really. I remember getting dressed to go out on my regular patrol, and then…well, just bits and pieces of the ambulance ride, and then being in the emergency department for what seemed like a lot of hours, and then, well, just waking up now."

"You have been admitted to the inpatient unit while we assess your condition and arrive at a diagnosis, then determine an appropriate treatment plan."

"Can you take off these restraints?" Kennedy nodded at the straps on his left arm, across his belly, and on his ankles.

"Yes, after we observe you for another hour or so to make sure you're not a danger to yourself or others. This is standard treatment protocol for suspected PTSD patients, and especially important given that you've had a shock, literally, to your system."

"What do you mean, 'suspected PTSD patient'?"

"It's just an intake diagnosis at this point. Have you ever been diagnosed as having PTSD?"

"Yes, although not formally. It was suggested after I returned from the military."

"Why didn't you pursue treatment for it?"

Jason barked out a laugh. "Exactly how many decent jobs do you think a guy whose only experience is in the military could get with a PTSD warning label?"

"I understand. Please try to rest. We'll complete the diagnostic evaluation shortly, and I'll be back in about an hour to check on you. Here's your call button if you need anything before then."

Jason really needed to use the bathroom but figured he could wait another hour.

He settled back to construct a game plan. Jason's eyes periodically wandered past the half-drawn privacy curtain to his roommate, who hadn't stirred since Jason awoke. He wondered what the guy was here for but suspected he already knew—PTSD.

Jason pushed the red call button on the rectangular plastic box attached to a cord that ran somewhere behind his bed. Within a few seconds, his nurse entered the room, crepe soles scarcely making a sound. Jason made a mental note of the response time.

"Yes, Mr. Kennedy?"

"I need to pee. And I'd like to use the phone."

"I'll bring you a bedpan. I'm sorry, I can't let you up just yet until the doctor okays the removal of your restraints. You can discuss your use of the phone with him then."

Kennedy thought back to his Middle East deployment. One of the most basic rules in preparing a captured soldier for interrogation was to begin with subtle psychological manipulation. Isolation, lack of information, withholding of basic privileges, and, of course, physical restraints.

Interesting, Jason thought. *This is the kind of shit that can actually* create *PTSD. And here I am, in a state-of-the-art psych unit that uses the same shit on patients who already have PTSD. I might not be a medical professional, but it's pretty easy to see that something's wrong here. Really wrong.*

CHAPTER 66

John Ricker opened the door to allow the US marshals in, motioning for them to sit in the small living room area. Aaron Davis, the male agent who had introduced himself, looked calm and self-assured and was very polite. The woman looked vaguely familiar to him, although he couldn't quite place her. Aaron sat on the small, well-worn leather sofa, and Claire took the chair to his right. That left Ricker to choose either the sofa seat next to Davis or the armchair to Claire's right. He chose the armchair and faced Aaron. A small tumbler of amber-colored liquid sat on the coffee table, overlapping rings indicating that it had been lifted and replaced repeatedly.

"What is this about?"

"We'd like to ask you a few questions about a cold case we're following out of Chicago."

Ricker felt a sudden surge of panic as adrenaline flooded his veins. He felt himself blanch and hoped it wasn't visible to the US marshals facing him. Davis didn't notice, but Claire Wilheit did.

Ricker looked at Aaron and said nothing.

Davis continued. "We're investigating the death of an FBI agent in a fire that occurred about seven years ago during the time you were with the Chicago Bureau. Does this ring a bell?"

"Of course, it was a terrible tragedy. Everyone in the Bureau, and probably everyone in the public, heard about it. Terrible." He shook his head slightly as if recalling how terrible the tragedy really was.

"Just a bit of background here, Mr. Ricker." Aaron consulted a small notebook he'd pulled from his jacket pocket. "You were the agent in charge of Facilities and Logistics, were you not?"

Ricker felt sick. "Yes."

"Your responsibilities included assessing and arranging for all facility upgrades and modifications for FBI buildings and locations, correct?"

Dear God, thought Ricker, *do I need a lawyer?* Not trusting his voice, Ricker just nodded.

"Our records show that you had access to original blueprints for the annex building where the fire occurred. Is that correct?"

Ricker nodded once more.

"You realize that there's no statute of limitations on murder, don't you, Mr. Ricker?"

"But the fire was an accident—that was determined by the investigation."

"Which has now been reopened."

John Ricker slipped his hands under the outside of his thighs to hide their shaking. Claire noticed the move, and now so did Aaron.

"Mr. Ricker," began Aaron, opening his phone to access the photo Marian had taken. "Do you recognize this woman?"

Ricker needed only the briefest glance to see that it was the woman he knew as Nancy. His already gray pallor turned ashen. His nod was barely perceptible.

Claire spoke for the first time since entering. "Might we trouble you for a glass of water, Mr. Ricker?"

"Um, sure." Ricker practically leapt from his seat and hurried into the kitchen. They could hear him opening and shutting a cabinet and running water.

"It's the middle of the day, and he's already been drinking." She nodded toward the glass on the table. "So he's probably already nervous. And he's trembling, so I think he's decompensating. And he's not lawyering up." Claire spoke just above a whisper. "Let's push him harder—and call Perry."

Aaron gave her a short nod.

Ricker tried to compose himself while he filled the two water glasses, but it was hopeless. He was terrified. His hands still shook a little as he brought the waters back to the living room.

"There's someone else we'd like you to meet, Mr. Ricker. But in the meantime," Claire said, "we have a few more questions about how it is that you found your way to employment as the top security guy at AllMed."

By now, Ricker couldn't speak at all. Perspiration left large damp circles on the underarms of his shirt.

Davis stood to answer the single knock on the Ricker's front door.

A tall man entered and stepped into the room, slightly favoring his right leg.

"Hello, Noble."

What little color remained in Ricker's face disappeared as he stared at the man he only knew as Mack. He looked back at the female agent as the last coin dropped into the slot, and he recognized her as the therapist who was, he thought, killed in the recent explosion.

CHAPTER 67

Tuesday, January 16

Two floors down from the room occupied by Jason Kennedy, and through a hundred yards of locked hallway compartments, Stephen Chen entered the room whose only sign read, "Susan." He was greeted by the soft hum of the devices that monitored his mother's vitals, as well as the digital display on the wall behind her bed.

"Here you go, Mom, finally." He injected the syringe's contents into the IV port. "The first of three doses. You'll be awake and talking by the end of the week." He leaned over to kiss her smooth, dry forehead.

Chen hurried off to his office to review and finalize the preparations for this week's public announcement. He knew everything was in place, but as he'd learned over many years, double-checking plans always paid off. He couldn't think of a single time, either professionally or personally, where he'd wasted time by being certain.

Ricker had called in sick with the flu this morning. Christ, there couldn't have been a worse time for AllMed's head of security to be away than these next few days, but Ricker assured him that Smith could manage anything that needed attention and that he'd be available by phone or online if anything particularly troubling came up.

Chen had gone to great lengths to isolate himself from Smith and the other employees in the security division. He hoped the week would go smoothly and that there wouldn't be any need for him to meet personally with Smith.

Chen had given Ricker full autonomy to do whatever he deemed necessary to protect the secrecy of operations throughout the corporation, and especially those related to the proprietary research of the A1A labs. Chen had no need to know the details, and frankly, he didn't want to know. Which wasn't to say that he didn't have his suspicions. In retrospect, perhaps he'd delegated too much responsibility.

CHAPTER 68

Jason Kennedy watched the nurse replace the saline bag running into the IV port on the top of his left forearm.

His visit last night with the medical resident had lasted less than thirty minutes. The doctor explained that they believed he may have had an acute PTSD episode at the Brigade offices. It was important, the resident explained, to rule out an acute psychotic event, since often the symptoms of acute psychosis and acute PTSD presented in similar ways. If it was determined that Jason was suffering from PTSD, he would be put on a new, highly effective medication regimen that had demonstrated excellent results for patients. The IV drug therapy would last for three days as an inpatient, and then it was likely that he could continue to be seen as an outpatient for ongoing treatment and follow-up. But first, Jason would need to be under observation for another twelve hours or so. Assuming there were no indications of psychosis, Jason's medication therapy would start first thing Wednesday morning. He was assured that his supervisor at the Brigade would be kept up to date, and that if Jason wanted to call him in the morning, he could do so. Kennedy's nurse removed the restraints just before administering a strong sleeping agent. *I'm in the belly of the beast now, so let's rock and roll.* He gave in to a long, deep sleep.

Claire watched Ricker's composure complete its disintegration as the three of them drove in silence for the short ride to Davis's working apartment. Perry's arrival had shaken any last remnant of resolve Ricker might have been able to muster, and it had taken virtually no effort to persuade him to accompany them to Davis's place.

Ricker's "interview" lasted almost four hours on Monday night. Everything he said was on the record, with the three agents asking questions in an orderly way. Ricker was vaguely aware that the interview had been joined by an unseen individual via teleconferencing.

Claire focused on Perry as he asked questions in a careful, systematic manner, beginning with Ricker's relationship with the woman he knew as Nancy. Davis again showed him Malone's photo. Claire stepped in to continue the questioning as they had discussed. It was important to keep Ricker a little anxious, and responding to questions asked by different team members was a good way to keep him off balance.

"Mr. Ricker, this woman's name is Belinda Malone," said Claire. "How do you know her?"

Ricker seemed unsurprised.

"I met her in Chicago. She suddenly showed up at a meeting, introduced herself as Nancy, and we began to talk. And then one thing led to another. She was smart and beautiful, and I trusted her. I was falling in love with her, and I thought she felt the same."

"And how did that change?" asked Claire.

Ricker then described how she had stolen the documents and construction plans for the FBI annex from his home.

"I hadn't heard from her in years and just thought that she was part of my past. Then she suddenly shows up again and basically blackmails me. I have no idea why she wanted advance details about the timing of the Lucident press conference and announcement about the release of Lucidaire."

"Well, did you ask her?"

"Not directly, but she told me it was about money."

Claire looked at him, waiting for him to continue. A tried-and-true therapy method, it generally worked in a broad range of situations.

"So I told her I didn't have any money to pay, but she already knew that. She just wanted information and said she expected daily phone calls to let her know that everything was continuing on schedule."

"Thank you, Mr. Ricker. Why don't you take a break and rest for a while before we continue."

Ricker nodded and returned to the first bedroom down the hallway.

Claire and Perry were deep in a quiet discussion when Aaron returned with breakfast bagels and carryout sandwiches.

"Perry, why do you think Malone wanted that information?" asked Claire.

"I don't know. It seems peculiar, and it worries me."

"It concerns me as well, but we don't have the luxury of time right now to delve into it." Aaron continued. "But we'll definitely prioritize that as a problem as soon as we get past the immediate situation."

"Anna has already spoken with her contact. Based on what she heard last night, they've agreed to offer Ricker limited immunity for his testimony in front of a grand jury," Claire said. "We'll accompany him to DC later today. Anna's arranged a private charter."

"Excellent," said Aaron. "What about the others?"

"Kate will bring Kingston and Block to DC tomorrow. We'll help them prepare their testimony to the extent permitted, and we'll get Ricker to meet with the prosecutor. He's got a lot of evidence already, but we think that Ricker will be able to provide the smoking gun. You, Perry, and I will be our only other witnesses, assuming we're needed."

Perry smiled. "We won't need anything more."

"What do we know about Kennedy?"

"Nothing. But now that we know the grand jury's going to be in play, we need to get him out of there. And hope we're not too late."

"Let's wake Ricker up. We've got a lot of ground to cover before our flight."

"Perry, how would you like to proceed with the next session with Ricker?" asked Aaron.

"I think Claire should take the lead and indicate when either of us should step in. She appears less threatening, and her area of expertise is getting people to talk."

"That sounds good," said Aaron. "I'll go get Ricker."

Ricker joined the small group in the living room and took the cup of steaming coffee. *He looks ragged,* Claire thought, *but he'll no doubt look a whole lot worse by tomorrow. What a sniveling coward. But making judgments has no place here right now.* She turned her full attention to the man sitting across from her, energized by the progress her team had made in just a few hours' time. She was confident and looking forward to her own testimony. It would be easy because she only had to tell the truth. Funny how easily she'd stepped into this strange, fascinating role. *Of all the human puzzles I've ever encountered,* she thought, *this has been the most intricate. By a long shot.*

"Good news, Mr. Ricker," said Claire. "In exchange for your testimony, you'll be granted limited immunity for not only the FBI investigation but for your role at AllMed."

Ricker put his head into his hands, relieved beyond words. He wanted to cry.

"You'll need to talk to the FBI about your relationship with Ms. Malone in the near future. But right now, we need to talk about two former therapists on staff at Lucident, Jacob Morgan and Melanie Overstreet."

"Their names are familiar. I don't remember exactly when they worked for the clinic, though."

"They're dead," said Claire.

"What do you mean, they're dead?"

Claire watched Ricker's face turn from gray to a sick, greenish color. She ignored the question and continued.

"Okay. Let's get back to the therapists who were fired under Block's watch. Perry, would you please describe the sequence of events to Mr. Ricker?"

Perry continued with the line of questioning he was uniquely qualified to handle. After all, he was the one who'd had to intercept what would likely have been life-threatening circumstances for the departing therapists. All but the two he'd been unable to save.

"So, Mr. Ricker, we believe that someone at AllMed was responsible for both therapists' deaths," said Claire. "I'm sure you can understand our reasons, given the context. Perhaps you can also understand that I was fired in just the same way as the others. That placed me in the same kind of danger as our dead therapists. Do you understand?" Claire delivered this statement in a calm, unemotional manner, totally at odds with her suppressed fury.

Unfortunately for him, he did.

"Aaron, would you like to summarize things for Mr. Ricker?"

"Yes. If you answer every question truthfully, you'll be placed in a probationary witness protection program for three years. If you've observed all the program rules, you'll be allowed to live on your own, with only annual checks." Aaron stared directly at the former head of security. "If you violate the terms, even once, the immunity will become null and you will be prosecuted to the full extent of the law. You might escape the death penalty, but I wouldn't bet on it. Got it?"

"Yes, yes. Thank you."

Claire looked at the desperate, pathetic man in front of her. Professional training and years of experience enabled her to remain objective with her patients, and right now that's what she considered Ricker to be. But that discipline now teetered right on the edge of fury—as she realized how close she had come to disappearing.

CHAPTER 69

Wednesday, January 17

Since dinner the first night at sea, James Garrity and Stacy Atkins had been inseparable. They spent their nights in his cabin and their days at the ship's pool, laughing and talking almost nonstop. They'd gone on a culinary day trip during their dock at Portofino and a wine-tasting tour in the countryside at the next stop.

James couldn't believe his good fortune, all tumbling out of the brochure his financial adviser had placed in his hands just a few weeks ago. As a thank-you, he planned to send her and her husband on a romantic weekend at a resort in the Keys, a place he knew she'd talked about for years but had been too busy to explore.

"Tomorrow's our last night at sea, Stacy." He held out his champagne glass to toast her. "Look, I know it's not really possible to fall in love in four days, but it's definitely possible to fall in 'like,' and it's sure as shit possible to fall in 'lust.'" She beamed at him, taking a small sip. "I don't want this to end with the cruise."

"Neither do I." Stacy set her glass down on the linen tablecloth. She reached over to take his hand. "But I have some business to take care of back in Scottsdale. Curt's left me with a royal mess."

Over the past days (and nights), she'd described in great detail how she'd suspected he was involved with another woman for the past year, how he'd moved into a separate bedroom and was gone on "business" for days, sometimes weeks at a time.

Eventually, she'd explained, she had to admit that the marriage was over, but she just didn't have the strength to end it herself. She didn't know why he just didn't ask for a divorce, but after a while, she just figured he would when he was ready. Of course, once she'd discovered he'd plundered their life's savings, his delay made perfect sense. At this, Stacy had actually managed a tear. James's face was pained with compassion.

"I'll have to put the house on the market, and it will probably have to go into default since I can't afford the mortgage."

James said, "I can help you with that financially. I'd be happy to."

"I can't thank you enough, but I couldn't possibly allow you to do that. I inherited this mess, and I'll clean it up. Then I'll be free to make a new start." She smiled. "What I meant to say is to be free to continue this beautiful new start we've made together. And yes, James, I'd love to live in New York. I'm not sure about the winters, but I'll give it a shot. If they get too cold, then we can always take another cruise."

James's heart felt ready to burst. "Okay, that plan absolutely works for me. Now, what shall we do on our last excursion tomorrow?"

"Let's go to the museum the captain was telling us about and have some lunch. Then I'd like to do some shopping, pick up souvenirs, stuff like that, before we have to leave port."

CHAPTER 70

Wednesday, January 17

Stephen Chen turned his attention to the patient file from Monday's intake. Kennedy, Jason. Suspected PTSD. Chen was simultaneously furious and appalled at the lack of competency the security guard had shown in allowing his taser to be taken from him. *Thank God*, he thought, *that we don't have them carrying guns.* Chen had expressed his dissatisfaction in an email to John Ricker, who was still out with the flu. Ricker had been adamant that he was likewise very unhappy with the situation and promised immediate correction.

Chen felt sufficiently confident that Kennedy was a suitable candidate for A1A. Hospital staff had observed him carefully and concluded that his behavior was unlikely to be a result of psychosis alone and that his symptoms, medical history, and physical findings all supported a PTSD diagnosis. He made a notation to reclassify the diagnosis to malignant PTSD and signed the order for the first dose of A1A to be administered. The second and third doses would be administered on Thursday and Friday. Then, assuming all went as expected, Kennedy would be discharged to outpatient status for follow-up therapy and daily maintenance doses. He'd be the last patient to get A1A. As of next week, all of Chen's patients would be receiving Lucidaire. He smiled. There were times he had doubted whether it would all come together, but here he was, on the eve of the announcement.

Chen left to check on his mom once more before leaving the hospital. Her last initializing dose would be tomorrow morning, and then he'd begin the process of bringing her out of the induced coma.

CHAPTER 71

Laughing, Stacy piled four shoeboxes into James Garrity's arms. "Thanks so much, Jamie," she said. "I just want to pick up some handbags from some of the street vendors, so I'll meet you back on board ship."

He smiled. "Okay, I'll put these in your state room, and we'll have time for a cocktail before dinner. What time?"

She looked at the Patek Philippe on her right wrist, a gift from Curt several birthdays ago. She thought, *God, I'm glad I won't have to sell this sweet little thing after all.*

"It's a little after 2:15. I should be back on board by 3:30, or maybe 4:00 at the latest."

He kissed her on the mouth, his hand lingering at the small of her back. "Okay, Stace, see you then."

She turned and headed back to the small cluster of shops and open-air booths several blocks away. Stacy breathed deeply to take in the scents of the fresh-baked breads and artisan cheeses offered by market vendors. At the end of the fourth block, she found the small, wiry man who had murmured, "Designer bags, authentic, special prices for cruise passengers" when she had passed him an hour ago.

"Hello. I heard you mention your shop with the designer handbags?"

"Yes, I remember. This way, ma'am." He smiled, showing crooked yellow teeth and one barely visible gold cap. She followed him behind the street-front shop, and he invited her to step into his open-air jeep. "I take you to our beautiful showroom. You choose all handbags you like." He drove through narrow, curving streets, pointing out views of distant hills, maintaining a constant banter in broken English that required nothing from Stacy other than an occasional nod to make him think she was paying attention. After about fifteen minutes, he turned down a narrow alley and parked near a small stone building.

"My showroom, ma'am. I keep all my best leather goods here, only for special cruise guests."

She followed him inside and down a short staircase to his private shop, excited about her new accessories. She'd buy a special leather satchel for James, too. At the bottom of the stairs was an ancient wooden door with beautiful old hardware. Stacy's companion opened the door with a flourish. "After you, lady, if you please."

Ten minutes later the vendor returned to the street level, alone. Stacy's gorgeous watch and diamond stud earrings were tucked safely into his front pocket. He climbed into the jeep and tapped the steering wheel in time to a melody he was humming as he slowly pulled away from the building.

By 4:00 p.m., James Garrity was concerned. The ship was set to leave port at five o'clock for a sunset voyage before dinner on the last night of the cruise. He found the first mate and explained that Mrs. Atkins hadn't returned from shopping.

"We don't check everyone in until 4:30, sir, and I'm sure there's nothing to worry about. She knows about the check-in and departure time?"

"Yes, of course. But she said she'd be back no later than 3:30 or 4:00."

"Ah, but sir, you know women and shopping…I'm sure she'll be back in time."

James sat in a deck chair facing the entry ramp connecting the dock to the ship, waiting for 4:30 to arrive. He thought the first mate was taking his concern rather cavalierly. But unless she failed to be back by check-in, he couldn't do much.

By 4:50, he and the first mate were deep in animated discussion with the captain.

"I'm sorry, Mr. Garrity, we cannot hold the entire ship at dock to wait for one passenger. I have called for the police to meet us here, and you can file a report. They are very good, and it is most likely that she just lost track of time."

"That's not good enough." James was losing patience. "I do not want this ship to leave without her. You have to send out someone to look for her—she was just going to pick up a few souvenirs, and that was nearly three hours ago!"

Two portly Italian men in police uniforms stepped into the captain's office. They quickly took their report, the captain helping with some translation where needed.

"You must not worry, sir. Every year we have situations just like this, and I tell you there is no cause for concern." The older police officer looked at him. "People lose track of time, and they miss their departure. But this is a friendly village and very safe. We will find her, and we can fly her to meet you when you dock tomorrow. She will, of course, have to pay a fee for the flight, but that is easy to arrange." He smiled. "She will probably arrive back at Cinque Terre long before you do."

"I'll just wait here until you find her." Garrity directed his comment to the captain.

"Mr. Garrity, I'm afraid that won't be possible. Our insurance policies do not permit this, and you do not have the proper visa. Please return to deck and try to enjoy your last dinner on our beautiful ship. You will see your lovely lady friend when we dock tomorrow morning. I'm sure she will be waiting for you."

The moment the officers stepped onto the dock, the ship's horn blasted twice, indicating that the ramps were to be pulled in and that the ship was ready to leave port. The soft rumble of engine noise no longer had the quiet comfort of white noise James had become accustomed to hearing for the past five days. Now, it just sounded ominous.

CHAPTER 72

Anna Dixon and Senator Will Stratton were seated at the small conference table in Stratton's hotel suite. Across from them sat a federal prosecutor who had made his reputation in the late teens after successfully indicting and prosecuting two United States cabinet members for outright bribery. Peter Hughes was smart and experienced and focused.

"Let's go over Ricker's testimony with him one more time. He needs to understand that he is not to lie, not under any circumstance," said Hughes. "Any improvisation or embellishment he might want to offer has no place whatsoever in his appearance tomorrow."

"He knows." Anna said as she looked at the prosecutor. He wore reading glasses and looked every one of his sixty-six years, with thin, mostly gray hair and a paunch visible under his suit jacket. He was seasoned and relentless. "He's terrified. We'll pull his immunity in a split second if does anything to jeopardize the case."

"What about your other witnesses?" asked Stratton.

Anna smiled. "Block's role is to describe his assault and the little he remembers about his attempted abduction. He'll respond to questions about when and how he began to form suspicions about the hiring and termination practices within Lucident.

"Kingston will be good. He's solid and comes across as sincere, probably because he actually is a sincere guy. But we'll only use him if we think he's completely needed. Wilheit will be mainly providing background, limited to what she learned through her interaction with Kingston and her initial look-see into Block's digital records. She's as smart as they come and has no difficulty leaving her ego at the door. And again we'll only need her if Robert testifies and we think we still need more ammo. It will be up to you to decide whether and how to identify her role in the initial interview with Ricker."

"What about Perry and Davis?" Will Stratton asked.

Peter Hughes straightened in his chair and folded his hands in front of him on the small table. "Rock solid, both of them. Davis performed exactly as he needed to under his legal authority as a US marshal, and Perry knows the ins and outs of the entire security function. No concerns about them whatsoever. What have you heard about your guy on the inside?" Hughes's expression didn't change, but Anna could sense the concern in his tone.

Anna said, "One of my people is working on it right now. We'll have our agent out of the hospital first thing tomorrow morning. I don't want to do anything to tip our hand until the grand jury is ready to go, and a high-profile extraction's the last thing we need. We won't know if he can contribute anything to the case until we see what he learned since Sunday night."

"The grand jury is set for 4:00 p.m. Thursday, so if he isn't here by then, I'll have to proceed without him."

"Understood. It's possible we could get him here in time, but not likely. Let's make arrangements for him to appear telephonically just in case," said Anna. "Thanks, Peter."

Hughes nodded and picked up his notebook, leaving the hotel suite with a stride that conveyed a composed confidence.

Stratton looked at Dixon. "Please let me know the minute your agent is removed from the hospital."

"Absolutely." Dixon had a great deal of work to finalize and needed to be available to the Oversight Committee on the slim chance that she would be required at the press conference, scheduled for 3:00 Thursday on the steps of the Capitol. The day would be windy and ice cold, not enough to keep away the ravenous press corps, but just enough to avoid a prolonged Q and A. Dixon shook Stratton's hand and stood, leaving the older politician sitting at the table, already deep in thought.

Hughes spent the rest of the day organizing warrants and subpoenas as well as finalizing an emergency executive order to mobilize the federalized National Guard assigned to Arizona, assuming the indictment was handed down as he planned. He was confident, but not overly so. He'd had enough experience to know that even the best-planned case could go south in a hurry and that no detail was too small to gloss over.

He was choreographing a complicated ballet involving a number of dancers, and the timing had to be absolutely perfect. He had every reason to believe that lives hung in the balance.

CHAPTER 73

Thursday, January 18

Stephen Chen arrived at the labs well before sunup. The day would be long and completely occupied with the press conference and announcements. Other than to be an active observer, he had no direct role in interviews, which was exactly what he required. He knew that Michael Parker would be watching every detail of the Washington, DC pageantry from wherever he happened to be.

Chen's first order of business was to check in with his clinical director, Vivian Jaffe, on production at the in-house labs. Then he would begin his morning rounds, first visiting the secure unit to see his mother and administer her last initializing dose of A1A. After that, Chen would see the new patient, Kennedy. He would receive his second dose of A1A as soon as the morning nursing shift arrived at 7:00 a.m., so that was on schedule as well.

Jaffe was usually in the lab by 6:30 every morning, and she was there now.

"Dr. Chen." Jaffe stood. "Good morning."

"Good morning, Dr. Jaffe." Chen nodded, coming as close to a smile as he'd ever managed. "Where are we with production?"

"Everything is exactly on schedule. We have just over three hundred thousand doses on hand, and production is ongoing. We should be at a million doses by the first week in June."

"Excellent work, Dr. Jaffe. Exemplary."

"Thank you. Is there anything else before I get back to work?"

"Nothing, thanks. Enjoy the press conference."

She looked at him, nodding once before she turned back toward her office. Jaffe felt a little sick to her stomach but knew where she needed to focus. Her latest lab trial would be complete by now, and there were data to analyze. The last seven experiments had failed, but maybe this one would hold the key to developing the A1A version that would eliminate the dreadful side effects. At least, she thought, Chen was on board with her continuing research. She wasn't so sure about the US military, since captured soldiers would always represent security risks. It wasn't hard to envision a scenario where the powers that be would rather eliminate the security risk even if it resulted in collateral human damage. Jaffe shut down the computer in her office and turned to return to the lab. Her steps quickened with her rapidly growing sense of urgency.

CHAPTER 74

Marian Thomas was up early. She needed to finalize the medical power of attorney form and get the "proper" signatures along with the notary seals on the documents. Her schedule was thrown off track for twelve hours or so, after deciding that she should also have in hand an advance directive when she walked into the AVS hospital. The medical power of attorney would likely be enough, but she didn't want to take the chance that there would be any administrative delay in getting Kennedy out, and she might not have another chance.

The advance directive, dated retroactively, would be a duly notarized document stating Kennedy's written objections to hospitalization in any facility operated directly or indirectly by the AVS and to participation in any drug trials whatsoever. It might be overkill, but it never hurt to cover the bases. She wanted to be at the hospital within the hour.

Kennedy had already been out of pocket for three full days, and frankly, that was much too long.

At 9:15 a.m., Marian Thomas was in the AVS administrator's office, having filled out all the necessary forms for Jason Kennedy's discharge.

"We understand your position, Mrs. Thomas, but we absolutely cannot discharge Mr. Kennedy until he has been cleared by his admitting physician."

"No, sir, I don't think you *do* understand my position. I have presented you with a duly notarized medical power of attorney, as well as my nephew's signed and notarized advance directive, which specifically indicates that he refuses any admission to any hospital operated under the aegis of the AVS, and that he specifically refuses participation in any clinical drug trials that may be ongoing or developed.

"I want my nephew discharged *now*. If I don't see him here in fifteen minutes, the next call I make is to the news. And then the attorney general's office."

The administrator stood and offered a forced smile. "No need for that, Mrs. Thomas. Of course, we will be happy to comply with Mr. Kennedy's directives. Please have a seat in my outer office while I make arrangements."

The moment she left, his smile disappeared, and he called Stephen Chen. AllMed's press conference would take place in just a few hours, and he didn't want to be responsible for anything that might jeopardize its success. He knew he was already on shaky ground after the tasing debacle.

Chen hung up the phone and uttered a curse. The Kennedy incident demanded immediate attention and represented a necessary but frustrating delay in getting to his rounds. He stepped up his pace as he walked through the labs to Vivian Jaffe's office. He entered and closed the door.

"We may have a problem, Dr. Jaffe," said Chen. "Jason Kennedy, the Monday admit, has an aunt. She's demanding that he be discharged. She has every legal right to require it."

"Was he the patient that was tased in the ER fracas?"

"Yes. We put him under forty-eight hours' observation to make sure the incident in the ER had no lasting effects on him. We began the A1A initializing protocol yesterday."

Jaffe immediately saw the problem. "Did he receive a second dose?"

"Yes, it was scheduled for seven o'clock this morning."

"Dr. Chen, every single patient in our group, all four hundred and thirty of them, received the complete initializing sequence. We do *not* have a single instance of a patient who had only a partial dose."

"I just need your most educated guess as to what it might mean for him clinically."

"The best thing would be to finish the initializing protocol and put him on maintenance. But as to the effect on the patient, I just told you, I don't know," she said evenly. "I recommend strongly against discharging him prior to completing the protocol. I'm not in the guessing business."

Neither am I, thought Chen. *At least, not until now.*

Chen left for his office. He had to review several patients' files before he headed to the acute inpatient unit. He was so preoccupied he didn't notice the look of alarm on Jaffe's face.

CHAPTER 75

Stephen Chen considered the situation. He had no idea what the mental or physical effect would be on Kennedy. That wasn't going to change. What were the options? Kennedy's intake history and physical listed no immediate family. He wasn't sure who had been responsible for such a blunder—had Kennedy's aunt been listed, he wouldn't have been approved for A1A in the first place. He wasn't sure whether Ricker could have prevented the mistake if admission review systems had been tighter, but combined with the tasing incident, Chen was becoming convinced that, moving forward, Ricker wasn't the right man for this position. Today was the third day Ricker was out of the office. Chen remained focused. Ricker was an issue for another day.

One option would be to give Kennedy a third intravenous dose immediately and to discharge him with a thirty-day oral supply of A1A. That would be seen as the most ethical course of action at this point. Just have Kennedy's doctor explain to the aunt that it was important for him to continue the medication. The unapproved medication. He'd have to deal with the legal fallout of administering a drug after he'd been notified not to do so via Kennedy's advance directive. He wasn't sure whether the clinical trial, which technically hadn't been approved by the FDA until this week, would become an issue. They were probably okay on informed consent; after all, Kennedy was a psychiatric patient under emergency admission. On the plus side, Kennedy had a ninety percent chance of succeeding with the drug. There were countless medical conditions that would make patients jump at a ninety percent chance for a cure. *But*, thought Chen, *I'm not a desperate patient, and ten percent is way too high to risk everything I've worked toward my entire adult life. If Kennedy proved to be that one out of ten, everything would unravel. Everything.*

Scratch option one.

The second option that came to mind was simply to do nothing. Chen could adjust Kennedy's medical record to remove any record of treatment with A1A. Either Kennedy would be fine or he wouldn't. If the second dose was enough to raise the level of A1A in Kennedy's system to a therapeutic level, Kennedy would have about forty-eight hours before the side effects, if there were to be any, set in. There would be no way to prove that AllMed had any role in Kennedy's clinical outcome or, in the worst case, his suicide. And anyway, as Vivian Jaffe said, there was no way to predict whether two initializing doses would be enough to trigger any side effects at all. The best-case scenario would be for Kennedy to have no side effects, and he would go on with his life. No one would know he'd received A1A. The worst case would result in a death sentence for Kennedy. Either way, AllMed would be in the clear.

Option two was the only choice. Chen hurried to the inpatient unit that housed Jason Kennedy to alter his patient chart and to sign the discharge papers. *Maybe Kennedy would be lucky*, Chen thought, *maybe not*. Chen's creative excursion in medical records completed, he moved swiftly to the elevator. He needed to make sure his administrator was on board and that Kennedy's discharge would go smoothly.

Twenty minutes later, Jason Kennedy left the hospital with his aunt. Marian Thomas steered his wheelchair to her waiting car. They were headed to the air force base thirty miles to the northwest, where they would board a nonstop flight to Washington, DC.

Vivian Jaffe opened the electronic record: Kennedy, Jason. Discharged. She moved to the discharge orders. No prescriptions. But there was a physician's note, signed by Dr. Chen, which specifically stated: "No follow-up required."

She looked at the detailed notes in his patient file, searching for the pharmacy details. No record of A1A ever being administered. She knew immediately what Chen had done.

CHAPTER 76

Liz Malone stood on the private deck of the villa she'd rented in the Cayman Islands for the month. She'd just watched her computer screen as the numbers changed in her investment portfolio. The last batch of put options had cleared, and all she had to do was check in a little later, after the press conference, to watch wholesale panic hit the entire pharmaceutical industry.

The water before her was the brightest, clearest turquoise she had ever seen. She, as well as each of her partners, will have cleared nearly $18 million each as the put options became reality when the markets closed the following day. Now all she had to do was be patient. Her profits will have been made, and nothing in AllMed's future would be able to reverse it. Even the worst-case scenario was perfectly covered. If, for any reason, AllMed failed to get its drug treatment implemented nationwide, her fat cash position would let her buy the nearly worthless competing pharmaceutical stocks before they headed back up.

She had a windsurfing lesson scheduled later in the afternoon and had made a dinner reservation at the rooftop restaurant at the new hotel down the road. It seemed like a good way to celebrate.

CHAPTER 77

Thursday, January 18, 3:35 p.m.

"Members of the press, Congress, and the entirety of the American people, my apology for the delay this afternoon. Thank you for bearing with us on this very auspicious day.

"I stand here today with my colleagues from the American Veterans' Services, the chairman of the Joint Chiefs of Staff, and the secretary of Health and Human Services to announce an unprecedented breakthrough in the treatment of US veterans suffering from posttraumatic stress disorder, known as PTSD.

"Through a rare combination of the FDA's breakthrough therapy guidelines and mechanisms for fast-track review, the US Food and Drug Administration today granted accelerated approval for Lucidaire, developed through AllMed's research and development arm, Lucident Technologies.

"As many of you know, some eight million of our veterans are estimated to suffer from PTSD, with suicides rates now estimated to be about twenty-six patients per day."

The chairman of the Congressional Oversight Committee continued. "The chairman of the Joint Chiefs has personally pledged to have this revolutionary therapy available for AVS hospital patients nationwide, as well as priority distribution to our troops in the field worldwide within ninety days. We, your elected representatives, are proud to continue putting the health and well-being of our men and women in service ahead of bureaucratic obstacles that might otherwise delay the availability of a life-changing medication. General?"

Looking as if he'd just emerged from central casting with his steely gray hair, square jaw, and massive physical presence, the general stepped forward, ignoring the biting wind and freezing temperatures that were severe enough to find their way through his dress uniform.

"As many of you know, the main category of pharmaceutical treatment for our veterans suffering from PTSD has historically been limited to standard antidepressants. Today, that changes. God bless our men and women in service, and God bless the United States of America."

There were no fewer than thirty reporters in the audience. At least half of them shouldered their way to the front, shouting over one another to interject questions. The others were already reporting live with their camera crews. They'd all been waiting over an hour in the bitter cold.

"We won't be taking questions this afternoon, but our staff has prepared a detailed press release available in your briefing materials. In closing, I'd like to thank the members of the Congressional Oversight Committee for their insight and leadership in forging new and better ways to care for our veterans. The fact that this new drug was developed by the very corporation we selected to begin the essential privatization of health care for veterans validates the congressional wisdom and foresight in passing this law.

"Thank you for being here and for the flexibility in allowing us to share our announcement on this chilly day.

"God bless America."

Michael Parker watched the news from his Manhattan apartment. Wall Street was in a state of flat-out pandemonium at the eleventh-hour announcement. The stock values of every major pharmaceutical company in the world were plummeting as investors realized that the enormous profits they'd enjoyed for decades were about to come to a screeching halt. Orders to sell fueled more of the same, and the numbers on the news ticker tape were changing almost too fast to read. The New York Stock Exchange would be closing in a matter of minutes.

Michael Parker smiled as he turned off the television and picked up the phone.

"Yes, I'm watching as well…I'll send you my flight information as soon as we hang up…no, thank you, that won't be necessary. I have all the documents ready to go and will hand-deliver the last of the files when I arrive."

He had a plane to catch and expected to be in Chamonix by this time tomorrow. It should be a great skiing season.

CHAPTER 78

Anna Dixon and John Ricker stood in the chilly, cavernous hallway outside the courtroom where the grand jury was convened. Peter Hughes opened the courtroom door and said, "Mr. Ricker? We're ready for you." His words echoed in the empty corridor, bouncing off the marble floors and hard wooden benches. Ricker made a pathetic effort to appear confident, failed, and stepped into the courtroom. He looked like a frightened, cornered animal.

Dixon caught the press conference while she was in transit to the courthouse. Nothing unexpected there. She was completely unsurprised at the self-serving performance of the speakers. She moved down the hall to the small foyer where the three witness waiting areas were located. After heated discussion, she and Hughes had decided to move forward with Block, Aaron, and Perry as witnesses and to keep Wilheit and Kingston back. If Hughes decided he needed them, they'd be available, but after long consideration, he didn't really feel it would be necessary. Aaron Davis had Block's fully cloned laptop, and what the two social workers could offer was little more than what he already had. He didn't want to invite an inquiry into how two people incontrovertibly declared dead through DNA evidence were anything but. Ricker was the only person outside Dixon's group who had seen Wilheit, and the former FBI agent knew full well the consequences of stepping even one inch out of line.

She watched the courtroom door close. With any luck, they'd have an indictment in hand before 5:00 p.m. Which would be 3:00 p.m. in Arizona, enough time for Hughes to unleash the Phoenix group awaiting his go-ahead.

Dixon entered the room where Aaron Davis was engaged in quiet conversation with Claire Wilheit. They looked up as she walked in and took a seat.

"And now," she said, "we wait."

CHAPTER 79

Claire sat with Aaron Davis and Anna Dixon in the living room of the small apartment on Capitol Hill. Four computer screens were lit up, one connected to each of four body cameras worn by the team leaders of the dispatched National Guard units in Phoenix. At 4:30 p.m., the teams of National Guard members converged at the administrative offices of the American Veterans' Services hospital, brandishing their IDs and documents.

The first team demanded to see Dr. Chen and the hospital administrator.

Claire watched the team leader burst open the door to an interior administrative office. Stephen Chen was engaged in a tense discussion with his administrator and whirled around to see several uniformed men walk in past a shocked-looking secretary. Claire could hear the secretary's futile protest and watched Chen wave his hand to dismiss her.

"Stephen Chen, you are under arrest for fraud, suspected money laundering, assault and battery, and conspiracy to commit murder. You have the right to remain silent…"

"No! I have patients I have to see this afternoon!" Actually, there was only one patient he cared about, and she needed her third and final initializing dose today.

One of the uniformed men handcuffed Dr. Chen, while the other completed the Miranda warning. Chen was extremely agitated and his rising voice and angry threats accompanied his demand to see his patients. Dr. Chen wouldn't be seeing any patients today. In fact, it was unlikely that he would ever see another patient.

The second computer screen showed the next team group barging into the labs. "Vivian Jaffe, you are under arrest for suspected fraud and conspiracy to assault patients through the supply of illegally manufactured drugs. You have the right to remain silent…"

The third group was right behind, made up of several National Guard members as well as two researchers from the Centers for Disease Control and Prevention, who would remain on site to seize and secure the nearly half million stored doses of A1A.

Dixon's team turned its united focus on the fourth team, in many ways the most critical part of the operation. The fourth team was comprised of a pair of National Guard members and two psychiatrists from the University of Arizona's teaching and research hospital facility. The first three groups knew to a large degree what to expect. But the fourth team was left speechless when they entered the locked inpatient unit. Forty-one comatose patients, all on life support, greeted them without expression or any indication of life, other than the soft symphony of monitors in each patient's room. "God help us," murmured the physician in the lead. No one else spoke.

Nearly a dozen subpoenas were on the move. The only subject not yet served was one Belinda Elizabeth Malone. If she wasn't located by this time tomorrow, the federal prosecutor would go on national television identifying her as a person of interest in cases related to an FBI cold case and in the AllMed investigation. Surprisingly, that approach had historically proved to be a good one, and while there were always a lot of false positives in sightings, there was often a nice, shiny needle in the haystack.

CHAPTER 80

Friday, January 19

Claire woke to the smell of coffee in the apartment Anna Dixon had provided for the team. Had it really been two weeks since she'd woken up in her own bed? Bed? She didn't even have a house anymore. No clothes, no furniture, not even the freshly painted back screen door. No job, and apparently not even a name to go back to.

She pulled on her sweat pants, a sweatshirt, and a pair of thick socks and walked into the kitchen. Aaron Davis was toasting some bagels and setting out some cream cheese and jam.

"How are you doing this morning, Claire?"

She was on the verge of giving him a sarcastic response but just said, "I'm tired, Aaron. So incredibly tired."

He set a coffee mug in front of her and pulled a second stool up to the breakfast bar.

"This has been an unbelievable week, and you've been through an incredible ordeal. But despite that, your help has been invaluable. Anna said she'll call us later but wanted me to be sure to convey her thanks. Tell me what you're thinking."

She clasped both hands around the warm mug. "Aaron, I feel completely uprooted. Because I am. I've spent my whole adult life trying to gain some measure of control over it, but it seems that there's been someone to knock it off balance at every step."

He nodded at her as he placed the toasty bagels on the counter. He smiled and waited for her to continue.

That's the first time I've ever seen him smile, she thought. *It's a nice smile, a lot of deep smile lines that add character.*

"I'm thirty-two years old. I finally bought a place of my own, where I could control who visits or who doesn't. How late I stay up or how early I go to bed. It wasn't a big or fancy place, but it was mine. Now I have no money, and my insurance policy on the house is worthless, too, since dead people can't collect on insurance payments. I can't even collect my savings or my retirement account. My entire self-image has been built on independence, and snap, just like that, every part of it gone. My parents died several years ago, so I don't have any family."

"I thought Robert said you had a sister?"

"We don't speak." Claire gave him an abbreviated backstory about Stacy and the lawsuit. "You're familiar with the notion of the butterfly effect?"

"Oh," said Aaron, "indeed I am." He nodded with a slight smile.

"I mean, if I hadn't had to deal with that damn deposition, I would never have been at Lucident so late to begin with and wouldn't have met Robert and wouldn't be sitting in an apartment in Capitol Hill having coffee with someone I've only known for two weeks."

Aaron said, "Well, you could look at it this way: if you hadn't had to go back to your office and hadn't been at Robert's so late, you might have been home asleep when your house blew up."

Claire barked out a cynical laugh. "Right! I'll just have to send her a thank-you note. From the grave!"

Aaron laughed, too. "On the other hand, you don't have to deal with a deposition, and she'll probably have to pay her own legal fees."

She raised her coffee mug in a toast. "To legal fees—for someone else."

The brew was hot and strong, but the aroma's comfort was short-lived. Claire returned to reality.

"Do you think that with all the arrests and getting AllMed shut down, I'd ever be able to be Claire Wilheit again?"

Aaron's expression changed immediately. "Claire, it's always your decision about witness protection and how you choose to manage your identity. Even though we hope a lot of people will be going to prison, there are way too many unknowns for me to feel comfortable recommending you keep your identity.

"There's a network, potentially a big one, of money behind AllMed, not just the CEO and employees. It will be a long time until we know if members of Congress are involved and how deep that might be, but Anna thinks we could just be seeing the tip of the iceberg. It doesn't matter if you don't have Block's computer—it only matters whether someone thinks you saw its contents. We still have no idea who was responsible for the explosion or whether you were targeted. Not that I want to pry, but are you leaving behind a boyfriend or significant other?"

"Leaving behind? That sounds rather final, doesn't it?"

Aaron turned toward her, concerned over his choice of words, but relaxed when he saw her quirky half smile.

"Come on, Aaron, I'm just trying to find some dark humor here. So, no, I'm not leaving anyone behind. I just got myself out of the last relationship I was in and realized that I'm no better at picking men now than I was as a teenager."

Claire thought back again to the day she'd left the box of Don's things at her back stoop for him to retrieve. There was no point confronting him about anything, since she knew he'd use it as a reason to try to drag her into another stupid argument. When she got home, it was pretty easy for her to envision what had happened. He was royally pissed off. He was used to calling every shot, and the fact that it had been Claire, not him, who ended the relationship would have infuriated him. Which would have resulted in a sadly predictable temper tantrum. Which in turn resulted in the back screen being torn and the lower part of the door displaying splinter damage, probably from an angry kick. *Ironic, isn't it?* she thought. *The minute I put the last touch of paint on that screen door, finally putting him in my rearview mirror for good, fate blows up my world, literally in front of my eyes.*

"Aaron, I'm going out for a short run."

"Do you want company?"

"No. No, thanks, I just want to get some fresh air. I'll be back within the hour."

Aaron hung up after his conversation with Anna. There might be a way to help Claire with her finances. She had less than $30,000 equity in her house—the bulk of the insurance proceeds would go to the bank that held the mortgage; the remaining monies as well as her savings would go to her estate, whose beneficiary was a nonprofit organization that funded legal defense for prisoners on death row. It was an outgrowth of the Innocence Project and a worthy cause. Not that there was any shortage of worthy causes out there.

They'd discussed the pros and cons before bringing Claire into the conversation. Could Perry create a new will for Claire and backdate it? Easily. Change the beneficiary to Claire's new persona? Sure. Was there any risk to that? Very little. Alternately, Dixon's group could self-fund the $46,000 or so it would take to make Claire whole.

Anna and Aaron had also spoken at length as to whether they could see a future role for Claire in the group. Anna felt confident about the consulting group's future, especially after AllMed's exposure. Of course, it wouldn't be with the chairman of the Congressional Oversight Committee, who, after all, had a good likelihood of doing some jail time. But there was a lot of investigation to be done, and Will Stratton had complete confidence in her and her group. Claire was tough and resourceful and smart.

"Aaron, talk to her and just lay things out for her. Let's suggest a six-month engagement to see how we fit together. I can see an immediate, obvious role for her in jury selection processes. And I suspect there will be quite a few such opportunities coming up."

"Can you keep her from having to testify? Having her face and name out there is risky and further exposes the DNA problem, which would be a real can of worms. We have to assume there will be a lot of people who have a lot to lose watching every part of the AllMed trials."

"We don't think we'll need her testimony, so all should be good."

"Claire, Anna and I have spoken at length about the upcoming grand jury. We don't think that either you or Robert will need to testify."

"Are you worried that one of us will be recognized?"

"Frankly, yes. You are both supposed to be dead. In fact, your deaths have been completely confirmed, due to the DNA issue."

"That's perfectly fine with me. How is Robert doing? I never really had the chance to say goodbye." Claire took off her glasses and started cleaning them with the edge of her shirt. "Could you give him a message for me?"

"No, I'm sorry. Once someone enters our witness protection program, we are 100% invested in their anonymity."

"Oh. That makes sense. We only knew each other for a few days, under pretty horrendous circumstances. Still, I am kind of surprised that I could feel as strong a bond of friendship as I do."

"That's probably not unusual – you were both in a highly emotionally charged state and needed to depend on each other. That's something rarely tested, even among people who have been friends for years."

She replaced her glasses.

"I understand." She did.

CHAPTER 81

Friday, January 19, 10:00 a.m.

By quarter after ten on Friday morning, Liz Malone was on her third cup of coffee, fingers flying over her computer keyboard. How the fuck had things gone so far south so fast? One moment she was watching the stock market implode over the announcement about Lucidaire as her put options were perfectly positioned for the close of market Friday. And then the arrests and nonstop news about AllMed's growing scandal. The television in her living room blared.

"Sherry Billings for Channel 6 Network news, reporting live from Washington, DC. Dan, what do we have on the investigation?"

"Well, Sherry, not much, as the prosecution has been very close-mouthed about details but will hold a press conference tomorrow morning, along with the chairman of the Senate Ethics Committee.

"In the meantime, we have a video clip of the chairman of the Congressional Oversight Committee as he was arrested leaving his office last night. Let's run it."

The senator was red-faced and sputtering. "This is an outrage and a bald-faced political stunt to make me look bad. Every single charge will be dropped, and I will be looking at countersuits at the appropriate time. No further comment." He squared his shoulders and turned from the camera in a show of defiance.

"Thanks, Sherry, we'll be bringing you live updates throughout the day. Dan Scott, signing off."

Liz muted the television. She didn't need to hear the commentary; she could see the stock market fiasco flashing in front of her eyes as the ticker tape scrolled across the bottom of the screen. She called the house staff to have coffee and toast sent to her villa. She couldn't have stopped watching the not-so-slow-moving train wreck if she tried.

Dr. Vivian Jaffe and her attorney sat in a small interview room with Perry MacRae, the CDC physicians, and the local prosecutor. The red-eye flight from DC last night got Perry back to Phoenix at seven this morning. The attorneys were the only ones who didn't look exhausted. Chen's lawyers had shown up almost immediately, and he wasn't talking to anyone. Dr. Jaffe, her attorney in tow, though, was a different story.

"Gentlemen, I am happy to talk to you in an informal, off-the-record fashion."

Her attorney didn't look happy at all. "No, Dr. Jaffe, that is not possible. We aren't doing anything here 'off the record.'"

Jaffe's attorney quickly gathered his papers. He touched her arm to indicate that they were leaving the meeting.

She shook off his arm.

"Well, gentlemen. Here's what you need to know."

"Dr. Jaffe, I strongly advise you not to answer any further questions."

She ignored him.

"There are four hundred and thirty patients out there who must have their daily maintenance dosage of A1A, so it is imperative that you reach every one of them and make sure they have their medication. There are sufficient doses in stock to cover them for about eighteen months. But at that time, they're going to need additional A1A, which, if the labs are shut down, won't be happening. The better option would be to continue with the research I've been doing on a mitigating drug therapy. But they can't just be left out there."

"That's enough, Dr. Jaffe. Gentlemen, I think we're done here for the moment. Please excuse us. My client and I have much to discuss."

Vivian watched the others leave the room, then turned toward her attorney.

"Dr. Jaffe, again, I unequivocally recommend that you answer no further questions. None."

"Don't you get it? It's one thing to cut a few corners on FDA rules, but I never signed on for murder."

"Yes, I 'get it.' I also 'get' that my role is to help you stay out of trouble. In the best-case scenario, you will likely lose your medical license. In the worst case, you'll go to prison as an accessory to murder."

Actually, cutting corners on FDA rules was a very big thing, but it paled in comparison to what she saw Stephen Chen was willing to do when he decided to discharge Kennedy without letting him know about the drug he'd been getting. She couldn't actually prove that Kennedy had received A1A— not without a blood sample from a patient she could no longer access. At this point, it would be her word against Chen's, and neither of them had much credibility right now. And maybe never would. But she did know about the other patients in the program. At least there was that.

"We need to have a lot more discussion before you say anything else to the authorities. As far as anyone knows, you run the labs and oversee treatment protocols. It's not your responsibility if someone fails to follow them."

"I don't care. I'm a doctor, and I don't pass the buck on patients whose welfare I am involved in—even peripherally. I want you to talk to them about giving me leniency if I keep working to develop a drug to replace A1A and manage its side effects."

"Dr. Jaffe, let me be a bit more clear. You have no cards to play here, not a single one."

"I'll just have to find one, then."

Who am I kidding? she thought. *I couldn't get a job teaching fifth grade science at this point, let alone ever work in a pharmaceutical lab again.*

Liz Malone couldn't reach any of her partners. If they wanted to talk to her, they knew where to find her. She had only a few hours to put together orders to purchase as much stock as she could afford in the pharmaceutical companies whose demise she had been counting on just twenty-four hours ago. Before they bounced back too quickly and thoroughly. She had watched as each of the ten largest companies she'd bet against began to recover value. In another hour, they'd most likely be above her "strike" point before the contract expired at 4:30 today. Her entire contract for the puts would be forfeited. *I can't do anything about that now,* Liz thought. *I just need to do as much damage control as possible right now. I've got about forty grand in cash reserves, so I just need to figure out where to best invest it.*

CHAPTER 82

Even in winter, Washington, DC, was a beautiful city. Claire's run took her through beautiful old neighborhoods, restored brownstone apartments with brightly painted front doors, inviting porches and bay windows, and small front yards that she expected would become charming, well-tended gardens as soon as spring broke. She came to a stop at what looked like an old train station. The signage read, "Eastern Market." Bundled-up weekend vendors already had their wares on display at the forty or so outdoor booths that surrounded the building. She looked at the array of fresh vegetables, knitted goods, imported purses with Tibetan designs. She stepped into the market and was instantly rewarded with the scent of fresh-baked goods mingled with curries and some other spices she didn't recognize. She envied the shopkeepers, who, when they closed up for the evening, would go home to families or friends or maybe just their cats, and who could curl up with a good novel and forget the outside world. *They have no idea*, she thought, *how lucky they are.*

Back in the apartment, Claire pulled off her fleece jacket. She ran one hand through her tousled curls and handed a small brown bag to Aaron. "Look what I found," she said, "fresh-baked almond croissants."

He could smell them from inside the bag. "Fabulous, thanks." He took out a small plate from the kitchen cabinet. "I take it you found the Eastern Market?"

"I did, and it was a wonderful place, you wouldn't believe the food…"

He laughed. "I certainly would. It's been one of my favorite weekend haunts over the years." Getting down to business, he continued, "We have a late lunch scheduled with Anna and her colleague. So let's have a croissant, and you'll have a good hour to clean up if you want to before we have to leave."

He watched Claire wipe some powdered sugar from her mouth as she went to her room. He heard the shower running and smiled. She seemed to be energized by her run and, if he wasn't mistaken, might be in something approaching a good mood. Not there, but approaching it. Still, a huge improvement from where she'd been when he first met her in a formerly quiet Phoenix neighborhood two long weeks ago.

Anna Dixon was seated in the back of the restaurant at a small booth upholstered in a midcentury patterned fabric. The table was set for four. Aaron and Claire scooted in from the left.

Anna reached out to shake Claire's hand. "How are you feeling today?"

"Okay, thanks. I'm doing okay."

A silver-haired man of medium height slid into the booth next to Anna. "Sorry I'm a bit late, the traffic in this town…"

"Will, please meet Claire Wilheit. Claire, this is Senator Will Stratton."

They shook hands. Aaron greeted him as well.

"Ms. Wilheit, I'd like to personally thank you for all that you've done over the past number of days. I can't imagine how demanding this has been for you."

Up until that very moment, Claire would have bet her life that nothing more could have surprised her. Yet here she was in a quiet restaurant in the midst of a bustling, frenetic city with one of the best-known and respected statesmen of the past decade. She wasn't ordinarily the kind of person to be starstruck, but she couldn't think of anything to say in response. So she just nodded.

"Will, we've just started to talk about some of Claire's options from here on out. As I mentioned before, I think that there's a possible role for her with my consulting group. Either here in Washington or in the field, wherever we might be placed. Would you like to weigh in?"

Stratton began. "Ms. Wilheit—"

She interrupted. "No, Senator, Claire is fine, thanks."

"Claire. As you no doubt are beginning to realize, the AllMed investigation may very well become small potatoes once we delve into the roles of members of Congress and beyond. This investigation is a very, very big deal, and it will shake all of Washington, DC, as we know it. Anna's group has been instrumental in bringing this to fruition, and she—we—think you might be a good fit for the group. I'd like you to think about taking her up on her offer of employment, at least for the next six months, until you both have a chance to evaluate the fit." He was careful to make it clear that she alone would have to decide.

"I understand that you have been well briefed on the advisability of changing your identity?"

"Yes, I have. I get it. I don't like it, but I get it."

"The sequence of events is fortunate for us, for veterans of the United States, and for the potential to dig out some rot from the halls of Congress. I know that it's been unfortunate for you, and for that I am sorry. If I could turn back the clock, I would, but all I can offer you now are some options that I hope you'll find satisfactory.

"Please give it some thought, and let me know if you have any questions." He rose to leave. "My apologies, I can't stay for lunch. There seem to be some phone calls I need to make."

Aaron and Claire walked through the busy streets, matching the pace of the scores of Washingtonians rushing from what they must all view as one important place to the next. They took the escalator down into the Metro, a relief from the chilling wind on the surface streets. Aaron swiped his prepaid Metro cards, and they both passed through the turnstiles, heading back to the Capitol Hill apartment. The train was packed. They rode in silence, observing their train mates.

Back at the apartment, they left their jackets on the chair in the foyer.

"So what did you think of our meeting?" Aaron asked as he folded his gloves and put them on the small table near the door.

"Wow, I don't know what to think. He seems to be everything you'd think based on his public persona."

"Agree. But that's not a show. He's really that kind and sincere. And tough as nails."

"Was he trying to bullshit me?"

Aaron gave a hearty laugh. "Well, he *is* a politician. And I do think he wanted to convince you to join Anna's group and, even if you didn't, to go with the new identity for your own safety. But he's not going to demand that you do anything, and he'll respect your decision either way. Anyone who chooses to go into the kind of work we're doing clearly isn't in it for fame or riches. It's because the work matters to them."

"So you're saying that yes, he was playing me, but it's okay since we all know it?"

"Pretty much."

Claire threw her head back and laughed. "Fair enough. How do we start? Do I get to pick a name I always wanted?"

"No. We'll have the computer come up with half a dozen composite names, and you can choose one you feel will suit you. We've found that people who invent their own favorite names usually pick the name of a character or place they've been associated with, consciously or not, and that's a pretty poor way to stay under the radar."

"How do we do that?"

"I don't understand the technical details, but basically we would identify a dozen or so common last names, then pair them with random first names. We'll look for any combination of names or initials that might trigger a memory of yours—whether a childhood friend, school acquaintance, and the like—and eliminate those. Anyone with a similar name in any locations you've lived, same thing."

"So I can choose to be either Jane Doe or Jane Smith?"

"Not quite." Aaron grinned. "Eventually we'll end up with three or four possibilities and will let you choose."

Claire managed a weak smile. "Do I have to change the way I look?"

"That would be a good idea, yes. Fortunately, there seems to have been a bit of short-term karma in play—the only photo of you that has been made public, at least so far, is this one." He opened his computer to show her the picture of her in evening garb that had been all over the news.

Claire started to laugh. "That was my ill-fated blonde period. I let myself be convinced that I would be pretty if I was blonde and wore a lot of makeup and ended up resenting that boyfriend even more as a result. But it looks like he did me a favor after all."

Aaron was puzzled that Claire evidently didn't think of herself as pretty and wondered why. But this wasn't the time to delve into that—not now, and maybe not ever. After all, he was a retired—make that an un-retired—US marshal, not a shrink. He needed to focus on the tasks at hand.

"Claire, I also need to bring you up to date on your sister."

"My sister? We haven't had contact for years. Except through her lawyer, that is."

Aaron filled her in on the report filed by the Scottsdale Police Department, including Curt's unexplained departure, Stacy's sudden trip to Italy, her own mysterious disappearance, and the overall evaporation of what was once a substantial portfolio of wealth.

Claire's smile was gone.

"But that doesn't make sense. My final comments on the deposition in her lawsuit against me were due—just three days after my house blew up."

"None of it really makes sense. It all just looks very suspicious."

"Do you think she's gone for good?"

"I don't know. At this point, the Scottsdale PD think the most likely scenario is that your sister and her husband are enjoying their wealth on a tropical island somewhere without the risk of extradition. And that they devised a scheme to get out of the country along with their money."

"Why would they do that?"

"I don't know, Claire. We're not even sure that's what happened, but it could be anything—loans gone bad, the wrong people crossed, that kind of thing."

Claire stood and walked to the window. She would never wish anyone ill, even her wretched sister, yet she felt a tiny tinge of guilt at the sudden sense of freedom she felt. True, given Claire's confirmed death in the explosion, Stacy would never be able to get to her again. Maybe Stacy was dead, or had just run away, maybe from her asshole husband. Or maybe they did concoct some financial escape together—after all, scheming was one of Stacy's long suits. Stacy's disappearance just underscored Claire's sense of freedom. Regardless, she was Claire Wilheit and, notwithstanding her new identity, always would be. She took a deep breath and turned to face a concerned-looking Aaron. She smiled and watched him visibly relax.

"I'm going to wash my face and change clothes. Do you know of any good Italian restaurants for dinner? Preferably one without a stringent dress code."

CHAPTER 83

Jason Kennedy swallowed the small orange pill along with his morning vitamin. He poured a cup of black coffee and thought back to the untenable position in which he'd been placed nearly ten days ago. God only knew what would have happened to him had Vivian Jaffe not demanded to talk to him and Marian.

The arresting agents had no intention of allowing Jaffe to contact potential witnesses, but the scientist was relentless and persuasive, and the arresting officers eventually put her in touch with Anna Dixon. Jaffe had explained very concisely and clearly Kennedy's dilemma.

"Mr. Kennedy has what may well be a life-and-death choice here, and frankly, I'm not sure how I'd advise him. If he chooses not to take the third initializing dose, he may fall by default into the group of patients for whom treatment failed. You all know what that may mean." They all did. They'd seen the surreal patient ward housing forty-one comatose patients. In the past days, two patients had died of brain hemorrhages most likely resulting from the A1A treatment. One was a seventy-seven-year-old veteran of the Iraq war, who had been receiving the A1A medication for several months. The autopsy results wouldn't be available for another week at the earliest, but his medical record listed underlying cardiac issues and that was likely a contributing cause if not the actual cause of death. The other fatality was an aging female veteran who had been an Army surgeon. Her records indicated that she was the only patient in Chen's unit who had failed to receive the third initializing dose. Her autopsy results would likewise take some number of days, but the collaborating physicians felt confident that A1A had caused her death.

"If he elects to complete the initializing process, he can stay on the maintenance dose for as long as necessary, until a mitigating drug can be developed. I've made progress on that, but obviously, the research has now ended.

"There are enough doses of daily maintenance to last Mr. Kennedy and the other four hundred outpatients almost eighteen months. Assuming no intervening mortalities, of course."

Given the army surgeon's death, Kennedy's choice was basically no choice at all. He would complete the course of medication, returning to the hospital so that Dr. Jaffe's assistant could administer it. He liked nothing about his situation, but the decision had ultimately been the one most likely to minimize the downside. One out of ten odds on the medication failing? That's better than one out of six chambers holding a bullet in a game of Russian roulette, but not much. Whether eighteen months was enough time, he just had no way of knowing, and neither did anyone else. He'd seen a lot of bombs go off during his deployment but living with a time bomb was an entirely different game.

———————————————————

Ben Wolf sat in the Scottsdale Police Department conference room with his detectives and Stan Deering.

"Stacy Atkins mysteriously disappears in Italy without a trace. Less than a week after she cleared out the rest of their assets."

"How about that," said Beverly Genn. "I'd say she and Curt got away pretty clean. God knows what they were running from, but there's no law that says American citizens are prohibited from taking their own assets out of the banking system."

"They must have had a good reason to leave the country."

"No doubt," said Wolf. "But without a complaint from anyone or a request to reopen the investigation, I'd say we're done on this one."

"What about James Garrity, her male friend from the cruise?" asked Genn. "The guy who claims he fell in love with her?"

"We have explained the sequence of events to him, and he is devastated. But he does understand that he was likely played by a con artist and her husband, and that adds to the sting of rejection," said Detective Martinez. "I feel really bad for the guy. He seems like a decent fellow."

"Me, too," said Genn. "He's too distraught to realize it yet, but in the end, I'd say he was pretty lucky. That woman was nothing but trouble."

CHAPTER 84

Claire and Aaron sat in the corner of a tiny Italian restaurant near Lincoln Park. Claire was refreshed after her shower and a change into some fresh clothes. She put her menu down.

"Aaron, do you think this is the end of A1A?"

"Most likely."

"But what if another researcher decides to keep going with it?"

"Claire, I think that's pretty remote. Other than Chen, Vivian Jaffe is the only other person in the company who understands the entire research and manufacturing process picture, and she doesn't want to see A1A out there any more than we do. Anyway, the FDA immediately rescinded its approval, and with the arrests and current mess in Congress, I'd say we're on pretty safe footing."

Claire set her glasses on the table and rubbed her forehead. "You're probably right. I just keep thinking what if we hadn't been able to stop it? You know AllMed would never have stopped with the veteran population, right? It would have just been a matter of time before its usage would expand to the far larger civilian population with PTSD."

"What do you mean?"

"Nobody really has a good handle on the numbers, or why different people can go through similar experiences and one will develop PTSD, and the other won't. But we are probably talking a potential market in the tens of millions of people. And it includes children."

Aaron stared at her. "Pretty sobering thought. But there's no point to us worrying about something that is just so unlikely to happen."

Claire nodded. "I guess not."

The waiter's return ended the conversation.

"Can you give us jut a few more minutes with our menus?" Aaron asked.

"Of course, sir."

Claire set her menu to the side of her place setting. "On another topic - I can't thank you enough for covering my financial losses, Aaron."

"You're welcome, but Anna is the one who approved it, and Perry is the guy who will make it happen. We'll need to cement a new identity for you as soon as possible so that your will can be backdated and the 'new you' becomes your sole beneficiary. I wish there was more we could do."

"Aaron, come on. I know you had a big part in this decision, so just say, 'You're welcome, Claire.'"

"You're welcome, Claire."

She grinned. He grinned back.

"So, what do you think I have to do to change my appearance?" Claire's serious expression had returned.

"Just like everything else involved in the process of creating a new identity, it needs to be something that you're comfortable with. Hair color and style are the obvious first steps. Different glasses. Or maybe contact lenses. Clothing."

Claire closed her eyes and ran her hands through her hair. She sighed.

"This is starting to remind me of that old boyfriend who wanted me in the role of Eliza Doolittle or him in the role of Pygmalion. Something like that."

"Claire, I understand your having that kind of response. Still, these circumstances are so fundamentally different…"

"I know Aaron, it's just my visceral reaction to the situation." She sighed. "Do I need to get plastic surgery?"

"You can, although it's not necessary. Facial recognition software has become so advanced that anything less than radical facial and skull reconstruction has become basically pointless. Even the smallest scars left from plastic surgery are easily identified. But people aren't going to be looking for you. You know, because you're dead.

"Anyway, I think you should at least consider some minor facial surgery. There's always a chance you'll run into an old friend or colleague someday. Given that, the superficial changes in your outer appearance and especially some small change to your features will render you unrecognizable to most people who might know you."

"Plastic surgery sounds too extreme for me. I'll put off that decision."

"That sounds fine. There's not the same sense of urgency, because as I said, nobody actively looks for dead people."

"Where will I live?"

"To start with, you'll stay in DC. The proverbial shit is going to hit the proverbial fan, and Anna will need both of us here."

"So for the next six months, I'll be here?"

"Yep."

"I'm gonna need some warmer clothes. This place is cold."

Aaron smiled. "So you'll be able to get a jump-start on your new look."

"That's certainly a positive way to look at it. Well, I guess this is kind of my new birthday, so let's indulge. In the most fattening stuff on the menu. Plus dessert. Plus wine."

"Perfect plan, Claire. But we should start with the wine first, don't you think?" He signaled the waiter.

"Yes, sir, have you made a selection from the wine menu?"

Before Aaron could speak, Claire jumped in. "Yes, we have. It's my birthday." And she proceeded to order.

CHAPTER 85

Gregory Sapozhnikoff enjoyed the brisk walk from Geneva's Four Seasons Hotel, opting for some exercise and fresh air rather than risk suffering a ride in an aging taxi that smelled of cigarette smoke and God only knows what else. He brushed a dusting of snow from the shoulder of his overcoat as he handed it to the young staffer who greeted him at the door of the Russian Consulate.

"Please, sir, right this way."

The Consul General stepped out from behind his desk and offered a warm, enthusiastic handshake to the man who'd left his Michael Parker passport in the safe deposit box at a Credit Suisse branch a couple of blocks away.

"Welcome, Gregory, excellent work. Please have a seat."

"Thanks, Ivan." Sapozhnikoff smiled back. It was good to be on friendly turf. "What can you tell me about the status of our laboratories in Moscow?"

"All in excellent condition, my friend. With your final set of research files in place, they're estimating full production within thirty days and an ongoing capacity of half a million doses per quarter."

Gregory stood to leave. He would be back at his ski lodge by dinnertime. Six inches of powder were forecast overnight, and tomorrow should be a glorious day on the slopes.

"Thank you, Ivan."

"While I can't say anything formally, you can be sure that your patriotism will be well rewarded."

It had better be, thought Sapozhnikoff. *I just handed my government the gift of the century.* He returned to the lobby and retrieved his outerwear from the staffer on duty. Donning his coat and gloves, Gregory Sapozhnikoff stepped out into the winter air.

As things turned out, the battle victory he thought he'd gained back in the States was a complete loss. It would have been nice if things had worked out differently, but he had won the larger war. While Stephen Chen's arrest no doubt posed a risk to Michael Parker, it offered no such legal exposure for Gregory Sapozhnikoff. The Central Park apartment was never at risk, since the Parker moniker showed up nowhere in property or ownership records. He liked that spot and was pleased that he could continue to keep it. Of course, he'd lose his initial investment in AllMed, but in the scheme of things, it would amount to little more than an investment hiccup. He'd recoup the loss many times over, just not in the United States. At least not in the short run. He believed in contingency plans, and he believed in playing the long game. He'd used the Michael Parker passport for the last time.

Governments were not to be trusted, and Sapozhnikoff had hedged that bet well. He was under no illusion that Moscow would honor its relationship with him, at least after the initial rollout of the Russian version of A1A. Then he could orchestrate some very lucrative international competition. He's already set the foundation for one such contingency plan in Indonesia. After all the machinations, chest-thumping, threats, and politics, money was still money, and power was still power.

He flagged a taxi. "Airport, please."

<<<<>>>>
The end

YOUR FREE COPY OF "SKYBOX", my short-short story, is just waiting for you to download!

Just follow this link: https://preview.mailerlite.com/a6y6p7

What is a "short-short" story? For me, it was taking on the challenge of writing a complete story in just 1500 words. As Mark Twain famously said: "I'd have written you a shorter letter, but I didn't have the time."

Did you enjoy reading "Collateral Carnage"? You can make a difference to me as an author.

Until writing "Collateral Carnage", I didn't realize how vitally important reviews are for authors, especially self-published authors. We don't have big publishing houses with enormous marketing budgets behind us. We can't put billboard-sized ads on the sides of city buses (well we could, if we loved the idea of second mortgages).

But what we can do is nourish relationships with our readers.

Honest reviews matter, because they help other readers find my books. If you enjoyed "Collateral Carnage", I would so appreciate your taking a few minutes to write a review on my book's Amazon page. Just hop on over there https://www.amazon.com/dp/B07TSL17GT/

I'd also like to welcome you to my website, ChrisSaperAuthor.com. Come visit at your leisure! As I add more works to my portfolio, you'll be able to find them on my website.

Thanks so much, and I'll see you online :)

Acknowledgements

There are so many people who have been generous and beyond helpful to me in bringing *Collateral Carnage* to fruition. My deep appreciation to John M Raines, MD; to my amazing editors: Lourdes Venard, Comma Sense Editing, Kate Schomaker, copyediting, and the folks over at Reedsy. Thanks to Bill Dooling Photography, for making me look better than I do; to artist Charles Thomas for his insight into how put options work; and to Shelley Stark Kingrey, Creative marketing consultant, writer/producer. My special thanks also go to Lyne Harmon, Licensed Psychologist, for sharing her insight and expertise in treating PTSD patients.

Thanks also to my valued Beta readers, whose honest critiques have helped me make the manuscript so much stronger. Mark Dawson's Self-Publishing 101 has been an amazing resource and one I can readily recommend to other self-publishing writers. And of course, to the many authors whose works I've loved over the decades, including Brett Battles, Stephen King, Steven Konkoly, Jonathan Maberry and so many others. I just wish they would write faster.

Disclaimer

This book is entirely a work of fiction. All names, characters, businesses, events and incidents are products of the author's imagination. Any resemblance to actual persons, living or dead, is purely coincidental and completely unintentional.

About the author

Author Chris Saper counts herself lucky to have had three pretty diverse careers, and what has made them so much fun for her is what they've all had in common: big, beautiful, giant puzzles just waiting to be solved.

Author Chris Saper first arrived in Arizona in the late 70's with a fresh new master's degree in health services management from the University of Missouri. In her first role as health care executive in Phoenix, Saper was tasked with implementing the nation-wide categorization of hospitals in Central Arizona to modernize and standardize prehospital protocols so that patients were assured of timely care and delivery to hospitals that offered the right level of care, including Trauma Centers, High-risk Neonatal Centers and the like. Later, Saper was tapped as a strategic planner for a multihospital system in Arizona, and then, as the Associate Administrator whose role was to implement the opening of Phoenix Children's Hospital in 1983. Great puzzles: lots of pieces and most of them moving.

In 1996, Chris revisited her bachelor's degree in fine arts, set on a way-back burner for seventeen years, and embarked on a 28+ year career as a commission portrait painter. And what more is a canvas than a big white puzzle whose pieces aren't even yet in existence? During the course of her portrait career, Saper has authored four books and four DVDs on the practice of fine art portraiture, also available here on Amazon.

Though long retired from health care, Chris has never stopped being intensely interested in patient care, the role of health insurance and the mechanisms by which patients in need are treated, or worse, fail to be treated.

She considers the health care industry, especially the lobbying functions its components embrace, to be facing its greatest challenge: to provide access to excellence in patient care, positive outcomes and safety in the ways that patients are managed.

The Arizona VA hospital has had some of the worst press imaginable and has been the subject of Congressional hearings and promised oversight. But it isn't alone. Just open the news, and you can see for yourself.

"Collateral Carnage" is Chris's first novel.